The Dreams We Bring

BY TOM K. REYNOLDS

ISBN: 979-8-218-43077-1

Author's note: This is a work of speculative fiction.

Acknowledgments

This book is dedicated to all the wonderful neighborhood theaters in Seattle that are now gone, especially the Harvard Exit and the Seven Gables. Thanks for the memories.

One person who was instrumental in helping me with the research for my book was Ruth Hayler. Ruth was a fixture in the Seattle movie scene as a theater manager, film booker and programmer, and publicity agent. Ruth loved movies and seeing films in theaters, and she worked her entire career for what was essentially the same company under different names, Randy Findley's Movie House, the Seven Gables Theater Company, and eventually Landmark Theaters. She was also a regular programmer for the annual Seattle International Film Festival. Whatever I got right in my description of the operations of a small independent theater probably came from my discussions with Ruth. Whatever is fiction or fantasy probably comes from me.

My special thanks to my wife Claudia McNeill, for doing a first copy edit which included reading aloud parts of the book to me, to help identify writing problems. In addition, she reviewed and corrected the final copy edit and helped prepare the manuscript for the internal designer. Her patience was essential in what turned out to be an over four-year project.

Finally, I want to thank Stephanie Ogle, Dale Carter, Doughlas Remy, and Benjamin Chamberlain. At various times, each of you offered me encouragement and/or assistance as I researched and then wrote this book. Thanks for your interest and help.

Contents

Part 1   **Beginnings** 1

Chapter 1   Now Playing at the Magic Lantern 5

Chapter 2   You've Got to Have a Dream 16

Chapter 3   A Man and a Woman 21

Chapter 4   Astronomy Club. 28

Chapter 5   The Trouble with Woody 32

Chapter 6   Starting Over. 38

Chapter 7   Café Talk 46

Chapter 8   Black and White in Mexico 52

Chapter 9   Rules of Grammar. 56

Chapter 10   Happy New Year 60

Part 2   **Keeping the Faith** 67

Chapter 11   All Things Old and Wonderful. 69

Chapter 12   The Spanish Tutor 75

Chapter 13   Surprise! Surprise!. 78

Chapter 14   Breathing Space. 93

Chapter 15   New Faces, Old Faces, Big Plans. 100

Chapter 16   The Big Picture. 109

Chapter 17 La Marcha 117

Chapter 18 On the Bench 125

Chapter 19 La Festival de Cine .128

Chapter 20 The Manifesto 132

Part 3   **The Summer of Film** 145

Chapter 21 The Waiting Game .147

Chapter 22 The Man Who Loved to Show Movies . .156

Chapter 23 Topsy Turvy 164

Chapter 24 Friends 178

Chapter 25 Local Sightings 186

Chapter 26 Film Studies 190

Chapter 27 The Women Who Make Movies 196

Chapter 28 Finding Her Voice .209

Chapter 29 Poster Art 215

PART 4   **The Story Goes On** 231

Chapter 30 Cinema is a Strange Creature 235

Chapter 31 Lady Bird 243

Chapter 32 After the Storm 257

Chapter 33 Things of Importance 265

Chapter 34 The Road Ahead .270

Chapter 35 The Unexpected 277

Chapter 36 Falling Apart 285

Chapter 37 Brainstorm 294

Chapter 38 Judgment Day 303

Chapter 39 The Dreams We Bring 313

Credits 329

PART 1

Beginnings

Scott Ryan
Journal Entry
June 1, 2017

This Theater is Closing

Laura and I stared in shock at the notice posted on the wall across from the theater office. How could this be? None of the staff had any information. They had only been notified of the closure the day before. The theater was to stop operation after Sunday's showings.

Before the movie started, we stood around in the salon and all the talk was about the closure. The other movie patrons, mostly long-time regulars like ourselves, a few going back to when the theater opened in 1978, were upset like us.

"It's because of all the streaming," said a stocky middle-aged man with a crew cut.

"They should have maintained the place better," responded a younger woman in designer jeans.

"They are closing all their theaters," said an older woman with silver hair and glasses. "You can tell when a place is in trouble when the staff acts like they don't care. The staff here used to be so friendly."

"Nobody goes to movie theaters anymore. The ticket prices are too high and the food costs too much," said a tall young man, who was there with his girlfriend. Then his cell phone rang, and he walked over to the big window that looked out on the street below to take his call.

All through the film, a Terence Davies' film about Emily Dickinson, I kept thinking—this can't be happening. How can this be happening?

I have seen many other Seattle neighborhood theaters go out of business since 2015. But I never thought it would happen to this little jewel of a place. Laura and I have come here regularly for about 15 years. We've seen films at other places in town, but this was our go-to theater, the place we always thought about first when we wanted to see a movie. Often, we had dinner at the little vegetarian restaurant about ten blocks north, and then we walked to the theater to see a seven o'clock show.

As we came out of the theater that last time, most of the folks we passed were talking about their experiences seeing movies here, the films they had seen, and what they liked best about them. Often, I heard the word "loved" when they spoke about a particular film or performance. A few mentioned when they had started to notice that the building was deteriorating, but most were remembering this or that great movie experience they had over so many years at this cozy little place.

"How sad," someone said as we got to the sidewalk in front of the theater.

Looking up at the theater marquee, I just kept saying to myself, "This can't be happening."

Laura gently stroked my left arm and looked sympathetic.

"I'm sorry," she said.

I looked at her, and mustering as much determination as I could, I said, "I can't let this happen."

CHAPTER 1

Now Playing at the Magic Lantern

"The first movie I couldn't forget was the restored version of Alfred Hitchcock's *Vertigo*," Dad says. "I saw it in 1996 and it blew my mind."

We are in the Magic Lantern's small office this afternoon waiting for a reporter from the *Cascadian* to show up. It has been four days since Dad re-opened the Magic Lantern, and he is really trying to get the word out. The weekly *Cascadian*, the one newspaper left in Seattle that regularly lists movie show times, is sending a reporter to the theater to do a story about the opening. Since we students have an early dismissal from school, Dad has roped me into working in the office while he talks to the reporter.

I remember the day in May when Dad brought me here to see the building. The outside walls were covered with graffiti, a chain-link fence having been added just recently, but too late to stop the vandalism outside. I kept thinking to myself—this place is a mess.

"You're going to buy this place?" I asked. "Does Mom know?"

Dad ignored my questions and immediately started talking about his dream for the Magic Lantern. "When there was talk about this building being torn down—and given the way things are right now with all the neighborhood theaters closing—I just couldn't let this place disappear without a fight.

"And the inside is in better shape than the exterior. It'll need to be cleaned and there are some plumbing problems. You probably don't remember being here. But we came a lot, and this place used to be one of the nicest little theaters in the city."

"Hello!" a voice says, and a girl appears at the office door.

"Mr. Ryan? I'm Ana Perez from the *Cascadian.*"

She is standing in the doorway, and her wavy black hair immediately catches my attention. She looks pretty young to be a reporter. She can't be much older than me. Her skin is golden brown and she's got a nice figure. Dad glances at me, and I realize that I'm staring at the reporter. So, I quickly go back to sorting the mail.

"We were expecting you. Come in, sit down, and you can call me Scott."

She sits and then immediately starts peppering Dad with questions. "What is your plan for this place, Mr. Ryan?"

I scan the room while they talk. There are some old movie posters on the back wall and a pile of bills and invoices on Dad's desk. He repainted everything, including the office, and put in new lights. But the office still feels sort of dingy. Maybe that's how an old movie house is supposed to feel.

"We're going to show both independent and foreign films, along with some archival stuff, Ms. Perez." Dad hands her one of the flyers showing the films he plans to screen in September, which she glances at while he talks.

"We'll have some mini-festivals—mostly, I think, built around particular directors' work. We're having a Woody Allen festival in October." He smiles as he tells her about the mini-festivals, and she smiles back. You can tell this idea excites him.

When she looks up from the flyer, her hazel eyes catch the light and seem to flash. They're amazing.

"With so many people streaming films, and so many neighborhood theaters closing, how do you expect to make this place work?"

I've been wondering the same thing since Dad announced that he was going to buy and reopen a theater on the edge of the University District. At first it seemed like a cool idea—owning and running a movie theater. But then I wondered, would it really work?

"Let me show you around," Dad says, and he and the girl walk into a big room just beyond the office, which Dad calls the "salon." The salon has three sofas, an old projector sitting on a tall table, and a low table partially covered with movie flyers and memorabilia.

I grab some movie marketing material, postcards and flyers, and follow them. The salon is where people are meant to hang out between films. A previous owner hosted an annual foreign film poster sale in the room, and French, German, and Italian film posters still cover part of the walls. The room screams out "old-fashioned movie theater." Despite having been cleaned and painted, the room still feels dark.

I put the stuff I brought out on the table and try to look busy rearranging materials while I wait for what I know is coming—Dad's elevator speech.

"You know," Dad pauses for emphasis. Then he motions for her to sit down on the big red sofa, the centerpiece of the salon.

"We've lost so many of these great movie houses in the neighborhoods and downtown that I think people—at least the ones I've spoken to—are ready for someone to bring some back. They want to have the experience again of going out to a great movie house and seeing a good movie on a big screen. And that's what we're going to give them: popcorn, soda, candy, and great movies."

I've heard this speech in various versions many times over the last four months as Dad explained, or tried to explain, his dream, first to Mom and then to friends.

After a pause he asks, "Don't you enjoy going out to the movies?"

"It's never been a big part of my life," the girl says without hesitation. "I remember going to that theater in Greenwood a couple of times with my grandparents. But I can't afford to go myself, and I don't really have the time. So now I mostly stream stuff with friends."

Her answer seems to catch Dad by surprise. He thinks everybody likes going out to the movies, and he thinks that streaming services shouldn't be able to show first-run films.

Dad doesn't respond, and the girl moves on to her questions. She's not shy.

"With two other theaters still open in the district, and so many theaters closing citywide, is there really a market for another one?"

This girl is asking some tough questions.

"I think so," Dad says. "We're going to offer an eight-dollar ticket for everybody, less than any other major venue in the city. We'll also offer a membership, and the cost of tickets to members will be five dollars. We'll run films six days a week with matinees and, I hope, workshops and special events."

This is his standard answer to any tough questions. We'll keep our prices low, sign up members who will become regulars at the showings, offer specials and mini-festivals, and show the most exciting schedule of films in North Seattle.

"That means you'll be in competition with Film Festival in Queen Anne and the Film Forum on Capitol Hill."

"There's no place in the north end that does what we're going to be doing, and no place that has such a good house. This place is steeped in Seattle theater history. It was the first of the neighborhood theaters that became such a prominent part of the Seattle movie-going scene, starting in the 1960s. The Historic Preservation Board recognized this when they designated it a historic building last fall."

Dad pauses, and then before the girl can ask anything else he adds, "So, I don't see us competing with the festival venues. We'll be giving people in North Seattle another venue for watching movies, a great older theater with eclectic, exciting programming."

Dad's cell phone rings, which is probably the only thing that could have stopped him from talking. "Hello," he says, and the look on his face changes. "I've got to put you on hold while I go into the office."

Dad turns to me and says, "Jackson, take Ms. Perez and show her the concession area and the theater seating. You can answer any other questions she has."

Dad is like this. Since the theater opened, I have sometimes found myself selling tickets, or working at the concession stand, or putting toilet paper in the restrooms. Often it is something that Dad intended to do, but then got pulled away to "more important things."

"Thanks, Mr. Ryan, Do you mind if I take some pictures?"

"Fine," Dad says with a wave of his hand. He is obviously anxious to get back to his phone call.

Ms. Perez extends her hand to me. "Hi," she says.

"Hi, I'm Jackson." I suddenly feel a little tongue-tied.

"I know," she responds, again with that big, warm smile.

We shake hands. I'm so stupid. Of course she knows my name. Dad just said it.

At the concession stand we stop and talk.

"So, Jackson, since we're on a first-name basis, you can call me Ana."

"Ana, that's an interesting name."

"It means 'graceful girl.'"

For a minute, I think she might be blushing, and then she asks, "What school do you go to?"

"I'm a junior at Truman. You?"

"St. Frances. I'm a junior too."

"How did you get a job at the *Cascadian*?"

"I interned there for the summer."

"Oh, nice. They're actually letting you write a story?"

She smiles again. She really has a great smile. Then she pauses, as if she is considering how much more she wants to say.

"They're between movie critics, so I volunteered to do this interview and write the story with some pictures. I want to be a writer."

"That's awesome. I scribble some myself."

Ana looks a bit puzzled. "That's a funny word to describe your writing."

"'Scribblers' is an old-fashioned name for writers," I explain. "Particularly those who were considered second-rate, or disreputable."

"You don't look disreputable to me."

Now I blush. "Well, thanks." I don't know what else to say, but I manage to smile back.

"Second-rate?"

"Probably, right now, but I love to write."

"What do you think about your father reopening this theater?"

The truth is I don't know what to think. Sometimes this whole idea seems crazy to me. At other times, I think I should be proud of what Dad's trying to do. So, I just shrug and say, "Let me show you the theater."

By far the best thing about the Magic Lantern is the screening room, with its low red theater seats, chandelier lights that disappear into the ceiling when the movie starts, and a painted Grecian scene, which covers the movie screen and means people don't have to stare at a blank screen while they sit around waiting for the previews to start.

Ana seems immediately charmed as she looks around the theater.

"What a nice little theater," she says. "I love the red seats." She pulls out her phone and starts taking pictures.

"Dad had everything cleaned before we opened and had the plumbing in the small downstairs bathrooms fixed. That took all summer. He did much of the work himself and then brought in some plumber friends to get the bathrooms working. But it was a struggle to get everything done on time."

"Are people coming, so far?"

"Well, it was the first weekend, so we weren't expecting much, but we were about two-thirds full for the Saturday night show. Our first film was by a French director, Claire something, someone Dad said was very popular. But most of the people who came, the ones I heard talking to Dad anyway, were old customers who wanted to support the reopening."

"It must be risky owning a theater today, what with all the streaming and everybody wanting to watch films at home."

"I don't know. Dad says it's just a matter of time until we have a steady attendance. But some of the movies he's talked about screening sound a little obscure, like foreign films, or movies by older directors. A lot of the people who've come so far are older too. Will we be able to attract a younger audience? I don't really know what to expect."

"You're not getting the college crowd?"

"Not yet," I say. "But like I said, it's only our first weekend."

Ana looks around the theater and then sits down in one of the chairs. "These seats are a bit low, aren't they?"

"Supposedly, they're just right for seeing the screen." That's what Dad always says to people who ask. But I find the chairs a little low myself.

Ana takes a few more pictures.

"Are you working here regularly?"

"Mostly on weekends. Dad's here most of the time because he runs the films himself. But he's trying to hire some college kids to work at the concession stand and maybe close on slow nights."

I pause and then ask a little flippantly, "Would you like a job?"

She smiles and shakes her head. We walk up to the screen and then back to look at the screening booth.

"So, your dad is the projectionist?"

I nod my head.

In the screening booth there are two projectors. I walk over to the newer looking one and say, "This is the digital projector we use for most of the newer films. It's pretty cool and easier to use than the older projector. That projector runs the older 35mm films."

I can tell that she would like me to say a little more about the projectors. But I don't really know much more. Dad has promised to teach me, but I have no idea when that will happen. With school starting, I have all I can do to keep up with my class work.

"Dad can tell you more about the projectors if you ask him."

We walk back to the office where Dad is sitting at his desk looking at his draft film schedule for October. He looks up and says, "What did you think, Ms. Perez?"

"The place is cozy and the red seats in the screening room are cool."

"They may seem a little low, but they are just right for looking at the screen."

I have to catch myself from saying that I already told Ana that.

"See, you like it and you haven't even seen a movie here," Dad says.

"Jackson says you actually show the films yourself."

"Yes, we have a digital projector. New films run on these projectors, and they are simple enough that managers can run them."

"You don't use a projectionist at all?"

"No. Some of the chains still employ them. The Puget Sound Film Festival employs one to run their 35mm films. But it's hard to have a career as a projectionist today. We do have a second 35mm projector, and we may have to use it for one or two of the films in the Woody fest."

Dad pauses and then says, "Honestly, I'm just learning myself how to work the 35mm machine. An old projectionist friend of mine will be coming by in early October to go over its operation and do some test runs to see how it's working."

"So that means you have to be here every day the theater is open to run films."

"Right now," Dad says. "But down the road Jackson will be able to run the digital machine."

He nods toward me, and I immediately wonder what he means by that. But I don't say anything.

After a moment Ana asks, "Do you have anything else you'd like to say about your hopes or dreams for the Magic Lantern? Something I can maybe end my story with?"

"I'd like to let the public know that we want the Magic Lantern to become the film center for North Seattle. We hope it will be a place people talk about and regularly attend to see exciting films. A place where we can have filmmakers come to speak and maybe film workshops. A place where the little parking lot is filled almost every night. When people mention the Magic Lantern, I want them to say that it is the best place to see a movie north of the ship canal."

Ana nods and seems to be writing down everything Dad is saying in her little notebook. Then she glances at her watch.

"Thanks, Mr. Ryan. I've got to get going if I'm going to catch my bus."

"Well, thank you, Ms. Perez, for coming and for writing a story about our efforts to restore a little bit of film culture here in North Seattle. And remember, next time we see each other you can just call me Scott."

She smiles at Dad and then turns and smiles at me. "Nice to meet you, Jackson."

"Nice to meet you too, Ana," I say. And I watch her walk down the battered wooden steps to the street. If we stay in the movie business, those steps are going to need some repair too. She looks graceful walking away with her black hair bobbing up and down. She's not exactly beautiful, but she's so interesting. And then there is that smile. I should have said something else to her, something about seeing her again. But now it's too late.

"She'll be back, Jackson," Dad says from behind me. "Now that she's seen this wonderful little movie house, and she understands what we're doing here, she'll be back."

Chapter 2

You've Got to Have a Dream

"Scott's always been a dreamer," Mom said when we finally had a talk about Dad's buying the Magic Lantern. "When he first came into that little gallery I worked at in Ballard, I was immediately attracted to his energy. He wanted to change the world. He had such dreams. He was an exciting guy."

Mom seemed a little wistful as she thought about that first meeting with Dad.

She was another "graceful girl," taller than Dad. He called her "statuesque." She had thick blond hair and people always looked her way when she came into a room.

"Laura is just classy," Dad had told me once. "When I met her, my first thought was, "What a classy babe."

"Scott came out here because he wanted to be somewhere 'clean, fresh, and new.' He was working as a sales person and part-time actor when we met, but he wanted to have his own green business. Being sustainable was really all he talked about, and after a

16

while he settled on the idea of starting an environmental consulting firm. Which he did."

"That green thing really confused me," I said. "He bought a hybrid car and talked about putting solar panels on the house. But I can't see him marching in a demonstration about climate change or living totally off the grid."

"Remember, he joined a climate action group at your uncle's church. But that wasn't really what he wanted. 'Too much talk and too much politics,' he said. He wanted to give people tools to help them cut their carbon footprint, and he wanted to do it in his own way."

"Yeah, I remember him lecturing us about our carbon footprint before he bought the heat pump. I guess he is kind of a wizard when it comes to business, but do you think people want to come to a 250-seat, single-screen theater and watch obscure films?"

"He might surprise us, Jackson. Remember, he took a risk before with his business and pulled it off. Nobody thought someone without any experience in the field could successfully start an environmental consulting firm. But he did his homework, volunteered where he had to, and ended up knowing, and in some cases employing, most of the experts in the field here in Seattle. Eventually his firm was considered the best in town."

"But he had to sell that business to buy this theater, right?"

"Well, yes, but we'll still have money in the bank—enough, I hope, for your first couple years of college."

Mom likes to talk as though the college thing is a given. Even though I wasn't sure where, or even if, I wanted to go, I had wondered about the college money.

"And he can go back to being a consultant if things don't work out with the theater."

I wondered if it was going to be that simple. Dad was working every day at the theater, at least until he could hire some staff. He wanted me to work Friday nights, most weekends, even weeknights as needed, and to learn to run the projector. With that kind of schedule I wasn't ever going to be able to get all my homework done, let alone do anything fun.

"Are you worried about having to work on weekends?"

I shrugged. "A little, yes, because well ... because for one thing, what's going to happen to the Astronomy Club?"

I had started the Astronomy Club at Truman during my sophomore year and had been its president ever since. My grade point average is, well, average. Good enough to get me into one of the second-rung state colleges, but not into the University or any of the good private schools, in or out of state. But being in the Astronomy Club and on the baseball team might improve my chances of getting into a good college, at least in-state.

"Don't you meet on Thursday afternoons?"

"Yeah, but most of our activities are on weekends."

"Well, you've got to help your dad until he can hire a few college kids to usher and work the concession stand. Can't Ellen step in?"

Ellen Hara helped me start the Astronomy Club and is probably my best friend. We both love stargazing and talking about what we see through a telescope or the newest NASA mission. We've been friends since middle school. I know she could take over the group and run the meetings, but it's my group. The more I thought about it, the more I realized that Dad's owning a movie theater would really limit my participation in the Astronomy Club.

"Maybe I can run our afternoon meetings. But the weekend activities like the monthly Saturday night sky party at Swanson Park I'll have to miss. Can't you help out?"

Mom frowned, and I could tell I had stepped on her toes.

"I'm going to cut my open hours to Thursday through Sunday to help with the bookkeeping, and maybe I'll work a night or two selling tickets. But I've got a gallery to run, and weekends are my busiest time. We'll all have to chip in, at least for a while."

"Why is running a theater like this one so important to Dad anyway?"

"It's always been one of his dreams. Ever since I've known Scott, he's been movie crazy. Our first real date was going to see *Shakespeare in Love* at that theater on 45th Street. It ran there for almost four months. In those days, it seemed like everybody was going to the movies and talking about films, and Scott got caught up in all that excitement.

"But it didn't seem like a real possibility, certainly not when he was running his company. In the end, he thought it would be a bigger challenge and he just wanted to do it."

Mom paused and she looked a little worried. "He really does know a lot about movies, honey. That first year, after we were married, he taught a film appreciation course at the Seattle Art School, the college for aspiring artists on Capitol Hill."

I could tell she was thinking some of the same stuff I was, but trying to be more positive. This sort of situation made me wish that I had some older brothers or sisters. More kids to share the work and worry. But my parents are busy people. At least, that's what Mom told me once when I asked her why they hadn't had a bigger family.

"Too busy to have sex?" I'd asked.

"No," she shot back, "too busy not to use birth control."

We talked about these things in our family. But we really hadn't talked about Dad's buying and running this old theater, and all that might mean. And now that it had happened, it seemed like we were stuck, stuck in Dad's dream, for better or worse.

CHAPTER 3

A Man and a Woman

Truman is only about a mile north of the theater. But I miss the bus, or rather it is completely full by the time I get to the bus stop. So, I speed walk south along 15th Avenue and then through Judkins Park to Eisenhower Avenue, south past a comedy club, the last video store in town, a soup kitchen with its line of desperate looking people, and the library, to the crosswalk right across the street from the theater.

I'm late, so I run across the street after the light changes and bump into a man standing with his back to the crosswalk, looking up at the Magic Lantern's marquee.

"Sorry," I say, a little annoyed.

"Oh," the man says in surprise. He's dressed in what looks like an old-fashioned grey suit—you don't see many people wearing suits in Seattle. He's tall and bulky, with a slightly hunched posture, and has a puffy face with thinning hair pushed back on the top of his head.

Something about him reminds me of the character in that old Christmas movie, about a department store Santa Claus who gets fired for insisting that he's the real thing, and then wins a court case against the store.

Before I can get completely past him, the man asks, "Is it really open again?"

"Yes," I say. "We opened two weeks ago."

The man gets a dreamy look on his face and he smiles. He stares back at the marquee. "Wonderful," he says.

What a strange man, I think to myself. Then I turn and run up the steps into the theater.

When Dad asked me to come by the theater after school on Tuesday to meet with him and our new film buyer, I was surprised. But maybe I shouldn't have been because he's started to treat me like his assistant.

It's 3:30 when I walk into the office. Dad is talking to a well-dressed older woman.

"Jackson," Dad says, "this is Genevieve Rolland, our film buyer."

The woman smiles and stands up. It's a confident smile. She's slender and wearing a long print dress, dark dress shoes, and a colorful scarf around her neck. Her dark hair is streaked with silver.

She extends her thin hand for me to shake. "Nice to meet you, Jackson." She has a bit of an accent.

"We're very lucky that Genevieve was willing to work with us. She's considered the best film buyer in the city."

"Scott's being kind," the woman says.

"Sorry I'm late," I say. "I had to walk."

"Well, you're here now so let's get to it," Dad says as Genevieve and I sit down. "We've run into a few snags with some of the films. We worked out a couple while we were waiting. The big problem involves the new Spike Lee film, which the distributor wants us to take for a month.

"It's a film about a Black policeman who joins the Ku Klux Klan to spy on the group. I thought we would have it run right after the Woody Allen retrospective. It seems like it would give us a guaranteed audience to jump-start our fall season."

I'd think Dad would be ecstatic about a four-week run. But apparently there is some kind of a problem.

"Genevieve," he says, "give us your opinion about what a four-week run of this film would mean."

"October will just be your second full month in operation. It's likely this film will do well with a certain audience, but it's going to be showing at two other theaters in the city, including Queen Anne. I think you'll likely have a good audience for a couple weeks, but I'm not sure you can sustain that for four weeks."

"I have the same concerns," says Dad. "Booking the film for two weeks seems like the safe thing to do."

"I would agree," the film buyer says, "except we probably can't."

"Why?" Dad asks.

"The distributor wants the minimum length of run for all theaters to be four weeks."

"Can't you talk them down to two weeks?"

"I'll try, but as a new theater, we don't have much leverage. We were late asking to run the film, and it's already getting good national press. It has a big-name director with a national following, and a Black star. There has even been a little Oscar buzz about the film. So, the distributor assumes that theaters should be able to successfully market the film for four weeks."

"Won't streaming the film syphon off some of the audience?" Dad asks.

"Probably," Genevieve says, "but again we're not in a strong position to negotiate with the distributor. At least they're committed to showing their films in theaters."

Dad shifts in his chair. I can tell that he is unhappy with the situation.

"I wanted that film to show right after the Allen Fest. It should bring in a younger audience and get the media talking about us before the holidays. We should be able to make a profit for two weeks. But a four-week run, competing with other theaters in the city! I'm not sure that will work. Isn't there anything we can do?"

"We could fight them on this. But they could decline to sell to us the next time we request a film that they're distributing. On the other hand, if we agree to the four-week run, and the film isn't making money, we can't stop running the film early unless we pay a penalty."

"It sounds like we're caught between our needs and the wishes of the distributor. But I guess we need to be cautious about picking fights with distributors right now," Dad says finally.

Genevieve nods her head in agreement.

"Okay, talk to the distributor, but don't push them too hard. If they'll only agree to a four-week run, we'll just have to run it for four weeks. Luckily, we've got the Woody Allen Retrospective to serve as a lead-in," Dad says.

There is a pause, and suddenly it feels like all the air has been sucked out of the room.

Then Genevieve says, "You know I'm skeptical about devoting two weeks of your October schedule to an Allen retrospective."

Dad looks frustrated. "Yes, we talked about this before."

"His audience is shrinking, especially with younger people and women."

"I see this as a draw for our older filmgoers some of whom may have first seen major Allen films at this theater fifteen or twenty years ago," Dad replies. "I want to bring all those people back to us, and then build on that by showing great new films, like *BlacKkKlansman*, to attract younger people."

"A week might be fine, but two weeks of Woody Allen could turn out to be a negative for the theater."

I can tell that Dad is really unhappy to be disagreeing with the film buyer. "We've already bought the Allen films, right?"

"Yes," Genevieve says. "But I think I could negotiate us down to six films from seven, and if you screened each for just one night instead of two, we could cut back to a week. I also have a good idea for a replacement film for that second week—the Coen brothers' new film."

"The western?" You can hear the skepticism in Dad's voice.

Although Dad isn't a big fan of the Coen brothers, I can't help but wonder if a new Coen Brothers film wouldn't be a better draw than a bunch of old films by a director nobody cares about anymore. But I can sense that Dad is determined to run the Allen retrospective.

He gives an audible sigh, and I can tell that the discussion is over.

"Let's go with the original plan," he says. "I want to reintroduce Allen to this film community. Regardless of his personal problems, I think when folks see some of his films, they will recognize how great they are."

"Okay," says the film buyer as she gets up to leave. "I'll get back to you after I talk to the distributor."

"Genevieve really knows her stuff," Dad tells me after she leaves. "She's worked for the film festival and for the big theater chain that used to run a lot of Seattle's neighborhood theaters. She knows all the distributors and can usually talk them into giving her whatever she wants, if it's reasonable."

He's looking at me, but I feel like he is actually talking to himself.

"Is working with distributors really that hard?" I ask.

"It can be. We're lucky to have Genevieve on our side."

Obviously, he and Genevieve have different views on the Woody Fest, but I could tell they were both worried about the theater making enough money. And from what I have heard I wonder if, even with a good new film, there isn't just a delicate balance between the length of a run and the success of a run that can be hard to determine. And then with older films, it seems like it might be even harder to put people in the seats. So again, I'm asking myself, how is Dad ever going to make this old theater into a successful business?

"However long our run of the Lee film turns out to be—two weeks or four—we're going to have to work to build an audience, starting with this film. So, Jackson, I need to have you contact the *Cascadian* and see how much it would cost to have an advertisement put in the paper on both the Allen Festival and the Lee film for the next three weeks.

"In the meantime, I'm going to contact a friend of mine at Seattle University about doing a Q and A on Allen the first Saturday night of the Woody Fest, and maybe I'll also call a film critic I know to see if he can speak on the second weekend. Anyway, we need to really ramp up the level of our publicity."

It sounds like Dad's theater dream is already in trouble. The reason he wanted me here today is that he has more work for me to do. What he hasn't explained is where I can get the time to be a publicity person for the theater.

"Oh, and we need to get someone in to help me work on upgrading the website. If you've got any ideas, or know anyone who builds websites, let me know."

After Genevieve leaves, I want to ask him about her comments on the Woody Allen retrospective, but before I can decide, he grabs his iPhone and walks into the salon to make a call.

CHAPTER 4

Astronomy Club

"**Y**ou won't be able to pick me up?" Marc Wilson asks.

I've just told the five semi-regular members of the Astronomy Club at our October meeting that I'm not going to be able to attend Saturday night stargazing for a while.

I have my license, but no car. In the past either Mom or Dad always let me use one of their cars, usually the old Toyota, so that one Saturday a month when the Seattle Astronomy Society held their star party at Swanson Park north of the city, I could go and pick up some of the other members. Now, having to work Saturdays is going to seriously limit what I can do with the club.

"I can pick you up," Ellen tells Marc.

"How long are you going to have to work weekends at your dad's theater?" Sherry Jefferson asks.

"I'm hoping just until January," I say. I'm being optimistic though. I know it might be longer, but I don't want it to seem like I'm leaving the group for

28

good. It's my group and I really need it, along with baseball, to put on my list of extracurricular activities if I do decide to apply to any colleges.

"So, we're still going to meet on Thursday?" Marc asks. "Because that's really the only afternoon I can meet."

Marc is an honors student and plays trumpet in the band. Ellen is also in the Math Club and in advanced placement in physics and biology. Sherry edits the student newspaper and is Junior Class vice president. Jonnie Rodriguez is president of the Chess Club. The truth is everybody in our club is a brainiac, except me.

"Yes," I say, "Thursdays as usual and we'll still cover the same things at our meetings. Our astronomy-related activities, like the monthly star party, and citizen science projects in astronomy."

"I finally got my bronze level certification," says Johnnie, the newest member of the club.

Everybody in the club is working to get an Astronomy League certification by volunteering to identify astronomical objects, like galaxies and exoplanets, as part of various online crowd-sourced astronomy projects, like Galaxy Zoo 4, Radio Galaxy Zoo, and Planet Hunter.

We congratulate Johnnie. We know how much time it takes to get the one hundred contributions necessary to qualify for a bronze certificate.

Even though everyone in the club is excited about being citizen scientists, most of us are too busy to spend much time actually doing the work. For every club member except maybe me, the goal is to get into a good college with substantial financial aid. The other possible exception to this is Ellen, who apparently doesn't sleep much, and who has made over five hundred contributions to various astronomy projects and earned a coveted silver certification.

When the meeting is over, Ellen catches up to me as I'm headed for the bus.

"Don't worry about the club," she says. "It's likely that one or more of the Saturday star parties over the winter will get cancelled because of the weather."

She is right about that. Winter weather in Seattle wasn't made for stargazing—too many cloudy, rainy, or just plain grey days. But sometimes, particularly in February, we get some clear, crisp weather—hot chocolate days Ellen calls them—and if you get that kind of weather on a star party night, it is perfect for stargazing.

"Yes, I know, but you and I started this group, and I hate missing meetings. Anyway, I want to have things I can list on my resume if I decide I want to apply to some local colleges, and the Astronomy Club will look really good."

"The best thing you could do if you're going to apply to schools is to get your grades up and not worry so much about anything else."

Ellen always says what she thinks. We've been through this before. For Ellen school is easy, while I often find my mind wandering to things I'm more interested in, like stargazing and baseball.

"Yeah, yeah," I say with a shrug.

"You read a lot, so I know you're not dumb. But it's your junior year, and if you don't bring your grades up this year, your chances of getting into a decent school are slim."

"That's easy for you to say. You know exactly what you want to do, and what colleges you want to apply for."

Since middle school Ellen has been saying that she wants to be an astrobiologist—that was before most people knew what an astrobiologist was.

We reach the bus stop just in time. My bus is coming.

I look at her not knowing what else to say. The college thing has kind of divided us.

"Do you want to keep walking to the next stop?" she asks.

"I've got to get home to study." Then I realize how ironic that sounds.

"Okay. Oh, I could sub for you at the theater some Saturday night if you wanted take the opportunity to attend the stargazing."

"I'm not sure how that would work. I'm not sure what Dad would say. He has to pay everyone who works at the theater. Something about state rules."

Besides, I'm not sure I want Ellen working at the Magic Lantern, although she might be the right person to help Dad upgrade our awful website.

My bus arrives.

"Well, ask him," she says. "And tell him I know how to use an electronic cash register. I work at my aunt's dress shop every summer. See you tomorrow."

"Bye," I say.

Sitting in a side seat at the back of the bus, I watch Ellen fade into the distance. Sometimes it's frustrating to have a friend as smart as Ellen, but other times I feel like she is my only really true friend. Because who else besides my parents cares enough to argue with me about my grades?

CHAPTER 5

The Trouble with Woody

The headline for Ana Perez's article in the *Cascadian* reads:

**Reopened U-District Theater Hopes to be
North Seattle's Film Center**

Her article is pretty good, no errors in the quotes, and it captures the feel of Dad's dream.

We'll be screening seven films in what Dad is calling our Woody Fest—three of his early films, one mid-career mystery-comedy, and three of his later works. Dad still thinks it's a good idea, despite Genevieve's skepticism. But as it turns out, Genevieve isn't the only staff member who thinks that the Woody Fest is a bad idea.

"Why Woody Allen?" Raji, a college kid Dad just hired to work concessions, asked when he saw the flyer for the October films.

"Allen's early and mid-career films are great," Dad tells him. "And we're going to show some of his best.

When people see how great the writing is and what great performances he gets from actors, they'll understand why his films can be of interest to us even today."

"Yes, but Woody Allen?" Raji says sarcastically. "He's passé and unpopular because of Mia Farrow's accusations about his personal life. Nobody I know will come to see an Allen Film."

"You'll see," Dad says. Then he turns and walks back toward the office.

The strain of putting on the Allen retrospective is starting to show on Dad, despite his efforts to stay positive. The fact that the Woody Fest could be trouble is underscored when we find out that the *Cascadian* ran an article very critical of Allen. The article, which came out a week before the first film in the Woody Fest, mentions the retrospective, but by inference it discourages people from seeing anything by the director.

"And you haven't even included any of his really funny films," Raji says almost under his breath, as Dad disappears into his office. "And how could you leave out *Annie Hall*?"

I doubt Dad heard him. He hired Raji partly because of his interest in movies, partly because he seemed to have a very flexible schedule. But Dad thinks he knows more about films than any of us. He has a plan, and he is going to follow it regardless of what anyone else thinks.

September was warm and dry, but at the start of October the weather shifted, and for the next four weeks it was cool, cloudy, and rained a lot.

The first film in the Allen festival is *Manhattan* on a Friday night. I barely make it to the theater by 6:30, the start time for theater staff when there is a show at 7:00.

"Jackson, you're here," Dad says, sounding slightly irritated when I walk into the office. "Good. So, you sell tickets and then help Raji with concessions after the previews start. I'm doing a short introduction to the series, and then I'll start the film. After that I'll check with you as I get a chance."

This has become my job when Mom isn't here—which is turning out to be often. I sell tickets and help with concessions while Dad runs the film. Raji was hired to work on Thursday nights and week-ends and is picking up an additional shift tonight. Mom is only working on Tuesdays and Wednesdays, and I am supposed to work just on Thursdays, Fridays, and Saturdays. But sometimes—like when Dad wants to introduce films or Raji can't work—whenever we need more help, I end up working more nights. Dad's schedule is already eating into my homework time.

I unlock the theater door and open the ticket sale window. Nobody comes in for about twenty minutes. Then three or four older couples arrive, and after that about eight other people. Following an old movie the-ater routine, people find their seats—not much of a problem tonight—and then folks come out to buy concessions.

By 7:05 everyone is seated, and Dad begins his in-troduction. I stand just inside the heavy curtain that closes off the screening room from concessions and listen. He talks about why he decided to reintroduce Allen to local filmgoers. He admits that the films se-lected are among his favorites, but he also feels they are among Allen's best and good examples of the "arc of his career." Dad knows a lot, and I feel a little sad that only twenty people are here to appreciate what he has to say.

Dad doesn't stop by concessions when he leaves the projection booth. He just walks back to his office and closes the door behind him.

For the next two nights, Dad and I stand by the door as the films end, handing out film schedules and taking comments. On Saturday night, Dad's friend, Dr. Bishop, makes a short presentation about the importance of *Annie Hall* and *Manhattan* to both Allen's career and American film in the 1970s. Saturday's crowd is a little larger, about thirty-five people. Dad is smiling again as he takes comments at the door.

"Scott, good to see you," a stocky man says as he and a woman stop to talk to Dad on their way out of the theater.

"Hi, George," Dad says.

"Great to see this old place open again," the man says.

Dad smiles, and goes into his speech about how it is so important to preserve neighborhood theaters, and how he just couldn't see this building go to seed.

"Small crowd tonight," the man continues. "How's attendance been so far?"

"About as I expected. People are just realizing that the theater has reopened. But as the word spreads, we'll see the attendance jump."

Then Dad says, "I didn't know you were a Woody Allen fan."

"I saw most of his big films in the '70s and '80s. *Manhattan* was one of my favorites, great ambience."

George introduces his wife, Margaret, to Dad, and they shake hands.

"Are you an Allen fan?" Dad asks her.

"Not really. I saw *Annie Hall* when I was in college. But I thought he was an acquired taste. You know, New York upper middle class, and I was from a working-class family. So, it didn't seem very relevant to my world, although the music was great."

Dad nods. There's a pause, and I can tell that Margaret wants to say something else. Before Dad can start talking again, she adds, "The music in this film is certainly great too—better than the music in *Annie Hall*—and it's a real loving portrait of New York City in the '70s. But, the main character's relationship with the girl, Tracy, was disturbing, even at the time, and particularly in light of what's happened in Allen's life since the early 1990s."

"Yes," Dad says, "it certainly reveals a passion for younger women."

After an awkward pause he says, "It was good to see you both," and hands Margaret a film schedule. "And I hope we'll see you back again soon."

Scott Ryan
Journal Entry
October 21, 2018

I should have listened to Genevieve. After all, isn't that what you have a good film buyer for, to help you select films? Apparently, nobody wants to see Allen's films these days, especially not in a theater, and not even the good ones. And to start with Manhattan *was a mistake, even though it's one of Allen's most complete films. Trying to sell it to the "Me Too" generation! Big mistake. I should have done the conventional thing and started the series off with* Annie Hall.

But I do feel disappointed. I saw and loved Annie Hall, Manhattan, *and* Stardust Memories *in my twenties. After I came to Seattle, I saw most of his newer films on video or DVD. And when I learned that the original owner of the Magic Lantern had an arrangement with Allen to preview his films in Seattle, I thought there would be a built-in audience here of older movie goers who would love to see some of Allen's best films in a theater again.*

Still, not all the news is bad. Most of the comments on Sunday after the second screening of Hannah and Her Sisters *were positive, and I'm still hoping for a strong turnout for at least* Manhattan Murder Mystery *and* Blue Jasmine. *Maybe we can still salvage something with a few of the other films, and with a lot of luck maybe we can break even.*

Chapter 6

Starting Over

"**I** think the festival has done pretty well considering," Dad says as he, Mom, and I sit talking in the office on Sunday nine days into the Allen mini-festival.

Really? I say to myself.

"*Hannah and Her Sisters* did fine the first weekend of the festival, and *Manhattan Murder Mystery* got a surprisingly good audience on the first night of its run," he adds.

But then Dad had trouble with the 35mm projector on the Wednesday night showings of *Manhattan Murder Mystery* and *The Purple Rose of Cairo*, and both shows were about twenty minutes late in getting started. Not great publicity for the theater. I saw the second showing of *Purple Rose of Cairo*, and I think there were maybe thirty people in the seats. Too bad, because that was an interesting film, a fantasy of sorts, about a woman who escapes the drudgery of her life for a couple hours at the movies.

I decide to speak up. "Yeah, but did we have more than fifty people in the theater for any of the films except *Hannah and Her Sisters*?"

"We got a good article in the *Times* about the festival," Dad says, unfazed by my comment.

I read that article too but didn't think it was that positive. The critic questioned the relevance of an Allen retrospective, when there were so many other good directors whose current work deserved more attention.

"We'll get a bigger audience for *Blue Jasmine*," Dad says. "That's Allen's best late film. Cate Blanchett won an Oscar for her performance."

Neither Mom nor I say anything, and Dad must have sensed that we are wondering if he knows what he is doing.

So, after a pause he says, "It's important to keep showing great movies. They're part of our film culture, and we want the Magic Lantern to be known as a theater that shows great movies, old and new."

Dad really seems to believe that he can save the Magic Lantern by showing almost anything that is a "good movie," despite its age or the popularity of the director. I don't get it.

"We all need to keep faith in what we're doing. The theater's been open for barely two months, and there's bound to be some ups and downs until everybody understands what we're trying to do."

And then with a burst of energy he adds, "Now we need to go full steam ahead into promoting our fall holiday films. We have a very strong schedule of films coming up. *BlacKkKlansman* will run four weeks. We're going to run *Manhattan Murder Mystery* again on Wednesday and Thursday nights as a lead-up to the Lee movie.

"For our agreeing to show the Lee film for four weeks, Genevieve got a promise from the distributor to give us a great film to run the first two weeks of December. We'll be announcing the name of that film soon. So, I want you to think of this as a new start, after a bit of a stumble. And now I need to focus on finding someone to help me with the website."

I haven't seen Ana Perez since her visit to the Magic Lantern as a reporter in September. But I've thought about her a lot.

Then at the Saturday night showing of the Spike Lee film, a girl wearing a green dress catches my eye as she goes into the screening room with two other girls to get seats. It's Ana, I'm sure of it.

The theater is practically full. It looks like our biggest audience so far, about two hundred people, and we're close to being overwhelmed. So, as Dad would say, it's "all hands on deck." Mom got one of her two assistants to close her shop so she could work selling tickets.

Raji and I are working on concessions, with Mom spelling Raji as needed. Ellen—who Dad agreed could work a couple of weekends until he could hire another person—is taking tickets at the door and helping people find seats. There's no time to talk to anybody, including Ana, before the film starts.

I keep thinking about Ana all through the movie, and as the film ends, I leave concessions and walk over by a little table that has a free water pitcher and some theater schedule flyers on it, right across from the entrance to the screening room. People are talking about the film as they come out, which is a good sign.

Then Ana appears, and at the same moment I see her, she sees me.

"Hi, Jackson. I thought I'd probably see you here."

"Hi, Ana. Yeah, I'm always here on Saturdays. In fact, it seems like I'm always here, period. That was a nice story you wrote for the *Cascadian*. Dad commented on it."

She smiles. "Thank you. My story on your theater was the last one I did. I wanted to continue working part-time, but I need to concentrate on school and grades. My grandparents keep saying, 'You can't let your grades slip, Ana.'"

"Are your grades slipping?"

"Not really. My GPA is 3.75."

"That's pretty high. Of course, getting into college is competitive, but a 3.75 GPA should get you into most of the state schools."

"Well, maybe," Ana says. "But I'm a little nervous about the whole process—getting accepted and affording wherever I want to go."

Over Ana's shoulder, I notice the two girls Ana came with, and then I see Genevieve talking to a tall, heavyset man who looks familiar.

"Are you doing a lot of extracurricular stuff? The schools want to see that kind of stuff on your applications."

"As much as I can."

Now I remember where I saw the man before. He is the person I ran into outside the Magic Lantern almost a month ago. I was in a hurry that day because I had a meeting with Dad and Genevieve.

"A good crowd tonight," Ana says.

"This is our best crowd so far, and last night was almost as good. Dad thinks our attendance will consistently pick up with this film, so tonight is a good sign."

I want to seem upbeat in front of Ana, and that is what Dad thinks.

"That's great." There is a pause, neither of us seeming to know what else to say.

"How did you like the film?" I ask finally.

"It was exciting, maybe a little too violent at the end."

"The lead actors were hot," yells one of her friends.

"That's my friend Sonja—she's the short one," Ana says, motioning toward her two friends. "Sonja says Spike Lee is an important Black director, but she thinks his films are pretty violent."

"Ah, a film critic," I say a little sarcastically.

Ana smiles again. "She wants to be an actress."

"Well, he is an important Black director, I guess, and we were lucky to be able to screen this film. It's the start of our fall programming, and we need to start getting bigger houses and building a following."

Ana looks a little confused. "You want to make this a bigger house?"

"That's theater talk," I say.

Ana laughs, a light, soft laugh.

"It's just a term that refers to the number of seats in a theater. So, when we talk about the size of the house, we're talking about the number of people in the seats, or the attendance."

"Oh," she says, and then nods.

"Ana, give him your phone number and let's go." It's Sonja again.

"Well, I've got to get going. We need to catch the bus back to Green Lake. It was nice to see you again, Jackson, and I'm glad the theater is doing well."

She's leaving, but I know that I want to see her again, so I blurt out, "I think your friend is right. Can I have your cell number?"

Then I stand there amazed at myself.

Ana gets that "I don't know what to say" look on her face. The crowd is thinning out. She looks toward her friends and then back at me.

"The thing is I don't date."

"You don't date?" I feel confused. How should I respond? I don't know what to say.

She looks perplexed, but then she reaches into her shoulder bag, pulls out a slip of paper and writes something on it.

"Here," she says and hands me the card. "Call me and I can explain."

I look down at the card. It's her cell number. I look up and she smiles sheepishly.

"Bye," Ana says, and before I know what's happened, she's walking out of the theater with her two friends.

"Nice crowd, Jackson."

It's Genevieve. I put Ana's number in my shirt pocket, and then turn around to face her.

"It's encouraging to see such a good turnout," she says, as a few of the remaining customers walk past us. Four or five people are still hanging out, talking in the salon, or looking at the movie posters by the front door.

I nod my head in agreement.

"And I heard a number of people say they liked having the theater open again, which is good to hear."

I notice Dad is talking to his movie critic friend by the front door. Then as the critic leaves, and with the theater finally empty, he joins us.

"A good night," he says, and then Genevieve mentions some of the positive comments she heard after the film ended.

"Very encouraging," Dad says, and now he's smiling. "Richard did a nice introduction, and he is going to put a review in his paper."

"There's this one man," Genevieve says, "an older man, who was so excited about the theater being open again, and he asked me so many questions that I had a hard time getting away from him."

"I'm sure that's just because you're so charming," Dad says. "And we can't complain about people being excited about us being open."

Genevieve shakes her head in acknowledgement. "Well, he seemed extraordinarily interested in the theater and also in you."

"In me?" Dad says.

"Yes."

"Oh, he's probably one of those historic building fanatics who wants to know how the Magic Lantern got landmark status. Did you recognize this guy?"

Genevieve shrugs. "He looked familiar, but I couldn't place him. He might be someone I've met at the film festival, someone who recognizes me as a programmer. But I'm not sure."

"I think he was the guy I ran into outside the theater about a month or ago, just after we opened," I say.

"Did you talk to him?" Genevieve asks.

"Not really. I was on my way to our meeting about getting this film."

Dad looks more interested. I think he's on the watch for supporters, people he might tap to do word-of-mouth advertising for the theater.

So I say, "I saw him out of the corner of my eye when he was talking to you, and I think he is the same guy. At least, he was wearing what looked like the same old suit he had on when I saw him outside the theater."

"You didn't say anything to him?" Dad says.

"Not much. He was just staring up at the theater marquee, and he asked me if the theater was really open like he couldn't believe it."

"He's probably a former customer who's just happy to see us open again," Dad says. "Those are the people I'm counting on to help us keep the doors open, until we can build a larger audience. We need those people, so if either of you see him again, give him my card, and let him know I'd be happy to talk with him."

Raji brings Dad the cash and receipts from the concession till, and I see Ellen waiting for me at the theater door. She is going to drive me home, so I don't have to wait for Dad or take the bus.

It has been a good weekend for the Magic Lantern. Dad is both happy and relieved. But what will happen as we get into November? Running this film for four weeks isn't a certain draw. Still, by the time Ellen drops me off at home, my mind is no longer on Dad or the theater or any of the customers. It's on the phone number I have in my shirt pocket, Ana's cell number. I wonder when I should call her.

Chapter 7

Café Talk

Ellen calls me early. She wants to meet at the Picasso Café after school. She won't say why, but I figure it has something to do with the Astronomy Club.

The Picasso is close to where I live, a short two-bus trip from Truman, in a middle-class neighborhood of older retirees and younger professionals and their kids, on a hill in northeast Seattle.

The café has an open, artsy feel with prints of Picasso paintings on the walls, and eight small tables big enough for two or maybe three people, along with a very small bar where a few people can stand and drink coffee, along with a couple of outside tables by the parking lot. It's a cool, grey day so we sit inside.

The place can be pretty busy, but it's late afternoon and it's easy to get a table. After we get coffee and sit down, Ellen, in typical Ellen fashion, gets right to what she wants to talk about.

"I may be working on the theater website," she says.

This idea catches me by surprise.

"I'm coming by the theater to talk with your dad about it on Saturday."

"You have the time to do that?"

"Sure. My parents will have to agree to letting me work a few hours a week. But the website stuff should be fun. It's a WordPress site, and from what Scott says, I will just be adding a few things and correcting a few others. Frankly, WordPress is fairly simple, and I'm surprised your dad can't make the necessary changes himself."

"Dad's an idea man. He uses email and he texts. But when it comes to designing anything, somebody else has always done the work."

I'm not sure how I feel about Ellen working at the Magic Lantern. Will that be fun or confusing for me? She has done programming, and she's always up for a challenge. I remember when we first learned that we could help identify distant galaxies by volunteering for Galaxy Zoo. While I was reluctant, she couldn't wait to get started. It was Ellen who pushed me to get involved, working with me until I got comfortable picking galaxies out of the pictures we had to review.

"Of course, he'll have his own ideas about what he wants and he'll want to look at whatever you do," I say, trying not to sound too sarcastic.

"Well, I can certainly make the site easier to navigate, and I'll also reload some of the film information and pictures to make it look better. But from looking at the website briefly Saturday night, while you were chatting up that girl Ana ... " She pauses to smile at me. "I think Scott will like about anything I do."

Was my interest that obvious when I was talking with Ana on Saturday night? I feel a little irritated.

"So, who was the girl?" Ellen asks.

"Her name is Ana Perez."

"She is a Latina, right? I didn't recognize her from Truman?"

"I guess," I say. "But I didn't ask her. She goes to St. Frances."

"A good Catholic school," Ellen remarks. "So, where did you two meet?"

"She came to the theater at the end of September because she was doing a story on our opening for the *Cascadian*."

"I remember that story. She works for the *Cascadian*?"

"She was a summer intern. She wants to be a writer, or maybe a journalist."

"Sounds like you two have something in common."

I'm getting a little tired of Ellen's questioning. But two can play at that game.

"So how is that guy you were interested in, the basketball player?"

"Oh, Charlie? Nothing really happened there," she says.

"I didn't know you were interested in sports, or guys who played sports."

"Actually, I met Charlie in AP Physics."

"Oh, that figures."

Ellen fidgets in her seat, and I can tell that we both want to move the conversation to something else, so I say, "Are you going to the star party on Saturday night?"

"If it doesn't rain. Anyway, do you have any ideas for things to change or add to the website?"

"Well, off the top of my head, the main complaint I've heard is that when people click on the picture of a particular film, they don't always get complete information, not the complete description, or even the film times. But I've never really seen that happen myself. The other thing some people have asked for is the ability to buy tickets online, but I know Dad doesn't want to do that."

"Oh," Ellen says, "why's that?"

"I don't think he wants to deal with the whole charge card, debit card thing."

She shakes her head. "If you are at the theater Saturday afternoon, I can show you what I'm doing and get your reactions."

"Oh, I'll be there. I've got to work both Saturday showings this week. I'll check with you after the matinee starts."

Then, out of the blue, Ellen brings up applying for college.

"A bunch of us are going to get together over the Christmas holidays to talk about visiting and applying to schools. You should join us."

"Isn't it a bit early for that? And who are 'us'?"

"Mostly kids from various AP classes, but there will be a few other kids there, too."

I know that crowd. They're all overachievers who are guaranteed to get into a good school, probably with financial aid.

"It's not too early. Most of us will be visiting schools this spring, and if you want to compete for the good schools, you need to be thinking ahead about things like application deadlines and financial aid."

"I doubt I'll be going to any of the really good schools," I say sarcastically.

"Don't you have at least a 3.0 GPA?" Ana asks.

I nod. It's closer to 2.9, but I don't mention that. "I'm not even sure I want to go to college."

"Why not? You're smart enough, and you'll have a lot more options for work if you get at least a BA—a lot more."

"That's fine for you. You know what you want to do, and you're really smart. But I have to work really hard to get B's, even in my best classes like writing and chemistry."

I pause and then add, "The only things I'm really interested in are astronomy and writing."

"You need to set some goals."

Easier said than done, I think. My parents just assume that college is in my future, but they have never pushed me very hard in terms of grades.

"You know neither of my parents finished college," I say, "and they both have done all right. And, now that I'm spending so much time at the Magic Lantern, who knows what is going to happen to my grades."

"I thought the deal was that they wanted you to work as long as it didn't affect your grades," Ellen says.

"That was supposed to be the deal, but ... " I just shrug.

Talking about homework makes me realize that I have a lot to do.

"And speaking of homework," I say. "I've got to go so I can get an hour of work in before dinner."

"Well, think about it, the holiday get-together I mean. It will be at my house. You really need to get serious about college."

We leave the café. Ellen is driving and I walk west four blocks to our big old house perched on the slope of a hill looking west across the north part of Seattle.

As I walk, I realize I'm pretty confused. I like thinking of myself as a citizen scientist, but going to college to major in science seems way beyond me. So where does that leave me in terms of college? Dad's got his big dream of making the Magic Lantern a success. But what are my dreams? I feel paralyzed when I try to make a decision about college. I can't even decide about calling Ana, and I realize that she is a lot like Ellen. Her biggest dream right now is to get into a good college.

Chapter 8

Black and White in Mexico

We're going to screen a Mexican film, *Roma*, the first two weeks in December. I couldn't believe it when Genevieve told us. This was the film we got from the distributor for running the Spike Lee film for four weeks. But who is going to come to see a Mexican film right before Christmas?

Attendance dropped off the fourth week we screened the Lee film, just as Dad had feared. *Puzzle*, the film that followed, didn't do much better. The audience was mostly women with a few couples. But Mom really enjoyed that film, which she described as "a small, quiet film about a housewife finding her calling."

Our audience increased a bit toward the end of *Puzzle*'s run. Dad felt that was because women who saw the film told their friends about it.

Dad, of course, was really excited about *Roma*, a film by a famous Mexican director, set in the early 1970s around Mexico City. He had me post the *New York Times* review, calling the film a "masterpiece of

52

memory" on the lobby wall across from the ticket window.[1]

I got more interested when Raji raved about another film that I loved, *Gravity*, and it turned out that Alfonso Cuarón, the director of *Roma*, was also the director of that film. I remember seeing *Gravity* with Dad and how amazed we were by the special effects and the overall excitement of the story.

Then Genevieve mentioned *Roma*'s beautiful black and white cinematography when I ran into her on Friday, the first night of the film's run.

I said, "You think people will come out to see a black and white film?"

"In some ways it's a throwback, but it really works for this story, and the reviews have been great."

I have to admit the *New York Times* review made it sound pretty interesting. But had I ever seen a black and white film I liked? *The Bride of Frankenstein* was the only film that came to mind. And why did I like that film? It was the setting and the story.

Despite my misgivings, the initial Friday and Saturday night showings of *Roma* were essentially sellouts. On Saturday night we actually had to turn two latecomers away. After the screenings, all I heard were positive comments from people leaving the theater.

"What a beautiful film."

"What a powerful story."

"Masterful evocation of time and place."

"Such a great performance by the actress who portrayed Cleo."

Today, the last Sunday of the *Roma* run, I decide to come in and catch the matinee because I'm not scheduled to work. After another big house on Saturday, the matinee audience is relatively small, and I end up sitting next to Genevieve, who's here to watch the film a second time.

By the time it is over, I tell Genevieve that I can see why the film is popular. It held my attention all the way through, and the black and white cinematography seemed different, more alive than what I've seen in the past.

All in all, it has been a good solid run, and Dad is happy. Tonight, he stands by the door saying good night to people as they leave, smiling and chatting with anybody who wants to talk. It feels so different from the way it felt when we stood there and listened to customers during the Woody Fest.

As the last customer leaves, Dad motions for everybody to come into the office. I want to go home, but now I can't leave.

"This is a big two weeks for us, a big two weeks for movies in Seattle," he says as the five of us, Genevieve, Raji, Ellen, Mom, and I, crowd into the office.

"I feel like having this film—and thanks to Genevieve for getting it for us—and getting this kind of turnout to see it here is going to be the best publicity we could get. People are going to be talking about the Magic Lantern from now on. Can we get this film back in the spring? I'm thinking about having a short Cuarón festival sometime, and it would be great to have this included."

"I'll look into it," says Genevieve. "But we need to be careful. Having too many retrospectives can give the Magic Lantern the reputation of being just another revival house."

"You think so?" Dad asks. "It would just be for a week."

Then before Genevieve can respond, he adds, "We're taking some chances here—I realize that. But it's all to move us toward our goal of making the Magic Lantern the go-to theater to see all kinds of movies."

Genevieve nods but doesn't say anything, and Dad quickly moves to another subject.

"Okay, on Tuesday we begin our holiday films. And check out our new theater website. Ellen," he nods toward her, "Jackson's friend, has added a few things and made it easier to navigate. Anything to say, Ellen?"

"Just take a look at the website, and let me know what you think and if there are other things you would like me to add," Ellen says.

"Oh, and Ellen will be joining our team here on Sundays. She'll be working the matinees, taking tickets, occasionally working concessions, and doing computer maintenance."

CHAPTER 9

Rules of Grammar

I've struggled to learn any language besides English. There isn't a language requirement at Truman. But there is a two-year requirement in most state and private colleges as part of their BA programs, and my parents, especially Mom, thought it would be good for me to take a language class.

"It will broaden you," she said. "And it will help you get interested in the world, and when you travel it's great to know another language, particularly if you go to Europe."

Mom is fluent in French. She lived in Paris for a summer as an art exchange student. And my parents spent their honeymoon traveling around France. I have the impression that Paris was a special place to her.

So, of course, I took French I as a sophomore. The teacher was this cute petite brunette with a sexy French accent, who turned out to be the toughest teacher I ever had.

Ms. Denis's class was all about learning the French rules of grammar, and I was lost from almost the first day. For Ms. Denis, the rules of grammar were the fundamentals, without which you could not learn to speak French properly. When I went to her for help about four weeks into the class, she was less than sympathetic.

"Are you working on your vocabulary four or five hours each week, Monsieur Ryan? If not, you won't get through this class."

Ms. Denis has high, high standards. She looked at the book where she had written the grades for everyone's quizzes. Then she added, "I can assign a second-year French student to help you, but you'll have to be willing to meet with that person regularly until you catch up. You are behind, and if you don't start working harder right now, you probably won't pass the class."

I knew she was probably right. But when I found out that Ms. Denis was known as the hardest grader at Truman, something no one had told me until after I'd signed up for her class, there was only one real option. I dropped out of French 1 and took an incomplete.

As the year came to an end, a confluence of needs—my frustration with learning a language and my desire to see Ana—merged, allowing me to do both.

I was nervous about calling Ana and uncertain about what to say if I did. I didn't really know much about her. We didn't attend the same school. As far as I knew, we had no common friends or common interests, except for writing. But still, I couldn't get her out of my mind.

When I did call her, she was busy and she made it clear that there was no possibility that we could meet for a date, even a coffee date. The rules her grandparents had set down were strict.

"And," she said, "I don't want to lie to them."

"Okay, I can understand that," I said. But it was still frustrating.

There was a long silence and then she asked, "What is your worst subject?"

"My worst subject?"

"You know, the one you really struggle with."

"French," I said. "I don't know if I'll ever be able to learn a foreign language."

There was a pause and then Ana said, "Switch to Spanish."

"Switch to Spanish?"

"Yes. When you register for the spring quarter, register for Spanish."

I was baffled. What was she talking about? "How will that help us get together?"

"I can't date. I have an agreement *con mi abuela y abuelo*. But I can study with other students, and I can volunteer as a tutor."

What was she getting at? "*Mi abuela and abuelo*?" I asked.

"My grandmother and grandfather," Ana said.

"You're suggesting you'll tutor me in Spanish?"

"Why not? You can get a head start on learning a language, and it will give us a reason to get together. Of course, we'll have to meet after school. But there is a nice little coffeehouse by Green Lake, and if it isn't too cold or rainy, maybe we can sit by the lake."

"And your abuela and abuelo will go along with this?"

"As long as I'm really trying to teach you some Spanish."

Wow. This wasn't exactly how I envisioned us getting together. But at least I was going to learn Spanish from a very pretty tutor.

Scott Ryan
Journal Entry
December 26, 2018

It's going to be Happy New Year for the Magic Lantern.

Roma *saved* us. The theater would have been in financial trouble without that film. With it we broke even for the four months we've been open. I keep looking at the figures to see if I've missed anything. I haven't gotten all the December bills, but I think we'll be okay unless we have an unexpected expense.

We've had some good crowds for a remake of Mary Poppins *which* has turned out to be a surprisingly good Christmas film, and I'm thinking we'll at least break even starting the new year with a film on Ruth Bader Ginsberg. She's very popular in liberal Seattle, particularly with women.

So, I won't have to dip into my emergency fund to keep us going into the new year. It helped that I was able to keep staffing costs so low. But I'm worried about January and February. They can be slow months attendance-wise

With the schedule set into March, I've got to try to hire another staff person. Ellen Hara is a good addition to the team, but she'll mostly be working on the website. And my family, especially Jackson, is going to revolt if I can't cut their hours. The problem, of course, is money. We need at least one other employee, at least one. But that person won't replace all of Jackson's hours. He seems ambivalent about going to college, so I had hoped he would get excited about helping me run the theater. I wonder if he'd like to be assistant manager? So far, he doesn't seem to care if the theater survives or not.

CHAPTER 10

Happy New Year

Raji went out of town for fourteen days in the middle of December, so I had to work additional hours at the theater, which meant that I had to miss another monthly star party at Swanson Park.

Ellen said it was spectacular, a perfect night for stargazing, clear and cold. Everybody else in the Astronomy Club was there, because that Saturday was the height of the annual Geminid meteor shower. Looking north through her small telescope, she counted thirty meteors in less than two hours. Members of the Seattle Astronomy Society let Astronomy Club members look through their big telescopes. They drank hot chocolate—both Ellen and Marc brought big thermos bottles—and had a great time. What a bummer, I missed the whole thing.

I'm getting really frustrated with the amount I'm working. I don't have time to do anything fun, and I'm barely getting my homework done.

When I see the films scheduled for the first two months of 2019, I again scratch my head and wonder.

We will be screening a rom-com spoof for the first two weeks in January—that's okay. But then two foreign films, one a Polish love story set in the late 1940s and filmed in black and white, and the other a Lebanese story about a 12-year-old boy growing up in the Beirut slums.

"Scott likes to show critically acclaimed, quality films," Genevieve says, when I ask her why she scheduled these two films.

"These films are critically acclaimed?"

"As a matter of fact, both are nominated for the Oscar for Best Foreign Film."

"Do you think we'll get an audience for these films?"

"We'll see," is Genevieve's response.

So, I guess that is the strategy. Show these two rather obscure foreign language nominees in the run up to the Oscars?

The rom-com brought in a decent crowd, mostly women, and mostly on the weekends. We started running previews for the two foreign films right after Christmas. Both the local papers reviewed the films, and Dad had Ellen add a special website page on them, including reviews. Of course, we posted all the good reviews we could find across from the office.

The film community did turn out for the German film, *Cold War*. Two movie critics, the former owner of a film bookstore on Capitol Hill, a couple of well-known local actors, a retired screenwriter, and a large group of people who call themselves "supporters" of the Magic Lantern showed up for screenings on the first weekend of its run. After that first weekend though, the crowds got smaller.

"This is such a good film, old-fashioned storytelling combined with beautiful cinematography. I thought after the first weekend that word of mouth would keep people coming even during the week," Dad said to me on the final Friday night of the German film's run. "Now I think maybe January is just a tough month to get people out to the movies. People are tapped out after the holidays. They're getting back to work and don't have the time or money to see a movie."

He paused and then added. "You know your mom and I would always go to the movies during the winter. We saw some of our best films in January, February, and March."

"That's was the past," I wanted to say. But I didn't.

On the last Sunday of its run, I decided to see *Cold War*. The previous Saturday night we had close to two hundred people in the seats, but on Sunday we were back well under fifty people for each show.

I wasn't sure I'd like it. After all, who wants to see a black and white film set in Eastern Europe after World War Two. But after seeing and liking *Roma*, I figured I'd take a chance, and what a surprise! I was totally transported to a different place and time. Again, the black and white photography seemed just right for the time and the story, which was really just an old-fashioned romance.

Unfortunately, the follow-up Lebanese film turned out to be a bomb.

"It's really a festival film," Genevieve told me when I saw her on the Friday night the film opened. It had been a cold day and we had gotten about an inch of snow, so Dad conjectured that the sparse crowd that evening was due to the weather.

But our first Saturday night crowd is only a little better. Dad is selling tickets and I notice he has stopped to talk with a tall man who looks familiar. For a moment, I think it's that strange man I first saw standing outside the theater in September, and then again at the Saturday night showing of *Roma*. But when he turns toward me, I realize it is somebody else completely—Uncle Peter.

Peter Bergmeier is Mom's brother and a Unitarian minister. He is tall, a six-footer, and solidly built. He is with three other people, one of whom I recognize as being from the church. The other two, a man and a woman, look Middle Eastern. I sell a customer two big bags of popcorn, and when I look up again Peter is standing at the concession stand.

"Hi, Jackson. Having a slow evening?"

"I think it's the weather," I say, channeling Dad.

"Yes, it was icy driving here. But a film like this should still have a bigger audience."

I don't know quite how to respond. Is he lamenting that not enough people are interested in films about poor people struggling in the Middle East, or is he suggesting that Dad isn't doing a good job of marketing the film?

There is a pause and then Peter asks, "Are you working here a lot?"

"Mostly on Thursday and Friday nights, and Saturdays."

"Wow, that's quite a bit. How's school going?"

"Okay." I don't want to say too much to Peter. I like him, but he and Dad don't always see eye to eye on the church. We attended his church for a while, and I was in the coming-of-age program. But about two years ago Dad lost interest, and then Mom and I quit going regularly. Dad said there wasn't much spiritual in the church anymore, and that it was mostly about activism and being angry at the world. And anyway, activism was part of his work.

Occasionally, Mom will still attend a service now and then, mainly to support her brother. I miss a few of the coming-of-age kids, but Ellen and Carlos are the only two I've really stayed connected with.

"I mentioned to Scott that we are having a big immigrant justice program the second Sunday in March, and I wanted to invite all three of you to come."

"Right now, Dad is totally involved in running the Magic Lantern," I say.

"I can see that. But it shouldn't stop your family from learning about our shameful national policy toward immigrants," Peter says. "And, a couple of your old friends from the coming-of-age group will be helping with the program. So, it would be a chance for you to catch up with them at the coffee hour."

I feel pressured to say something, but luckily, at that moment a woman comes out of the screening room to buy popcorn and a couple of sodas.

"I've got to get back to work," I tell Peter.

"Yes, and I've got to get a seat before the show starts. Nice to see you again, Jackson, and I hope I'll see you at church in March."

After the film starts, I walk back into the office. Dad is counting the tickets sold and not looking very happy.

"Damn weather," he says as I walk in. "We need to catch a break from this weather."

"You think it's the weather?"

"If people are on the fence about seeing a movie, Jackson, the weather can make a difference if they come or stay home."

Maybe that's true, at least partially. But even though it got good reviews, I've heard a few customers call it pretty dark and depressing. It's a serious film, and not a real crowd pleaser. So, I wonder how many people are really waiting at home for the weather to improve before they come to the theater.

"I don't know," says Dad. "You'd think people would enjoy coming inside to see a challenging movie especially when it's cold outside."

Then after a pause he adds, "Well, not to worry. I think we'll pick up a bigger audience as word of mouth about this film gets out to our regulars, and if that doesn't happen, we've got the Oscar-nominated shorts coming next, and people like the shorts."

Unfortunately, we didn't get a break in the weather. Instead, things got a lot worse.

PART 2

Keeping the Faith

Chapter 11

All Things Old and Wonderful

The last weekend of the Lebanese film it snowed. We got over six inches of snow on Friday. School closed early, and I helped Dad shovel off the steps and the sidewalk by the theater. Only ten people showed up for the seven o'clock show. Another inch and a half of snow fell on Saturday, but for the Saturday matinee we had our biggest audience, about thirty-five people. I guess some people just wanted to get out of the house.

Three and a half inches fell on Sunday, enough to slow everything in the city to a crawl. Monday, it snowed again, adding about six more inches to the total, and even though it turned to rain in the evening, our audiences for the remaining three days of the film's run were tiny. The local media called the event a "snowpocalypse." For the Magic Lantern it was a disaster.

With the Oscar ceremony coming at the end of February, Genevieve had scheduled the two 2019 Oscar-nominated short films programs, or shorts, to follow the two foreign-nominated films. One of the shorts programs covered the animated shorts nominees, and the other covered live-action shorts nominees. The shorts were to run right through the Oscars, and Dad's prediction that these would "get an audience" proved, at least partially, right.

Every year the shorts programs have a different mix of short films and a different feel—sometimes light, sometimes dark or moody, sometimes startling.

"The shorts programs have something for everyone," Dad told the staff. "You may not like everything in a shorts program, but you're bound to see one or two shorts you do like."

This year, the live action shorts were mostly dark and edgy, while the animated shorts were either light and funny or sad. But both programs attracted a good audience, and many people bought tickets for both shows. I caught both programs and liked the animated best.

As I'm walking out of the animated shorts program on Friday afternoon, heading to concessions to help Raji, someone taps me on my shoulder from behind.

"Excuse me."

I turn around and am face-to-face with a tall, middle-aged man with a stoop. I recognize him immediately. He's the guy I first saw outside the Magic Lantern in September and whom I've caught glances of again at various screenings.

"Excuse me, but don't you work here?"

"Yes, I'm the owner's son." I refuse to call myself the assistant manager.

Hearing this, the man seems to brighten up. "Oh, good, very good." He reaches out and hands me a business card.

"My name is Mr. Belvedere."

I look at the card and read:

Winston Belvedere, All Things Old and Wonderful.

"I want to thank your father, Mr. Ryan, and you, too, for continuing to show the shorts programs. My wife and I would come to see them every year, and I was afraid that when the theater closed, I'd never be able to see them again."

I glance back at the card. After "All Things Old and Wonderful," it says, "antiques and collectibles." This Winston Belvedere must be a dealer.

"Well, we're glad you liked the shorts. There's something for everybody in the shorts programs," I say. I'm sounding just like Dad now. "But you know, you could just stop by the office and talk to him yourself. I know he'd like to meet you."

"Oh, I'm in a bit of a hurry. I'm meeting a special customer at my shop in five minutes. Maybe the next time I'm here," Mr. Belvedere says. "But thank you, and please thank your dad." Now he's smiling.

I notice that customers coming in for the second show are lining up at the concessions stand. I need to help Raji. I turn back to hand the man his business card, but he's gone. I don't see Mr. Belvedere anywhere. So, I stuff the card in my pocket. I'll give it to Dad later.

On Saturday afternoon, the day before the Oscars, I find the card in my pocket and give it to Dad while he is standing at the door, talking to customers coming in for the matinee. He glances at it and says, "Do you know this guy?"

"He's the man I first saw outside the theater right after we'd opened, the guy Genevieve mentioned as talking her ear off at one of the showings of the Spike Lee film."

"So, why didn't you ask him to stop by the office? I always like to chat with our regulars."

"I did, but when I turned around to see how Raji was doing at concessions, Mr. Belvedere just vanished."

"Vanished, huh. Well, if you see him again, would you bring him to the office?"

Dad can be so irritating sometimes.

I have quit trying to guess which films are going to get a good audience and which are going to flop.

During the shorts fest, Dad gave Ellen, Raji, and me packs of little yellow cards that he wanted us to hand out to customers. "Suggestion cards," he called them. Any cards we got back, he would look at, maybe write a comment on, and then he'd have me post them on a bulletin board he was putting up on one side of the lobby.

"Just looking for movie suggestions," Dad said when I asked why we were doing this.

"You never know when some customer might have an idea for a film he or she has seen or read about that possibly we could show, or has some other idea for publicity we might want to use."

This seems like an idea of limited value to me. After all, what do we have a film programmer for?

"You're missing the point," Raji says, when I talk with him later at concessions. "It's just basic market- ing. You get the customers involved in giving the management ideas, or at least that's the idea you give them. Scott can use or not use the suggestions, but he can post some of the interesting and positive comments. And people, some people anyway, will feel more involved."

Simple marketing? "I think improving the website would be more effective," I say.

"Sure, positive comments need to go on the website," Raji continues, "but I bet he's already thinking of that."

Despite his success in running a business, in many ways it seems to me that Dad is living in the past. The more I know about the movie scene, the more it seems that technology is the future, and trying to save old-fashioned theaters like the Magic Lantern with old-fashioned ideas like suggestion cards is probably a waste of time.

On the last Sunday of the shorts program, Dad gets all the staff together, including Mom, in the early afternoon.

"I want everybody to get involved in publicizing our spring schedule," he says.

Ellen immediately offers to set up a Facebook page for the theater, and at Dad's request she agrees to add a suggestion form and positive comments to the Magic Lantern website. Raji will find some places on the university campus to post film schedule flyers. Even Mom is going to contact some of the neighborhood weekly newspapers to see if they will add an article about the spring schedule.

But when it's my turn to commit to doing something, I balk.

"I don't have the time. I'm just getting my homework done, and I barely survived my finals at the end of the quarter because I didn't have enough time on weekends to study."

That's true. If Ellen hadn't helped me cram for my math final, I probably wouldn't have passed. As it was, I barely got a B-minus.

Now everybody is looking at me. But I don't care. I can't spend any more time doing things for the theater.

"Well, Jackson," Dad says. I can tell by his tone of voice that he isn't happy with me. "I guess we can cut you a bit of slack because you're in the theater a lot already. But you are the assistant manager, and I'll still want you to mention coming attractions to any customers you talk to. You should also mention the website, as well as the Facebook page once it's up and running. We all need to be involved in promoting the theater."

Then, before I can ask how I got to be the assistant manager, Mom adds, "Maybe the three of us should talk about Jackson's schedule when we get a chance."

There is a pause. It isn't clear how Dad is going to react to Mom's suggestion. He's not smiling, but then he says, "Okay, I think that's a good idea."

CHAPTER 12

The Spanish Tutor

Ana and I can't get together for a study date until February. Ana is focusing on her classes, along with her other school activities, until she's comfortable that she's not behind.

I'm not sure what I expected, but the day we meet is cold, so we end up sitting in a little coffeehouse a couple blocks from Green Lake, and we mostly talk about ... well, Spanish. Then, after almost an hour of reviewing tense and verb endings, she finally asks me about my writing.

"I've been writing since I was a kid," I say. "I surprised my parents by writing a science fiction novel when I was in fifth grade."

"A whole novel?"

"Well, a short novel. At least I called it a novel. It was about forty pages."

She smiles. "What was it called?"

"A Mars Adventure. It was called A Mars Adventure."

"What was the story about?"

"The first colonists land on Mars, they plant some food, and then they're attacked by Martian zombies."

She laughs. It's a quiet laugh, but I like it. "Sounds like something a fifth-grade boy would want to read."

"That's right," I say. Now we're both smiling. "I actually sent it to a publisher."

"Really? What did they say?"

"That it had been done before. But they wished me luck in my writing career."

"So, is that what you write about now?"

"Not really," I say. "Now mostly I write stories."

"About?"

"Mostly about kids in high school."

"Can I read one sometime?"

The only person who has read any of my stories is Ellen. She wants me to set up an online writing blog where I can post a few. But I'm not ready for that. In fact, I haven't finished anything since I started spending all my free time working at the Magic Lantern.

"Well maybe, after I learn enough Spanish to write one in Español." There's that smile again. I really don't know much about this girl, but I sure like that smile.

"So, what do you write?"

"Some stories, some poetry. Mostly about my family and about my dreams."

"So, can I read one of your stories?" I ask, making it sound a bit like a challenge.

"Maybe ... maybe when you've learned enough Spanish to get through the non-English parts."

She's not intimidated or defensive at all about her writing.

We're making some kind of connection. I'm not sure exactly what it is, but I feel both anxious and excited. And then out of the blue Ana has to leave.

Later, when I'm alone, I'm having trouble thinking about my homework because I keep thinking about Ana and her smile. I'd like to write a story about today and call it "The Spanish Tutor." But I feel like I'm in uncharted territory, trying to get to know a girl very different from me. I guess that's what the story would be about, getting to know somebody new, somebody special. Of course, I'd have to leave out the zombies.

C̲HAPTER 13

Surprise! Surprise!

Dad is in a meeting with Genevieve when I come in for my Friday shift. It's March 1st, the day after the last showing of the shorts program, and the new film, a Spanish language thriller, starts today. The weather has gotten almost spring-like, and Dad's hoping that will help, not hurt, attendance.

"Hey, Jackson, come into the office, will you?" It's Dad.

In the office, I notice a younger woman, very thin with blond hair, wearing a flowered blouse and grey jeans, sitting between Dad and Genevieve.

I smile at Genevieve who smiles back.

"Great news," Dad tells me. "We're going to be a festival venue this year."

"Wow," I say. "How did that happen?"

Before Dad can answer, the young woman does.

"Hi, Jackson, I'm Mandy Rose, a program coordinator for the film festival. We had a theater back out of being a venue. We knew Genevieve was working for your dad, so we checked with her, and I'm here to finalize the dates and the films you'll be showing."

"We're going to have the festival here for twenty-three days?" How is this going to affect me? The festival usually runs through finals week.

"Actually, for just one week," Dad says.

I don't know what to say. I never thought about the festival being at the Magic Lantern. But Dad is definitely excited.

"That's great," I say finally. And I know this will be good for the theater, but I'm also wondering how it will affect my work schedule.

Dad knows what I'm thinking. "And Jackson, unless you want to become a festival volunteer, this means you'll have the week off."

I feel a sudden sense of relief, a whole full week off. "Which week is that going to be?"

"It's the first week of the festival," Mandy Rose says. "May 17th through the 23rd."

That's even better. I'll be able to get a head start on studying for finals, something I really need to do. "Will it be just Dad and a bunch of festival volunteers working that week?"

"Actually," says Mandy Rose, "we'll bring in a festival venue manager, so Scott can have the week off too."

Before I can ask any more questions, Dad jumps in and says that he's going to have a meeting to discuss this with staff after he has more details.

"So please don't say anything to other staff yet about the Magic Lantern being a festival venue."

But despite Dad's request, when Raji and I are working at concessions just after the seven o'clock show starts, he asks me how my work schedule is affecting my studies, and I blurt out that I'm happy I'll have the whole third week in May off.

"That's fantastic," Raji says. "But how is Scott going to staff the theater if you're not working at all?"

"I really can't say any more, and don't ask Scott. He'll be talking to staff when he gets ready."

Of course, this only makes Raji more curious. So, when I go to check the bathrooms and the concession area is empty, he goes to the office to talk with Dad. And when I see him again, he's bouncing around with nervous energy and smiling.

"What did Dad tell you?"

"Just that we're going to be a festival venue for a week. He wouldn't give me any details. He says he'll talk with staff later."

Then he adds, "But I'd love to work the film festival."

From what I heard at the meeting with Mandy Rose, it sounds like only festival volunteers will be able to work in the festival venues. But I don't tell that to Raji. Dad will explain what's going to happen to all the staff when he has more details. For now, I've already said too much. I'm not saying anything else to Raji or any of the other staff members.

When I see Dad after the show, I wonder if he'll be angry about my letting something slip to Raji about being a festival venue.

But all he says is, "Please don't tell anybody else about us being a festival venue until I make a formal announcement."

"The flowering trees are starting to bloom," Mom says on our way to church. It is the second Sunday in March and despite the grey sky and the threat of rain, spring is on the way.

In the past, Dad would be up and working out in the yard, preparing the gardens for planting on a Sunday morning in March. But today he's still asleep when we leave.

Dad is the one who likes to work outside, while Mom spends much of her free time in her small studio on the converted back porch. She likes it because it gives her loads of light.

Peter Bergmeier's church is a little over a mile from our house. With so much of our time and energy going to other things, mostly the theater, we haven't gone to church in almost a year. In the past, we've often walked, but not today.

The parking lot is almost full for the 9:30 service when we arrive.

"Hey, Jackson," someone says as we walk in the side door by the parking lot. It is Carlos Sanchez. I know him from the church's coming-of-age program.

"Hi, Carlos. How are you doing?"

"I'm fine. What's up with you? I haven't seen you for a while."

"Yeah," I say. "Been busy. Dad has reopened that rundown theater in the U District, the one just east of the freeway. And I'm working there some week nights and on weekends, which doesn't leave much time for me to do anything else but schoolwork—."

Mom interrupts. "Hi, Carlos, nice to see you."

Then she turns to me and says, "Jackson, I'll save you a seat on the right side of the sanctuary. Please try to get there before the singing starts."

I know Carlos from church and baseball. He goes to St. Francis, and I'm tempted right away to ask him if he knows Ana. But immediately the conversation turns to baseball.

Carlos would like to turn pro. I'll always be a second-string outfielder with a good arm and a so-so bat. But Carlos is a natural. After we met at the church, we realized we both loved playing the game, so we got together after our freshman season, just to practice at a public field by the community center in northeast Seattle. We even went to a couple baseball games together the year the Seattle team made it to the World Series.

"Are you going out for baseball?" he asks.

Immediately I feel upset, not at Carlos but at Dad.

"I went to both of the team tryouts last week," I say with a sigh. "I think I can probably make the team, but the question is, will I be able to play?"

"Why's that? Do you work on Fridays?"

"All Fridays and most weekends."

"That's too bad. Half of our games are on Fridays in the late afternoon."

"I know," I say. "I talked with Dad, but he won't promise me any time off until he can hire more staff, and I don't see that happening any time soon."

"Are you getting paid for this work?" Carlos asks.

"Minimum wage. But it's just taking up too much of my time. All I do is work, go to school, and then do homework."

"That's a bummer, but I guess you have to help your family."

"Yeah, Dad's started calling me his assistant manager."

"Congratulations," Carlos says.

"I hate it. It seems like it's mostly a way to justify how much I'm working."

"Well, look on the bright side—you get to see a lot of movies."

"That's true," I say. But that doesn't make me feel any better.

"I'm in the service," Carlos says as we get to the stairs that lead up to the church's main floor and the sanctuary.

"Oh," I say, surprised. "So, what's the service about?"

"Immigration, but with a focus on the Dreamers."

Carlos is a Dreamer? He seems just like all the other kids I know. Certainly, just like all the other kids I have met at church.

The chimes that sound the Call to Service ring. Now everybody who has been having coffee or chatting streams into the sanctuary.

"Talk to you later, Jackson," Carlos says, and he immediately heads straight down the main aisle toward the nave.

The sanctuary looks almost full, and at first, I don't see Mom.

But someone is waving at me from the middle of the center section of seats. It's Ellen and I wave back. Then I turn to look again for Mom, and this time I spot her on the right side of the sanctuary, just where she said she would be.

When the chimes ring again, the congregation settles down and the offering plate is passed around. Then the choir director leads the congregation in an opening song. At this church, the songs are almost never about God and seldom about faith. They are about justice, equality, and nature. When we first started attending, I remember thinking it was very odd to hear all these protest songs, what Mom called "ballads of the oppressed," at church.

"Today most Unitarians are humanists," Dad told me once. As if that would clear up my confusion about the music. He also said that Peter didn't have much of a sense of humor. But I don't think Dad came to church for the music, or to hear the minister tell jokes. He came because, for a while, he thought the church was going to be a force for environmental change in the city. But that didn't happen, or it didn't happen fast enough, or he just lost interest in doing churchy stuff after he decided to throw himself into opening the Magic Lantern.

Mom is the one who likes to sing, Mom and I. She has a great soprano voice, and she sang semi-professionally sometime in the past. I'm not sure when or with what groups. We spent two years in the family choir, a choir just for families or members of families in the church. Carlos and his sister were in that choir with us. I'm not sure why we quit. Maybe Mom's business took too much of her time, or maybe Dad's lagging interest made it harder for Mom to feel comfortable about going.

Today the opening song, by someone called Holly Near, is about being a gentle and an angry people. It's very singable. But I can't quite figure out how it's going to connect with a sermon on the Dreamers.

After the song, a young woman, maybe in her late twenties, presents a reading from the hymnal:

This is the mission of our faith:
To teach the fragile art of hospitality;
To revere both the critical mind and the generous
   heart;
To prove that diversity need not mean divisiveness;

And to witness to all that we must hold the whole world in our hands.[2]

Then Peter, in his black gown and multi-colored stole, steps up to the lectern. After greeting the congregation, he pauses for a moment to look over the congregation before he launches into his sermon.

Peter is in his element when he is preaching. Although he seldom mentions religion, he clearly sees his church as being on the side of the angels, and treats every sermon like a call to action for the congregation.

"America has always been of two minds about immigrants. On one hand, we have invited them to come here because we appreciate their energy and work ethic. On the other hand, we have targeted them as scapegoats for most of our social problems. Crime and poverty have been blamed on immigrants, and they have been criticized for not assimilating quickly enough into America's dominant culture, for not being able to speak English, and for having quirky or un-American customs or dress.

"America has a history of treating immigrants poorly, even when we have used them as cheap labor to do jobs that other Americans don't want to do.

"Being anti-immigrant has often been and still is a political tool. And attempts to reform our immigration system have been repeatedly derailed by calls to close our borders and increase deportations.

"Many innocent people, fleeing terror and repression in their home countries, have become trapped in this dysfunctional immigration system. Today the most tragic of these are the young people known as Dreamers."

I notice Carlos sitting with three other young people at the end of the first row in front of the chancel.

There is another guy who looks a bit older than the others and two girls. I can only see their backs, but I have this feeling that I know one of the girls.

"The Dreamers are young undocumented immigrants who were brought to the United States as children," says Peter. "The term takes its name from the bill in Congress, but it has a double meaning referring both to the undocumented youth and to their big hopes and dreams for a better future as American citizens. The Dreamers have lived and gone to school here. Some are old enough to have jobs and to pay taxes, and most identify as American."

"Today we have four young people with us who are Dreamers. They are here to tell us their individual stories and talk about the challenges they face, being undocumented in the United States."

Carlos and the other Dreamers stand up. I know I've seen the girl standing next to Carlos before. Is it Ana? I can't be sure. Then everybody except Carlos sits down while he walks up onto the chancel and joins the minister at the podium.

"Our first Dreamer is someone many of you know," Peter says. "Carlos Sanchez and his family are members of our church, and he is the youngest member of our Immigrant Justice Team."

Carlos smiles at the congregation. Then, for a moment, he fumbles with a piece of paper—I assume it's his notes—trying to put it down securely on the lectern in front of him. Finally, he looks back up at the congregation and speaks.

"My family came to the U.S. six years ago when the Obama administration instituted a new program called DACA that made it easier for undocumented immigrants to stay in the country. My father works as a carpenter, and my sister is going to college at the U and hopes eventually to become a doctor.

"My father initially struggled to get work, but my parents taught us that life would be better in the U.S. than it had been for them in El Salvador. Members of this church, some of them immigrants themselves, helped us use government assistance programs and get health care."

He mentions the coming-of-age program and the friends he has made at the church.

"Then in 2017, the new administration tried to kill DACA. My parents became scared. I heard them talking at night when they thought I was asleep. Initially, I didn't understand why, although I had heard about some of the bad things that had happened in El Salvador before we left. But then an uncle told me that he knew people who had been picked up and deported by ICE, the government's immigration office, and I began to understand that we could face deportation and even worse if the new administration was successful. For the first time, I understood that not all Americans welcomed immigrants like me. My dreams are to go to college and to play baseball, but my biggest dream is to become an American citizen."

As he finishes, the congregation spontaneously stands and applauds.

"Bravo, Carlos," yell members of the coming-of-age group.

Carlos' eyes are wet as he walks back to his seat. But my eyes are on the back of the girl who is next to him in line, and I realize what's so familiar about her. It's her green dress, the one she wore the night I saw her at the theater.

Peter introduces Ana, and she faces the congregation.

She smiles and launches right into her story. There's no timidity or self-consciousness.

"I came to America twelve years ago with my father. We lived in the Lake City area in a small apartment. My father had been a journalist in Honduras and had received a death threat, probably from the military, because they objected to his investigations into the killings of certain environmental and labor leaders. He continued to write for some newspapers and blogs after we came to this country, sometimes being critical of United States policies toward Honduras, but his main job was as a waiter in a fancy restaurant downtown.

"A few years after we got here, the immigration people came to his restaurant to check the immigration status of the workers. Something about my father's green card raised a red flag with the investigators. I don't know all the details. Eventually, they let him go. But after that he became increasingly afraid that he might be picked up again and deported. He even quit his writing.

"I guess to shield me and let me live as normal a life as possible, I started living with my grandparents in their house north of Green Lake, while he stayed in the tiny apartment in Lake City. Then two years ago he was stopped for speeding, and he was taken into custody. My grandparents knew a local immigration attorney who agreed to help. She met with my father and it looked like he was going to be released."

Ana's demeanor changes and she's not smiling anymore.

"But three weeks later we got a phone call. Father had been deported after a sham hearing in front of an immigration judge. The judge said he was in no danger of being killed if he returned to Honduras."

Now her voice cracks.

"He was taken in by old friends when he arrived in Tegucigalpa, but a few days later he disappeared."

Ana stops. I wonder if she's going to break down, but instead there's a fierceness in what she says next.

"My father is still missing. We don't know what happened to him. But we won't forget him, and we won't forget his dream of coming to America to build a better life and to work for justice in Honduras. Thank you for inviting us to come and speak to you as Dreamers."

Ana's head is down as she walks off the transept, but when she gets to her seat she looks up and our eyes meet. Her eyes brighten, but I can feel her sadness.

Ana is a Dreamer. So many questions pop into my mind. Is she afraid she'll be deported? Will she ever find her father? Ana is a Dreamer—that's all I can think about, so I don't hear much of the final two testaments.

Alfredo came to the United States to attend college and just stayed after he had to drop out of school. Claudia's family came across the border from Mexico after her hometown became a battleground for rival drug gangs.

After the four testaments, Peter has some closing words

"What has happened to the Dreamers makes us angry, and it should. It is a violation of American values and a violation of our values as a church."

The choir sings a final song, and the accompanist plays music as we all walk out of the sanctuary. Just outside the main door the Dreamers are standing with the minister, shaking hands and talking with members of the congregation.

"Wow!" I say to Carlos. "How come you never said anything?"

"What would I have said? I'm just trying to be a normal sixteen-year-old guy. I don't even see myself as being Salvadoran anymore, I see myself as being American."

"This must be awful scary."

"It is now, but none of us want to leave."

Ana is standing next to Carlos. She smiles as I reach her.

"Hi," I say. "I didn't know."

"How could you," she replies. "I never told you."

"Yeah. This is amazing, and you never said anything."

"It's not the kind of thing you tell to just everybody, although I'm not ashamed of it."

"I'm just an 'everybody'?"

She smiles. "No, you're my Spanish student." She pauses and then adds, "And I hope my new friend."

I don't know how to respond to that.

"But anyway, you know now. So, what do you think?"

I don't know what to say. Can I even understand what she has been through? The fear, with her father gone missing while she is living in a country that considers her illegal?

But I have to respond, so I say the first thing that comes into my mind.

"Are you afraid of being deported?"

"No, there are lots of people helping us, and we're going to fight, and keep fighting."

I should have expected that kind of answer. But still I wonder if sometimes she isn't just scared.

"I can believe that," I say.

I can tell that other folks behind me want to talk with Ana.

"We can talk more at your next Spanish lesson," she says.

I smile and then add, "I think it's fantastic what you're doing."

For the first time since I've known her, it seems like she doesn't quite know to respond.

"Thanks," she says.

Scott Ryan
Journal Entry
March 11, 2019

It's a real coup for us to be selected as a Film Festival venue, even if it's just for one week. To rent our theater for one week, the festival will pay us $2,500, and we'll get all the money from concessions. That should help us move into the summer in a strong financial position.

I hope everybody will buy into the Summer of Film idea. But all the staff need to be on board, and I'm worried about Jackson. I know Genevieve has some reservations about filling our summer schedule with too many older films and mini-festivals, and she favors the event being six weeks rather than eight. But we need to make a big splash this summer, and the Summer of Film is how we are going to do it. I'm leaning toward an eight- or nine-week event, at least from the July 4th weekend through Labor Day. And whatever we decide, I know Genevieve will get us the best films she can.

Chapter 14

Breathing Space

March comes in like a lion, weather-wise, and after a few days of mild weather, we start to get every kind of weather imaginable—sun, heavy rain and sometimes hail, fog, cold mornings occasionally turning into 60-degree days. With a hint of spring in the air and more daylight in the evening, attendance at the Magic Lantern increases.

We're showing the new *Captain Marvel* film the second two weeks of March. It isn't exactly a remake of the comic book but more like an original story, and it did particularly well the first week of its run.

On the first Sunday of its run, Dad, Mom, and I have an impromptu meeting about my schedule. Mom says she thinks we need to look at ways we can cut my hours.

"I agree," says Dad. "I am going to interview two college students next week, and I hope to hire one or both to work on Thursday nights and take some of the weekend shifts."

This will really help once the new people are hired and trained, but it doesn't answer all my questions because Raji mentioned to me that he had asked Dad for some time off around Memorial Day. That's right after our week as a festival venue and right before finals.

"So, what's my schedule going to be like after our week as a festival venue, the period around Memorial Day, and just before finals? Have you thought about that?"

Dad frowns. "Well, don't forget you'll have most of the festival venue week off. But I may need you to work a few additional shifts over the holiday weekend. Anyway, before you get upset about scheduling, let's wait and see how many people I'm able to hire and when they can work."

This seems to placate Mom, but I wonder. What does Dad mean by 'a few additional shifts'? Still, I feel like I can't complain. If he actually hires additional staff, that will be great, and having the festival week off is the best news I've gotten since the Magic Lantern opened. Maybe I can attend the May star party, or maybe I can even talk Ana into doing something besides a study date. It doesn't seem fair that her grandparents won't let her date, but I have a feeling that dating isn't Ana's first priority either.

"The other thing that I want to mention," Dad says, "is that I'm planning to have some more film retrospectives or mini-festivals over the summer."

This surprises me. I thought he had given up on this idea after the Woody Fest fiasco and Genevieve's strong resistance to his scheduling another mini-festival over the winter.

"So far, we've been doing okay, with some good programming and more publicity. And being a film festival venue is going to help us financially.

"But we still haven't differentiated ourselves from the other theaters in North Seattle. Being a festival venue should help with that. We need to leverage that event to expand our visibility. So, I'm envisioning what I call a Summer of Film at the Magic Lantern, a time when we'll have a few big films, one or two mini-festivals, maybe a film poster auction, and hopefully some workshops."

"Have you talked with Genevieve about this?" Mom asks.

I wonder if she's thinking what I'm thinking, that this is Dad's big idea, but that Genevieve can rein him in if she objects.

"We've talked, and she's going to see if she can get us a couple of big films for July and August."

"So, what does she think about more mini-festivals?"

"Well, she agrees with me that we need to do something special over the summer. We're a new theater, and the summer can be a slow time, particularly after the film festival. I wish we could have gotten a second week as a festival venue. But we're lucky to be able to host the festival at all."

Mom looks like she's thinking this over and then she asks, "But will being a festival venue for just a week help the theater financially?"

"Yes, definitely," Dad replies. "What I'm talking about for the summer will be more like retrospectives than mini-fests. And we need everybody on staff to be enthusiastic about the Summer of Film and to share that enthusiasm with customers as we get closer to the summer."

Dad looks over at me, and I can tell that this comment is directed at me. Then he adds, "Because it's not an exaggeration to say that the success of this could make or break this theater."

What a startling comment. Mom shifts in her chair and looks a bit worried. Has Dad gone crazy?

"Anyway, I want to have a June film calendar available by the end of April. When I have more details about films and events, I'll talk with the whole staff. But I wanted to give you both a heads-up about what I'm planning."

Dad seems to be set on this Summer of Film idea. But he also seems nervous, and after what happened in October, he has reason to be.

Screening the *Captain Marvel* movie was a big success, with full houses both weekends of its run. But even more important to me is that Ana has booked a meeting room at the northeast branch of the library for our next Spanish tutoring session. I just wish we could get a bit beyond my learning Spanish.

"You realize that I'm listing this as a volunteer activity, don't you?" she says when I ask why we're meeting at a library and not a coffee shop.

"Well, actually, I didn't," I say, trying to sound very in control. "But if that's the case, you need to teach me some Spanish."

So, for about a half hour we talk about Spanish verbs. We go over some simple phrases, and she talks to me a little about verb tenses. Then she hands me a couple of exercise sheets.

"Do these at home, and then we can go over them the next time I see you."

With that, the conversation turns to her immigration status and the whole situation with the Dreamers.

"You said you feel like an American, but isn't that hard when the government is cracking down on immigrants?"

"I have this group of people who know and support me—all my friends, my grandparents, and some of my teachers. Most other people don't know I'm a Dreamer."

"Really?"

She smiles and adds, "Yes, after all I don't wear a t-shirt that says Dreamer on it. But when someone like you asks, I tell them."

"You don't seem scared. I think I would be scared all the time."

"When my father was deported, I was scared. But then I realized that he wouldn't want me to give up on my dream. So, I can't let what this government does keep me from working hard. I've got this goal of going to college, and then becoming a writer like *mi padre*. I know that wherever he is, my father is thinking about me, and I want him to be proud of what I'm doing. Besides, maybe that woman will run for president again."

"You mean the one who ran last time and lost?" I say a bit sarcastically.

"Yes, that woman," Ana says right back at me. "I think having a woman president might make a difference."

There's a pause, and then Ana adds, "In America, you can be whatever you want to be as long as you're willing to fight for whatever that is."

As I listen to Ana, I can understand, in a way, how she feels because I don't really know where I'm going either. But Ana has one thing I don't. She has this crazy confidence in her future. After all that's happened to her, how did she get to be like that? That's what I want to ask her. But I don't get a chance.

It's four o'clock and Ana gets up. "Our time is up and I've got to leave," she says. "I've got something I want to show you, but not here."

We get coffee at a bakery about one block north of the library, and then we go sit on a bench in a pocket park close by, but away from all the street traffic.

Ana pulls a piece of paper out of her backpack and hands it to me. *Un Lugar Sin Muerte* is written on the top of the page.

"It's in free verse," Ana says quietly. "It means 'A Place without Death.'"

Un Lugar Sin Muerte

I remember playing in the garden,
mi madre's garden.
"Don't break the flowers, mi hija."
"Pick some for the table and come inside."
The flowers have wilted now.
Mi madre sleeps a lot.
"Your mother is very tired," mi padre says.
"Pick some flowers, and throw away the old ones."
The flowers sit in a vase next to her bed.
"Help your father," mi madre says.
"Is Mamá sick?"
"Yes," says mi padre.
The doctor comes to see mi madre.
He talks with mi padre by the flowers.
"Cancer," he says softly.

Mi padre says nothing.
Mi madre is going away.
I feel sad.
Las amigas come to our house bringing flowers.
Mi padre says nothing.
At the cemetery they put mi madre in a beautiful box.
"Mamá, don't leave me."
The priest speaks of eternity.
Mi padre and las amigas sprinkle flowers over the box.
I cry. Mi padre puts his hand on my shoulder.
"We must go now," he says.
I don't want to leave mi madre!
"Ana, we must leave this place of death."
I look up at mi padre, my eyes wet with tears.
"Where will we go?"
"We'll find a new home."
"A new home without Mamá?"
"A new home without death."
"Will it have a garden like Mamá's?"
"It will have a garden with flowers."
"And you can fill a vase for tu madre every day."[3]

I feel speechless. Ana looks very sad as she finishes.
Finally, I ask her to read it to me again.
"Wow!" I say finally.
"Yes? ... Anything else?"
"It's sad and ... it's good."
Now she smiles. "I think so, too."
I look back at the poem. This could be published.
Then she jars me out of my thoughts.
"You should come to the big May march with me,"
she says.

CHAPTER 15

New Faces, Old Faces, Big Plans

Dad asked me to "help" him train the two new employees on April 1st. It ends up being a kind of April Fools' joke. After he gives them the grand tour of the theater—which takes all of fifteen minutes—and then his elevator speech about how the Magic Lantern is going to be the center of movie culture in North Seattle, he hands the new employees over to me to do the actual training.

As it turns out, both new hires have some background with movie theaters. Clarice Perry's father was a projectionist, and Eric Robertson's grandfather owned and ran a movie theater in a Black neighborhood of Atlanta. I show them how to work the electronic cash register, how to fill out their time sheets, and how scheduling is handled. Staff have monthly schedules, and all schedule changes go through Dad.

I guessed from her colorful wardrobe that Clarice was either a design or a drama student. But it turns out she is neither. She's an architecture student, and she is very interested in the theater, especially the screening room with its chandelier lights and painted Grecian scene that hides the screen and the salon. But there is a real limit to how much I can tell her.

When we are in the auditorium, she says, "It looks like the building had additions. Do you know when that happened, and when the current auditorium and salon were installed?"

"The original building was built in 1925 as some kind of fraternal lodge. But I don't really know anything else."

What I do know is that there was a big report done on the theater before it got historic building status. I've never seen that report, but I think Dad has a copy. So I add, "Stop by the office on the way out and talk to Scott if you want to know more."

Clarice seems satisfied with that answer.

Eric Robertson is a business major and a movie fan. He especially likes action movies. He will be working Saturdays and filling in sometimes midweek, and Clarice will be working on Thursdays and alternating Sundays. I'll have to work with them for about two weeks or until each feels comfortable, which will make my work schedule unbearable. But after that they'll be working mostly with Raji or Ellen on Sundays.

So, if everything goes as planned, I hope I'll be working fewer hours in about three weeks. At least that's my hope. And that means I may be able to go to the big immigration march on May 1st. But I won't really know how adding two additional staff will actually change my schedule until the May schedule comes out.

There's a big staff meeting the second week in April, and Dad asks everybody to attend. He introduces Clarice and Eric and then asks how training is going. But the main topics are the film festival and publicity for the Summer of Film.

"The official film festival schedule comes out on May 1st," he says. "But I have a tentative list of the films that I expect will be screened at the Magic Lantern."

He hands the list to me and I pass it around. Eighteen films are going to be screened here during our week as a festival venue.

"I'm asking that you don't tell customers about what films we think will be screened here until the official schedule comes out. We'll have copies in the theater, and customers can pick them up whenever they're here to see a show.

"But the ever-creative Ellen has developed a post-card-size flyer you can hand to people attending films that tells them the Magic Lantern will be a film festival venue and lists the dates."

Ellen holds up a copy of the flyer.

"We'll have these in the office, and there will also be a stack by concessions," Dad says. "So, just a reminder, the Magic Lantern will be hosting the film festival for its first week, May 17th through May 23rd. Unless you're a festival volunteer, you won't be working that week."

Raji's hand shoots up. "I'm a festival member and I'd like to work most of that week at the festival. How can I sign up?"

"I can't sign you up myself, but for Magic Lantern staff who want to work that week, I have the name and cell phone number of the festival volunteer coordinator in my office. And I know that the festival still needs more volunteers. Anybody else volunteering or have questions about the festival?"

Eric raises his hand. "I plan to volunteer if I can get a schedule that will allow me to work here."

"You'll want to tell the volunteer coordinator that when you talk to her," Dad tells Eric. "Now, one other thing I need to tell you about our week hosting the festival. A festival manager will be running the theater that week."

Ellen looks in my direction, and I bet we're both thinking the same thing. Dad's not going to be running the theater for a week?

"I don't know who it will be yet, but he or she will be here the week before the festival to start learning about the building."

And then as if he can read my mind, Dad says, "I know I'm going to enjoy the week off. So, get caught up with whatever you must get caught up on, and come back refreshed because this is going to be a busy summer for Magic Lantern. Which brings me to the other programming event I want everybody to be aware of. We will be having a major event at the Magic Lantern this summer, an eight-week Summer of Film gala."

"Another film festival?" Raji asks.

"Not exactly, since we'll be devoting eight weeks to this. It will actually be bigger, a mixture of old and new films, with some films by local filmmakers, a couple series of the best films by important directors, some lectures, hopefully a film poster auction, and maybe a workshop for local people interested in making films. Genevieve and I are still working on nailing down the details. Any questions?"

Except for Genevieve and me, this has taken the staff by surprise.

Immediately, Eric asks, "Is it going to conflict with the festival?"

"No, it will start on July 5th and run for eight weeks. We'll have a schedule of films and events after the festival."

Since the Woody Fest debacle, Dad has left most of the scheduling to Genevieve. So the monthly film schedules have had better balance. But this Summer of Film thing is definitely Dad's idea, and I wonder if he knows what he is doing.

Nobody else says anything, although I'll bet they're wondering just like I am what this means for staff.

"People, this is going to be a very big event," Dad says finally. "So, if you're going to want time off during July or August, please, please, let me know about it as soon as you can."

Well, there's the first wrinkle—limiting last-minute requests for time off during July and August.

When the meeting ends, Raji and Eric stop by the office. I assume it's to get the information on the volunteer coordinator for the festival. As they leave, Dad asks me to step in to talk.

He says, "I'm hoping now that you'll have a week away from the theater when you can focus on your class work and pick those grades up a bit. B's will look better than C's if you decide you're going to apply for colleges."

He knows I haven't decided if I'm going to apply for admission anywhere. But Mom has been on him to give me more time off to study for just this reason.

"I plan to," I say.

"Good. But I will be counting on you to work more during the summer, especially during July and August, if we end up with a lot of unfilled shifts."

I've been focused on the school year and haven't thought much about the summer. But I'm not surprised. I've become Dad's go-to guy when he needs to fill a shift.

"Can't you ask some of the staff to fill in sometimes?"

Dad frowns. "I can, but I'll still need to have you here a lot this summer."

"Why's that?"

"You're my most experienced staff member, and you're my backup."

I don't say anything because I don't want to get into an argument with Dad when he's just hired more staff.

"Jackson, I can't overemphasize how important it is that the Summer of Film be a success."

"So, what does Genevieve think about this Summer of Film idea?"

"She's totally behind it," Dad says, but sounding a little irritated by my asking.

"Isn't the summer usually a slow time for theaters?"

"Yes, that's true. But we're making money from both the theater rental and the concessions during the festival—that's why I wish we could have been a festival venue for at least another week. But regardless, we really need to continue to find ways to distinguish the theater throughout the summer. I want the Magic Lantern to be the big show in town in July and August."

Then Dad slips back into a long version of his elevator speech.

"We need to do something big to keep people talking about the Magic Lantern. That something will be the Summer of Film, with director mini-festivals, critics and film historians doing Q and A's on certain films and directors, hopefully a daytime workshop for new filmmakers, and a poster auction. I'm even trying to put together a visit by a nationally known film critic."

He pauses and then adds, "So Jackson, I really need you to be positive about the Summer of Film and to be working hard with me to make it a success. Can you do that?"

"Okay," I say, sounding as noncommittal as I can. I'm not going to say more, or promise more. I'm just going to concentrate on school, and I'll think about the summer after the school year.

Leaving the theater, I run into Ellen sitting on the steps waiting for me.

"Sounds like your dad's got big plans for the summer," Ellen says. "You're going to be a busy boy."

"Yeah, now he's calling the summer festival a 'gala.' But does he really think we'll get a big audience for film and director retrospectives and lectures during the summer? It could be a gala flop. Anyway, I'm keeping quiet. I need to stay focused on having more time to study over the last five or six weeks of the quarter."

"You're right about that," Ellen says. "But you know, Scott could be right, too. He seems to know a lot more about movies and the movie business than anybody I know."

"Genevieve knows more," I say, "and she's got concerns about this Summer of Film idea."

Ellen scrunches up her mouth, as if she doesn't agree, and then changes the subject. "So, any chance you'll be at the star party next weekend?"

"Maybe. This Saturday should be my last Saturday shift for a while. But I've got two classes I'm worried about, and I need to spend as much time as I can studying."

"You know, that's good to hear," she says, "but come if you can because I'm probably not going to be there. We're going to Chicago for a school visit, and my parents want to go early to take me to the Field Museum."

Ellen likes the idea that I'm spending more time on studying. But she also knows that extracurricular activities, particularly school clubs, are important to have to put on your college applications.

"Do you want a ride home? I'm parked in the little lot behind the theater."

"That would be great," I say. "I've got to be back here at 1:30 because I'm working the two o'clock show, and I'd like to have something to eat."

On the drive home, I bring up going to the big immigration march. "Ana wants me to join her and a group of other teens in supporting the Dreamers at the May 1st immigration march."

"Oh, I think there is a group going from Truman, but everybody is concerned that the school district may count the time they miss as an unexcused absence."

"Really!"

"Nobody seems to know for sure, and the school district hasn't issued an official statement and probably won't until right before the march," Ellen says.

"That could be a problem. My parents may be hesitant to let me go anyway, and if it isn't an excused absence, they'll definitely say no."

"An unexcused absence will look bad on your record, especially if your grades are just so-so." Ellen says.

Dammit! I was looking at the march as a chance to get to know Ana better.

"I imagine that this march is pretty important to Ana since she is a Dreamer."

"Yes, and I'd like to go," I say.

"Do you support citizenship for all the Dreamers?"

"I guess. From what I've heard, it seems like they're being treated unfairly."

"Well, most of them have been living in the United States for years. But the whole immigration thing is complicated," Ellen says.

"Okay, it's complicated. But they've been here for years, going to school and even working, and they haven't been able to become citizens."

"Yes," Ellen says. "Just remember one march isn't going to change anything. But not spending as much time as you can now on getting good grades could hurt your ability to get into college and then to get a good job."

Ellen's right, but only if I decide I want to go to college.

"If I decide later that I want to go to college, I can always attend a community college, work hard, and then transfer."

Ellen doesn't respond, which is fine. Right now, I just need to figure out how I can talk my parents into letting me go to the May Day march.

Chapter 16

The Big Picture

I'm going to Saturday's April star party. On my way, I pick up Marc Wilson. The sunlight is almost gone when we get to Swanson Park.

It's a beautiful night for stargazing. There was a "pink" full moon on Thursday. Tonight, the moon is still basically full, but it is staying just above the horizon, which makes it a little easier to find other distant objects.

A bunch of older guys from the local Astronomical Society are already setting up their telescopes. Johnnie Rodriguez brings his own small scope. Ellen has one too, but she's gone to Chicago. The rest of us trade off looking through the big scopes of the Astronomy Society guys, and using our binoculars to see what we can. With a good set of binoculars, you can see a surprising number of objects, depending on the conditions of the sky and the amount of light pollution.

We get settled. Now that it's dark, everyone is using small, red LED flashlights to keep the park as dark as possible. There is a semi-circle of red lights around the north side of the park where we are all stargazing. Most of the objects we look at will be in the north part of the sky, essentially overhead, and are the least affected by light pollution from the city.

Johnnie is first in our group to identify something. "I'm looking at the Big Dipper," he says.

I want to get my own small telescope, but I haven't been able to save enough money to buy one. And when I asked Dad about loaning me the money, he just said wait until Christmas. But there was no telescope under the tree this year, only a couple of astronomy books and a SAT test guide. Maybe if I don't go to college right away, I can work and make enough money to buy myself a small telescope.

"I haven't seen you here since last summer," says Bradley Jones, one of the SAS guys.

Bradley was one of a small group of guys who came to a Sunday afternoon screening of *Apollo 11* at the end of March. I saw him come in, but we had a leak in the men's bathroom I had been asked to check out. I had closed the restroom and reported back to Dad, and by then the film was running. So, I never had an opportunity to talk with Bradley to see how he liked the movie.

"Yeah, I haven't been able to come. My dad bought the Magic Lantern in August, and outside of school I've been working mostly at the theater."

"So, you work there? I was there about a month ago to see *Apollo 11.*"

"Yeah, I'm sort of the assistant manager." But even as I say that, I'm thinking 'that's not true.' Despite what Dad says I'm really just his gofer. "What did you think of the film?"

"It was good. It was made up mostly of old news and NASA footage, which I really liked, and the interviews were interesting. Besides stargazing, I'm very interested in space exploration in general."

We both get back to stargazing. Using my Monarch 7 binoculars and my *Night Sky Field Guide*, I follow Johnnie's lead and find Ursa Major, aka the Great Bear, and the most prominent constellation in the spring night sky.[4] The Big Dipper, which is on one side of the constellation, can usually be seen with the naked eye. I follow the arc of the Dipper's handle south to a kite-shaped group of stars, the Boötes constellation, and there at the south end of the kite's tail is the red-orange glow of the brightest star in the northern night sky, Arcturus.

"Check out Arcturus," I say to no one in particular. "It's fantastic!"

Then I look north from Ursa Major to find Ursa Minor, a constellation commonly known as the Little Dipper. It's pretty hazy, but Bradley Jones offers to let me use his big refractor telescope to see it more clearly. The older guys are great about sharing with us what they know and letting us look through their scopes when our binoculars aren't powerful enough to see distant objects.

If you can see all four of the stars in the cup of the Little Dipper, you can generally see all the major stars and constellations in the spring night sky. Looking through the big telescope, I can see all four stars in the cup. But the one with the lowest brightness is still a bit hazy.

At the end of the handle of the Little Dipper, I find the North Star, Polaris.

"What are you looking at?" Sherry Jefferson asks.

"Polaris."

"Me, too."

"It's weird, you know, whenever I look at Polaris all the other stars seem to be moving around."

"That's because it lies in the direction of Earth's axis," Sherry says.

I know that. Sherry is a real science geek and she likes to show off her knowledge.

"It never moves in the northern sky, so it appears that all the other stars are moving around it," I say.

There is so much mythology about the constellations and the major stars, much of it coming from ancient times. Forty-eight of the eighty-eight known constellations were identified in the distant past.

I try to spot Venus or Mars, but Johnnie reminds me that right now Venus is only visible in the morning, and Mars isn't visible at all.

Sherry offers everyone hot chocolate from her thermos, but I'm too busy looking for objects to even answer her. It seems like it's been forever since I've been able to go stargazing, and I feel like I need to make up for lost time.

I look for Leo. It's easy to find in the spring sky. All I do is look slightly southwest from Ursa Major and there it is. The constellation actually has the outline of a lion, and its head and neck are an asterism, a pattern inside a constellation, which is called the Sickle.

On Leo's southwest side corner, I find Regulus, the brightest star in the constellation.

Sherry appears beside me. "What are you looking at?" she asks.

"Regulus."

"Ah, Leo the Lion, and its first-magnitude star Regulus," says Sherry. "Leo is one of the oldest constellations. It was first named in ancient Babylon."

I'm getting a little irritated that she thinks she needs to explain the constellations to me. "Yeah, but the idea of the lion comes from Greece. It was supposed to be a kind of monster lion killed by Hercules as part of his twelve labors."

Sherry and I never hang out, aside from the Astronomy Club. So, her coming over just to talk is kind of surprising.

Then out of the blue, she says, "I hear you're going to be coming to the big May Day march."

Sherry is also the only real activist in the Astronomy Club.

"Where did you hear that?"

She smiles. Sherry's not only smart, but with her blond hair and flashing smile, she's also hot. Too bad she's so irritating.

"Some people were talking about the march at school, and someone mentioned your name," she says.

Who would do that? Ana doesn't go to Truman, and I haven't mentioned it to anyone at school. Have I?

"Are you going?" Sherry asks again.

The only person I told I might go was Ellen. So, it must have been Ellen who mentioned that to Sherry.

"I don't know ... probably not. It's on a Wednesday, and I can't afford to have an unexcused absence. I'm not sure how my parents would feel about it anyway."

"Oh, I bet the school district will relent and excuse everyone who goes. There are a bunch of us going from Truman. And it's an important issue. You should come."

Sherry's pressing me, but I just shrug and go back to looking at the sky.

"I'm trying to find Spica," I say, as if that's a good reason not to give her a direct answer.

"Well, you should think about it."

After some more looking, I find Virgo just above the southern horizon, and there's Spica right in the middle of the constellation. But my Monarch isn't quite strong enough to clearly see the other stars because Virgo is so spread out that most of them are very faint.

Frustrated, I ask Bradley if I can look through his telescope again.

"I'm having trouble seeing most of the stars in Virgo," I say.

"Okay, but first, how would you like to see a star cluster?"

Bradley must be looking at star clusters. "Sure," I say.

"Let me see if I can find the star cluster in the Coma Berenices constellation."

Just north of the upper arm of Virgo is an area of the sky with some very faint stars. This is the Coma Berenices constellation. It is a dim constellation, and to the naked eye it's hardly visible. It makes a 90-degree angle almost straight above us in the sky, and even with good binoculars, Berenices can be very hard to see clearly except for its biggest star, Diadem, on its south end.

Bradley briefly adjusts the telescope and then motions for me to take a look.

At first, I don't notice anything except Diadem.

"Look at the upper end of the constellation, the upper west side of the 90-degree angle of stars," Bradley says.

I move north from Diadem and try to focus on that upper end of the constellation. But I still have trouble focusing on that arm.

"Look at Arcturus and then move your gaze to the right."

I find Arcturus and when I follow Bradley's instructions, the blurry smudge at the end of the north arm of the constellation suddenly becomes clear.

"Oh, I see them, a blurry clump of stars."

"That's Melotte 111. It's an open star cluster of about forty stars."

"I looked for the Pleiades star cluster when I was here in November of 2018," I say. "But there were too many clouds that night, and it was really cold, so I think most of us left early. Anyway, I wasn't able find that cluster."

"Maybe next November," Bradley says encouragingly. "But remember, there are a number of other deep space objects in Berenices, including some fantastic galaxies."

"Isn't the Black Eye Galaxy visible in Berenices?"

"Yes," Bradley says. "You want to see it?"

"I'd love to see it."

Bradley refocuses his telescope on an area just west of the center of the constellation.

"And there it is, M64, the Black Eye Galaxy," he says. "Take a look."

When I look, I immediately see a small, spiral galaxy, but its bright center and the dark cloud of gas in front of it show up clearly in the telescope. Looking for star clusters with a real telescope is … wow! "That's spectacular. I can almost feel its energy."

"Yeah, it's also called the Sleeping Beauty Galaxy. It's a favorite of a lot of regular stargazers."

First Marc and then Sherry come over and ask what we are looking at. Bradley explains, and Sherry goes back to her telescope to see if she can find the galaxy. Bradley lets Marc look at the Sleeping Beauty, and Bradley shows us a couple of other deep sky objects in the Coma Berenices constellation.

This is what I like so much about star parties. You not only get to see objects in our solar system and big stars like Arcturus or Polaris, but also star clusters and deeper space objects like the Black Eye Galaxy—objects that you can only see through a telescope.

Tonight was just exactly what a star party should be, clear skies and lots of telescopes, so everybody can really see different objects. I'll have fun telling Ellen about what I saw.

La Marcha

When I see Ellen again at school, the first thing I ask is if she told anyone that I was going to the immigration march.

"I sat with Sherry and some other girls for lunch one day last week," she says, "and they asked me if I was going. I said no, and then Sherry asked me about you, and I said you were thinking about it."

I'm a little upset that Ellen said anything.

"You can't say anything to people at school if you don't want it spread all around."

"Yeah, I know," Ellen says with a shrug. It isn't an apology, and I guess I can't really be mad at her. But now I'm feeling pressure to decide if I want to go.

Then out of the blue, Ana calls me five days before the immigration march.

"The school district has agreed to give students who attend the march an excused absence," she says.

I didn't expect that, and I don't know exactly what to say.

"Will you come?" she asks after a long pause.

"I'll talk with my parents."

"The group from St. Francis is going to meet up with the Truman group at Wilson Park, so we'd be able walk together, at least for a while."

She wants me to come. She wants me to come.

"Okay, I'll talk to my parents."

I want to go on the march. But I'm not looking forward to asking my parents.

A big sign hanging over the entrance announces:

The 20th Annual Seattle Immigration March.

Groups and individuals participating in the march are congregating at Wilson Park when we get there. The crowd is going to be huge.

People are talking, many of them are holding signs. I glance around and read:

Abolish ICE

Citizenship for the Dreamers

Stop Discrimination Against Immigrants

I feel both energized and anxious. I've never been to such a big protest march. My parents often talk about the huge 2003 anti-war march they participated in. Although I hadn't been born yet, Mom likes to talk about taking me with her when they marched because she was pregnant.

"How many people do you think are here?" Johnnie Rodriguez asks. Both Johnnie and Sherry are in the Truman group.

"I have no idea."

"I've heard that they expect 100,000 people," says somebody standing next to us with a sign that proclaims, "Open the Borders."

There are about thirty-five people here from Truman, student body officers like Sherry, basketball players, the usual activists' kids, some nerds and student body officers, and a few parents who are supposed to be chaperoning the school groups—what a laugh.

I'm feeling a little overwhelmed, and then I see Ana coming out of the crowd and walking toward us. She's waving her hand and saying something. But it's really hard to hear because of all the noise.

"Jackson," she says as she gets closer. "Is this your group from Truman?"

I nod, and then she turns and waves into the crowd, and almost immediately another group emerges and walks toward us. The St. Francis group is even bigger than ours, maybe one hundred people. But I don't see anybody else I know except for Carlos. As the two groups start to mingle, he walks over to me.

"You made it. Did you have trouble with your parents when you asked them about coming?" Carlos asks.

"Not really."

Actually, Mom was the most opposed. She was afraid that missing my afternoon classes would hurt my chances of improving my grades by the end of the year. But after I told her there was a group going from Truman, along with a large group from Peter's church, she said it was okay, as long as I could make up anything I missed.

"What are you going to do about the material you miss?" Ana asks.

"Ellen has agreed to share her math notes with me, and I'm in pretty good shape in that class. I didn't tell Mom I'd be missing a lab."

Ana looks concerned. "Labs are hard to make up."

That's true, but I wanted to come, so I'm here. Although now that I've committed myself, I'm feeling nervous about the whole thing. Surprisingly Dad was fine with my going, saying only that I needed to be back at the Magic Lantern by 6:00 p.m.

"I'm glad you came," Ana says. She's smiling now. She looks, well, really great in her jeans and a green shirt that highlights her soft brown complexion.

"Yeah, I'm glad I could come."

"Jackson!" someone calls.

It's Uncle Peter. His church group has come in behind us.

"Where are we headed?" I ask Carlos.

"The Federal Building."

There are a lot of older people in Peter's church group. I know most of them, and I wonder if they will be able to make it the mile and a half down the hill and north to the Federal Building.

"Is this your school group?" Peter asks.

"Yes, and the group from St. Francis."

Ana recognizes Peter from the church service on the Dreamers and smiles. "It's great to see so many people from your church here," she says.

"We've got your back," Peter says rather too proudly. "We support all the Dreamers."

Almost immediately, someone yells, "We're moving."

The St. Francis group forges ahead. I follow Ana, and Peter comes with us.

It's 1:15. For a moment, it's a kind of controlled chaos. People and groups jostle each other. Some people look confused. Maybe they've lost their friends or the groups they want to walk with. People raise their signs and banners. Peter's church has a big banner. Then suddenly everybody lurches forward, and we all head west down Pagoda Hill.

Along the march route, more people stand waving signs and shouting slogans. There are big signs and small signs, some homemade, some manufactured, in different shapes and different colors to match the variety of people marching.

Some of the people in the St. Francis group begin to sing songs, many in Spanish, about freedom and the fight for justice.

"Let's sing 'De Colores,'" Carlos yells out.

I've sung that song a number of times with the family choir at church, so I know the Spanish lyrics. It's supposedly the anthem of the United Farmworkers.

Carlos yells something to a guy with a guitar in the St. Francis group.

"I didn't bring my guitar," he says. "But I did bring these." And he starts handing out copies of the song to those around him.

Then almost everybody in the two groups begins to sing, and we are joined quickly by many of the people in the church group, some of whom I recognize from the family choir.

De colores, de colores
se visten los campos en la primavera.
De colores, de colores
son los pajaritos que vienen de afuera.[5]

I'm singing as loudly as I can; the same with Carlos, and when I look at Ana she is, too. Singing this song feels great.

When the song ends, we laugh and some people yell, "yes!"

Then somebody in the church group starts singing "Harriet Tubman," a song about the Underground Railroad. It has an added verse about Latin American immigrants, so it's perfect for the march. I glance around and notice that Peter has joined his other church members.

I think I'm the only person in the Truman group who knows this song. But most of the church group does, including Carlos, and they're able to sing it from memory. The song's message is clear: "get on board"—immigrants need a "lifeline" to help them.

As the music dies down, I ask Ana if this is her first march.

"I've come to this march for the last five ... " She stops to think for a moment. "Yes, for the last five years."

Everybody is feeling happy and energized when a small group of guys with different signs, including "Protect our Borders" and "Deport all illegals," come out of an alley right next to the march.

"Immigrants go home!" one of the men yells at the marchers.

"Racists!" someone from behind me yells.

Suddenly, there is a kind of standoff: the anti-immigrant guys yell at the marchers, and a few of the marchers step out of line to gesture and yell back at them. Carlos joins the latter group. Then a policeman steps between the groups. He tells the anti-immigrant group to stay back from the marchers and asks the marchers to keep moving.

"Does this happen a lot?" I ask Ana when we're walking again.

"It started happening after this president was elected. It seems like these people now feel emboldened to come out and harass us when we march."

"Can you believe those guys?" Carlos asks when he catches up with us.

"Kind of scary," I say.

"They don't scare me. I'm here to stay, and I'm not going to be intimidated by people like them."

"I can tell."

Ana smiles and slaps hands with Carlos.

I wonder how I would feel if I was an immigrant trying to live in the U.S. today. But I'm also shaken a bit by the closeness of the almost confrontation.

When we reach the Federal Building, there are speeches by some of the Dreamers, including Ana and other immigrants, some of whom have harrowing stories to tell of their experiences with ICE.

Then Peter gets up to speak.

"We need to have a peaceful revolution in the U.S., a revolution of the heart, to become a more welcoming country for all who want to come here."

It reminds me of what he said at the Sunday service for the Dreamers, and I wonder if this idea of a peaceful revolution is really possible. We learned in World History that revolutions tend to be very violent.

Anyway, hearing him talk, along with the stress from the standoff with the anti-immigrant guys, saps the energy I felt when we were singing.

It's almost 4:30 when the march starts to break up. Although a number of people want to talk with Ana, she comes back to where I've been standing at the edge of the crowd.

"Thanks for coming, Jackson," she says. "It was great to have you here."

"Well, I know how important this fight is to you, so I'm glad I could help." I suddenly want to say more but I don't.

"It's my dream, you know, like in the song."

She pauses for a minute. I'm a little confused.

"What song?"

"'De Colores.' It's my dream that all kinds of people will come together, all colors, like in the song. All religions, liberals and conservatives will come together to work for justice for the Dreamers. And when that is accomplished, these same people will work together to make everything else right, all the injustice, all the unfairness."

Wow, that's a big dream. But is that even possible? Then before I can respond, I get a big surprise.

"Can I give you a hug?" Ana says.

I'm tongue-tied for a moment. "Sure," I say finally.

We hug. It's nice. I try not to hug her too hard, but she feels really good.

Chapter 18

On the Bench

Mandy Rose is going to manage the Magic Lantern during the festival week, Dad tells the staff at the May meeting. Then he hands out a list of the films that will be screened at the Magic Lantern during our week as a festival venue.

"I thought Mandy was a programmer," I say immediately.

"She is, but she also has some experience managing festival venues, and she lives in the neighborhood, so it will be easy for her to get here and fill in if some volunteer shifts don't get covered."

Raji and Eric immediately begin riffling through the lists, which include very short film descriptions.

Dad gives everybody a chance to look at the lists, and then he adds, "Mandy will be here on May thirteenth while the theater is closed to get a feel for the building and the equipment. Each festival venue will have a projectionist, and I'm hoping that person will also be here on Monday."

After the meeting, I sit in the theater office, eating a sandwich and looking at the list of films. I don't recognize any, but I guess that's not a surprise since most are either new independent pictures or foreign language films.

Then I start thinking about my week off. I've got a lot of school stuff to get caught up on. But I quickly move to thinking about Ana, and I wonder if there's any way we can get together while I'm not working. Probably not. It's right before finals, and some classes have papers due before the holiday.

On Tuesday, I'm standing in the batter's box at the Truman-St. Francis baseball game. It's our last game of the season. We're leading eight to zero in the fifth inning when Carlos comes over from the other dugout.

"You guys are clobbering us," he says. "I wish we had a little more pitching."

"Yeah, I bet. We really hit that starter of yours. Can you believe Miller? Two home runs today."

"I don't remember seeing you at our first game in March."

"I had to work." Even thinking about how many games I missed because of work makes me angry.

"So, you're just sitting on the bench this year?" Carlos asks.

The team plays fifteen games. They're mostly on Thursday and Friday, and half were in March, so I wasn't even able to be at most of the games this year, much less play.

"I couldn't make it to most of the games until the second week in April, so Coach had to make me a reserve. He said he was sorry, but the team needed four regular outfielders. I've played a little more since Roy Hobbs got hurt."

"That Hobbs guy is something else—twelve home runs in how many games?"

"Ten," I say.

Before I can get up, our catcher grounds out and the fifth inning is over.

"A group of people from St. Francis are going to a film at your theater on Friday night."

"A festival film?" It has to be a festival film. "What's its title?"

"I'm not sure. It's a Mexican film. I think it might be a rom-com, but I'm not sure of the title."

I hadn't planned to see any of the festival films. I have other things to do—like schoolwork, lots of schoolwork—and I was looking forward to being away from the Magic Lantern for a whole week.

"So anyway," Carlos says, "I was thinking that you might be interested because Ana is coming."

"Ana's coming?"

"I think so."

I must look a little surprised because then Carlos says, "Give her a call. ... I've got to get back to our dugout. I'm up third if we can get anybody on."

CHAPTER 19

La Festival de Cine

It's still not dark when I get off the bus and head toward the Magic Lantern. Dad was on and off his phone all afternoon, working on things for the Summer of Film, I guess. I try not to listen to most of his conversations, but I overheard him say, "Thanks, Mr. Belvedere."

The first thing I notice when I'm at the intersection across from the theater is the long line of people waiting to see the second Friday night festival film, *The Good Girls*.

As I cross the street, I notice Carlos waving at me. Then I see Ana. She and Carlos are with about five other people, who look like students, and a couple of older women. This must be the St. Francis group. I join them in line.

"Hey, man, you made it," Carlos says. "Your first day off work and you're back to see a film."

Ana smiles at me.

I look up at the Magic Lantern. I just hope this is worth it, and I'm not talking about the film. "Wow, this is quite a line," I say. "It's good you guys got here early enough to have a decent place in line."

"It wouldn't be a film festival without a line at the venues," says one of the older women. I wonder if she's a regular festival goer.

"Do you see a lot of festival films?" I ask.

"I was a passholder for ten years, and I can remember standing in line to see a film at the Harvard Exit on Cap Hill when it was ninety degrees out, and the line ran completely around the block."

The woman smiles and adds, "I'm Helen Morales. I teach at St. Francis. And you are Jack ... and you work here, right?"

"I'm Jackson, and my father owns this theater."

"Oh, so don't you ever have lines when you're showing a popular film?"

"We've got a big room, called the salon, off the main entrance where people can wait if they get here early or are waiting for the theater to be cleaned before the second show. But I've never before seen more than ten people waiting outside to get tickets."

"The Festival likes to clear the theater between films," a man standing in front of us says. "They used to let passholders wait in the lobby, but they've stopped doing that."

"I can remember that," says Helen. "Those were the days when passholders had more power."

"I'm glad you could come," says Ana, breaking into the conversation and giving me a big smile.

We haven't talked since the day of the big march.

"So, what do you know about this film?" I ask.

"It's about a Mexican family living in Mexico City in the 1980s and dealing with a recession. Even in supposedly stable countries like Mexico, people have to deal with the ups and downs of capitalism."

"I thought your grandparents didn't let you go out socially?"

"Oh, no," she says, and I catch just a touch of a smile on her face. "It's okay as long as it's not a date. This is my break before I start studying for finals. It's a group activity. So, they are cool with it."

"I see." Now I'm smiling too. So, this still isn't a date, just a get-together with friends.

"They have the same goal for me that I have—get into a good college. They know I'm going to study as hard as I can, so they're okay with me doing some things with friends, so long as it doesn't affect my studies and I'm home by midnight."

This sounds reasonable, except for the rule about not dating. I don't know any other high school junior who's forbidden to date.

"Think you'll make it tonight?" I ask. "With a 9:30 start time, and ten minutes of marketing for the festival before it starts, it could be close."

"I'm driving her home," Helen says. "The film is ninety-three minutes, so we should be out of here by 11:15."

"Probably, but there will be about fifteen minutes of talk by one of the festival programmers, along with some previews, before the film begins."

"So, you're not working during the festival?" Helen asks.

"No, the festival uses its own volunteers. A couple of our staff will be working because they volunteered, but most of us have this week off."

As I turn back to Ana, the line starts to move. Suddenly, I feel disappointed. There's no chance I can ask Ana if she wants to have coffee with me after the film. She's right. This really isn't a date, not even close.

CHAPTER 20

The Manifesto

I ended up seeing two films at the festival with the group from St. Francis—the Mexican film, and a funny science fiction film from Cuba about a planetarium guide who gets a chance to travel to another planet. I liked the Cuban film the best. But mostly I was there to see Ana. We sat next to each other at the Cuban film on Sunday afternoon. I bought a big tub of popcorn and we shared it.

When the film ended we ran into Genevieve in the salon, and I introduced her to Ana.

"How did you like the film?" she asked Ana.

"It was funny. I mean the idea of leaving Earth to go somewhere else. But I kind of understood how Celeste felt. Sometimes you've got to leave where you were born to find a new place where you can be what you want to be."

Genevieve smiled as if she understood that feeling. "It sounds like it resonated with you."

Then, before I could say anything, Ana said she had to leave to catch her ride home. I noticed Helen Morales waiting in the lobby by the ticket booth.

"Nice to meet you, Genevieve."

"Nice to meet you too, Ana. I hope I'll see you again."

Ana said goodbye to me, smiled, and then she was gone.

I hadn't talked with Genevieve for weeks, and I just had to ask her about the program for Summer of Film. This, of course, was before I'd actually seen the program.

"So, Dad's really putting a lot of importance on this Summer of Film thing. Does it have a chance of being successful?"

Genevieve said, "I have to hand it to Scott. He's got a dream and he's willing to stick his neck out to make it happen." She paused as if deciding what else she wanted to say.

"The program is great. I'm amazed he got Jordan Walters, and we've also got a week of local filmmakers showing their own films and talking about them. Of course, it's summer and it can be hard to get people to come inside in Seattle when the weather is beautiful," she said.

Dad got Jordan Walters, the Chicago film critic, to come to speak? That should draw an audience.

"Jordan Walters. Wow, but isn't she expensive?"

"Yes, but I think Scott had to do something big to keep the attendance up over the summer. Having a major film critic come to introduce films signals film-goers that Scott is serious about making the Magic Lantern the theater in North Seattle where people come to watch movies. He has to take some risks if he wants to realize his dreams."

THE SUMMER OF FILM

The Magic Lantern Theater

July 5 – September 2 *(Closed Mondays)*

The mission of the **Magic Lantern Theater** is to present the best films for all ages, independent and commercial, foreign and domestic, by the best filmmakers of both the past and the present, for the entertainment of Seattle moviegoers. In this spirit, the Magic Lantern will be running an 8-week **SUMMER OF FILM** this summer.

❂❂❂❂❂❂

Starting July 5th and running through September 2nd, this theater will be showing some of the best films ever made, along with a few spectacular new ones. We will have mini-festivals on important directors and subjects, with experts talking about individual films, a week of films by local filmmakers, a movie poster auction, and a long weekend with **Jordan Walters**, the nationally known film critic from ***Film Perspectives Magazine*** and the ***Chicago Post Newspaper***, who will be leading off a 13-day mini-festival of films by major women directors.

❂❂❂❂❂❂

Come join us at the **Magic Lantern Theater** this summer for a celebration of film and of going to the movies.

* BE PREPARED TO BE AMAZED *

Scott Ryan, Magic Lantern Theater, owner/manager

Dad needed to make a statement that would catch people's attention, so at the top of the flyer introducing the Summer of Film he wrote a manifesto.

"It's my values statement for the Magic Lantern," Dad told me when I asked him about the manifesto. "But it's actually bigger than that. It's really a declaration of what I intend the Magic Lantern to be."

It's the first Saturday after our week as a festival venue, the holiday weekend. And because Dad can't be here until 5:00 p.m., I've had to open up and get the film started. But a big part of my job today is to put out the Summer of Film flyers, and to make sure everybody on today's staff gets a copy. Dad will start mentioning the event at tonight's showing.

"Cool, what a great mixture of films," says Raji after he reads the flyer. "Getting Jordan Walters—that's big—and he's written his own manifesto like Orson Welles' manifesto in *Citizen Kane*."

Certainly, the summer film program itself is pure Scott Ryan, full of the directors and films Dad likes.

Raji was scheduled to be off the whole holiday weekend, which meant I had to work again today. But despite being off, he came in today just to pick up the flyer. He's one staff member who is really juiced about the Summer of Film.

"I wonder how he got Jordan Walters," Eric says, looking at me as if I would know.

"Yes, I wonder that too." But what I'd really like to know is how much did she cost?

According to the flyer, Jordan Walters will be kicking off a thirteen-day program on female directors. She'll be here for the first four days of the retrospective and will give a short lecture on each night.

Walters is the only critic Dad regularly reads now that Roger Porter has retired. She's nationally known, has her own film blog, and has written two books, so a crowd should turn out to hear her speak. But it must be expensive to have her here for four days.

"So where are the film posters coming from for the auction?" Raji asks after noticing it listed on the flyer.

I wonder that too. We have a few stored in the salon, but they're not really saleable.

Our new film to start June is about the friendship between two teenage girls. Both Dad and Genevieve thought it had a chance to draw a younger audience, and as it turns out, it did fine that first weekend. Dad had a headache, so I came in to open up and show the film for the Sunday matinee. Running the digital projector isn't that hard. I actually enjoy it.

Unfortunately, at midweek there was hardly anybody in the seats. The same thing happened the second week of the run: good houses on Saturday and Sunday, but few people in the seats the rest of the week.

"It's the beginning of finals," Raji said, when we were talking about how small the houses were during the week. It didn't even help that the first full week of June was cool and rainy.

Out of the blue on Sunday, Ana calls to invite me over to her house to study for finals. I'm totally surprised, but of course I say yes.

"Be sure to bring along any notes you have from your Spanish class," she says at the end of our short conversation.

On Sunday, I take the bus to the Green Lake area and get off at a bus stop north of the lake. It's a sunny, warm day. Her house is a two-story older house in the middle of the block about three blocks from her high school. It has hardly any front yard, but there's an old-fashioned porch that runs across the front of the house.

Ana takes me through the house and out the back door where, it turns out, there is a great backyard, with a couple of trees—a Douglas fir and what looks like a spruce—a picnic table, a small flower garden on one side, and a bigger vegetable garden on the other. I immediately think of our backyard at home, or at least our backyard as it was before Dad bought the Magic Lantern.

Today, the only thing we have that tops what I'm seeing here is our bigleaf maple. We have a huge big-leaf that drops beautiful golden leaves every October, creating piles that Dad usually spends four or five days cleaning up and bagging. Of course, that didn't happen last fall because Dad couldn't get the time away from the theater, and between school and the theater, I couldn't either. So, the job fell to Mom. I thought she'd be upset about taking a week of her mornings to deal with the leaves. But if she was, she didn't complain.

We sit at the picnic table.

"Would you like anything to drink?" Ana asks. "We've got iced tea, diet Pepsi, and water."

"So, it was okay with your grandparents to invite me over?" I ask when we sit down.

"They're visiting friends in Tacoma," she says. "They'll be back after dinner. I told them you were coming over to study for finals, which you are."

"Okay," I say, sounding a little skeptical.

"I think you said you were having trouble studying for your Spanish final?"

"Yes, Spanish II."

She brings out some diet Pepsi and a bowl of corn chips.

"What are you struggling with?" Ana asks.

"Mostly conversations. I got a B on the midterm. But the last couple months Mr. Lopez has been instructing mostly in Spanish, and we're supposed to ask questions and answer questions in Spanish."

"That sounds frustrating."

"It is, but most of the class now is about conversation, not rules and memorization. So, I have to improve my Spanish speaking skills."

Ana looks over my Spanish conversation notes, and then she starts asking me simple questions, I guess to test how well I can respond. For the first few questions, I'm able to come up with a Spanish response. But soon I'm struggling.

"Why did you take a language?" She asks me after about a half hour.

"I have to take a language to get into in-state colleges."

"For most good out-of-state colleges, too," Ana says. "Have you decided if you want to go to college?"

"No, but I have to take classes this year that will be acceptable to in-state schools, at least."

"You're going to need to decide soon, aren't you? I've already visited two schools that I'm considering, and I'm visiting two more in the next couple of weeks."

"Mom wants me to decide this month, but I'm not really sure why I'd be going. Do you know what I mean?"

"Not really. Since I was old enough to think about it, I've known that I want to go to college, and I want to have a choice in the college I go to."

"Sometimes I think I should want that too. But sometimes I think I don't really care."

"You don't dream about doing something special after you get out of school?"

"I don't know. I actually like high school, even if my grades aren't great. Maybe I could just stay in high school. But I guess the one thing I'd like to work at after high school is astronomy."

"The U has a good astronomy program, doesn't it?"

"Yeah, but I'll never be able to get into the U. My grades won't be good enough, and I don't have enough strong extracurricular activities either."

"Well, wherever you apply, you'll want to have good enough grades to be accepted."

"That makes sense," I say. "I just wish I could get more excited about idea of going to college."

"You should visit some schools and find out about their programs. Maybe when you see some other campuses, you'll be more excited."

This actually sounds like a good idea, but I have to wonder where I'll get the time.

"How am I going to do that when I'm in school or working at the theater twenty-four hours a day?"

"I know you had a week of the festival off, and didn't your father hire some additional staff to give you more time to study?"

"Yeah, he hired two other college students to work weekends and a few other shifts. So, I am not going to be working quite as much. I think my parents, especially Mom, knew I needed more time to study. Anyway, I was almost caught up during the Festival. That is, with everything except for Spanish and Algebra II. How do you feel about math?"

Ana smiles, but I can tell that she doesn't want to volunteer to be my math tutor. So, before we run out of things to talk about, I bring up the Summer of Film.

"I brought you something." I pick up my backpack, take out a Summer of Film flyer, and hand it to her.

"What's the Summer of Film?"

"It's Dad's idea. Something he's got planned for the theater this summer."

Ana glances back at the flyer and reads Dad's manifesto. "How cool, a manifesto for the theater."

"Yeah, I just hope this isn't a complete disaster."

"Really, it sounds exciting. Why would it be a disaster?"

"Summer's not usually a great time for theaters, unless they are running a blockbuster movie like the Spiderman films. He's betting on this mix of old and new films, along with some films by local filmmakers, a film poster auction, and some guest speakers."

"He must have some reason he wants to try this."

"Remember what he said when you came to write a story about us in September? He wants to make the Magic Lantern the movie theater people talk about and think about when they want to go out to the movies, and he thinks that by having something big over the summer, when there aren't any other big movie events, he can grab people's attention."

"You don't think that will happen?"

"I don't know. But if Genevieve thinks it's risky, it must be risky."

Ana looks a little confused, and I realize that she doesn't remember meeting Genevieve at the film festival.

"You remember Genevieve? We talked with her after that Cuban film at the film festival."

"Oh, I remember her," Ana says after a minute. "She's the film programmer for the Magic Lantern."

"Yes, and she said this Summer of Film thing was risky."

"If she's the film programmer, can't she see that all the films for this Summer of Film thing are great?"

I start to tell Ana what Genevieve said that Sunday after she left. But now, as I remember that conversation, it's not as negative as I thought.

"She said that the film program was 'great' and ... she agreed that Dad needs to do something big if he wants to capture a bigger audience. But she also said she thinks he's taking a risk in doing such a big event in the summer."

Ana gets a serious look on her face.

"It sounds like Scott's got a dream and he's working to make it a reality."

"Yeah," I say. "I realize that, but unfortunately, this Summer of Film probably means I'll be working more at the theater in July and August, and that's going to affect how much time I have to think about college."

I may have just made a big mistake by bringing up the Summer of Film. Because now it feels like Ana is sympathizing with Dad, not me.

Ana looks at me and frowns.

"Anyway," I say, "I still think this summer program may backfire on him."

"You should be proud of your father," Ana answers right away.

Then I get it. Ana identifies with Dad's dream, or at least with Dad as a dreamer. Just like Dad, she's trying to make her dream happen. We go back to talking about college. But something about the afternoon has changed, and not for the better.

"Can I have this flyer?" she asks. "I'd like to show it to friends. Maybe I can generate some business for the Magic Lantern."

"Sure," I say. "The schedule is also on our webpage."

"Am I going to be able to continue my Spanish lessons over the summer?" I'd really like to see Ana over the summer.

"You'll have time for Spanish lessons?" She's referring to my saying that I may be working all the time in July and August.

Then she adds, "Let's wait and see if we've got the time. I've got visits to two colleges left, one right after finals, and I'm taking an advanced arts class during the second session of summer school."

"You're taking a summer school class? Don't you want to take some time off before your final year?"

"I've gotten kind of interested in the arts and I haven't had time to take any regular humanities classes, except journalism and creative writing. Also, colleges like applicants with a lot of interests, kids who haven't just excelled in straight academic classes, but who can show that they are well rounded."

"Rounded?" I ask. Then I say jokingly, "You mean like a ball?"

"Have a variety of interests," Ana says with a smile. I thought I'd lost her for a few minutes, but now that she's smiling it feels like the conversation has lightened up.

"I'll be taking a survey course on visual arts. You know, painting, sculpture, even film."

"Oh," I say, "'even film.' Well, that means you'll need to be spending a lot of time at a certain movie theater's Summer of Film program."

We both laugh.

"It was fun to see a couple of movies at the film festival, and I even liked standing in the line and listening to all the other people talking about what they'd seen and which films they liked and why."

"This will be just like the festival," I say, "except that it will be running for eight weeks." What I don't say is that many of the movies being shown were made before she was born, and some of the directors we'll be screening I've never heard of.

But now Ana has gotten curious.

"What are you showing?" she asks, and then glances back at the program flyer. "Women Directors in the Sound Era. That could be interesting."

Maybe this Summer of Film thing isn't such a bad idea after all. Maybe it will be a way for me to see Ana this summer, even if I'm spending most of my time this summer at the Magic Lantern.

Scott Ryan
Journal Entry
June 10, 2019

I'm taking a risk, but a bigger risk would be if I had just let Genevieve program a regular schedule of films for the summer. We have to use this summer window to increase our customer base. We have to try something big and bold.

I think we're in better shape with our publicity than we have been since we opened. The film critic for the local paper has agreed to do an article each week about the activities and films featured during the Summer of Film, a sort of coming attractions. Our Facebook page is looking better and better. Jackson's friend Ellen has done a great job. I spent a lot of time on distributing flyers to coffeehouses and bookstores in North Seattle and got the film festival to put them out at their venues. Raji has posted and distributed them all over the University District.

Staff-wise we're okay. Raji is taking off 10 days at the end of June, but he'll be back for his first shift on July 6. Then he'll be here essentially for the entire Summer of Film, and he's volunteered to take some extra shifts. Clarice and Eric will be gone for short periods, so Jackson and Ellen will need to work extra shifts. I've already mentioned this to both of them. It frustrates me that Jackson hasn't taken to his role as assistant manager. I'm concerned that he's been unwilling to grab this opportunity.

All that said, the Summer of Film is going to be big. It has to be.

PART 3

The Summer of Film

CHAPTER 21

The Waiting Game

Mom calls June "a waiting month." Local folklore says that summer in Seattle starts on July 5th, so most Seattleites spend June complaining about the weather and waiting for summer to arrive. Mom and I are exceptions. June's cool, cloudy days, mixed with some sun most afternoons, make June the best month of the year for us. Mom spends most of her free time working in her studio with its western exposure, and she likes the studio to be as cool as possible. I think our normal June weather fits my mood, particularly after school's out.

But today it's not cool. It's hot. It's the first day after my last final, and Mom catches me before I can leave to meet Ellen at the Picasso Café.

"Jackson, your dad and I have been talking, and we'd both like to sit down with you and make some decisions about your future."

I'm not surprised. Mom, in particular, has wanted me to have what she calls "a college plan."

She pauses, maybe expecting me to object. But I just nod and don't say anything.

"So, let's get together Monday afternoon, the three of us, and talk about college. With your dad working so much at the theater, I think we need to have a plan, so that you and I can visit some schools."

I was hoping that Mom would just let the college thing go. But no, she's determined, and when she's determined to see something happen, it usually does. So that means I've got to have something ready to say by Monday.

When I get to the café, Ellen is sitting at one of the outdoor tables drinking what looks like an iced vanilla soy latte. I get a tall iced tea and join her outside.

"What's the occasion?" I ask.

"The end of our junior year."

"So, another year of straight A's?" I ask.

"Maybe," she says. "I'll know next week when grades come out."

"You're just being modest."

"A.P. Calculus was a challenge this year. Yesterday was hot. I mean, it was in the 90s, and I had a problem staying focused on my review."

I'm always surprised when Ellen says she's struggling with any class, but especially a math class. I'm taking regular calculus next fall, and I'm expecting to really struggle. But to get work in astronomy, you have to have a strong background in math. It's not that I don't like math. I just find it hard. So, I'll have to work harder in my senior year if I expect any college to take me seriously as a potential astronomy major.

"Maybe you should just skip your senior year and go straight to college," I say.

"No, I want to hang around to see what you decide to do. That is, if you ever decide."

"Well then, you'll be happy to know that Mom just announced that she, Dad, and I are getting together on Monday to make me a college plan."

"That's great, Jackson. Better late than never. Have you decided where you'd like to apply?"

"I haven't decided anything," I say, trying to look exasperated. "So far, it's been Mom doing all the deciding."

"You know, it's great that your parents are interested enough in your future that they are pushing you toward college."

"Yeah, it's great," I say sarcastically.

"So have you done any thinking about where you'd like to go?"

"I'm still not sure I want to go anywhere. But if I do go, I'd want it to be somewhere I can major in astronomy."

"You know the University has a BS program with a major in astronomy," Ellen says. "That sounds perfect—in-state tuition and you can live at home."

"You forget one thing, honor student Ellen. My grades."

"Any chance that your final grades this year will bring up your GPA?"

"There's a chance. Having more time to study before the holiday helped, and working with Ana on my Spanish II conversation skills also helped. Dad even got Eric to work last Sunday, so I could spend the day studying. I feel like the tests on Monday and Tuesday went well. But even if I get all B's and an A or A minus in writing, that won't push my total GPA up much."

"You should still think about applying at the U, Jackson," Ellen says. "At least go over to the admissions office and talk with them."

It feels like Ellen is channeling Mom.

"Okay, Mom," I say sarcastically. "But if by some terrible mistake I don't actually get accepted at the University—hard as that is to believe—are there any other smaller schools that we could afford and that might allow me to major in astronomy?"

"There's a number of state colleges in the West that might have BS programs with a major or minor in Astronomy, and you'd probably have a chance of getting more financial aid at a less prestigious school."

I'm trying to visualize myself living someplace besides Western Washington. It's hard to do. Still, Ellen means well, and she's probably right. I need to do some research on schools, and I need to do it by Monday.

"The first film in the Summer of Film series will be a comedy about a Chinese family dealing with a grandmother's terminal illness," says Dad.

It's less than two weeks before the Summer of Film starts, and Dad has called a staff meeting to see that everyone has looked at the schedule and knows what he expects.

"Sounds like a film that will connect with a lot of different people," Raji remarks with his usual enthusiasm.

"It was a big hit at Sundance," says Genevieve. I'm a little surprised to see her at a regular staff meeting, but she's here today.

Dad says, "And thanks to Genevieve we've got this film for a full week before anyone else in town is screening it. I'm hoping that we'll get good crowds, especially for that first weekend right after the 4th.

"Then starting on July 12th we'll be screening a selection of documentaries, some with local connections and some that have won awards. And beginning on July 19th, we have one week of assorted films by local filmmakers, with seven local filmmakers coming to do Q and A's. During the day on Friday, July 26th, there will be a filmmakers workshop, and that evening we will start showing a new feature film by a local first-time director, which will run six days through the end of July."

As I hear Dad talk, I wonder about this type of programming. What size of an audience can we expect for films by mostly unknown local filmmakers? I hope he knows what he's doing.

Apparently, Dad has anticipated these concerns, and wants to head off any future criticism if the local filmmakers mini-fest doesn't draw well.

"You may wonder what kind of an audience we can reasonably expect to get for work by local filmmakers. So, Ellen, can you update everybody on where we stand with promoting the local filmmakers' portion of the Summer of Film schedule?"

And, no surprise, Ellen is ready with an answer.

"We're doing some special marketing to local film organizations like Film Forum, and the filmmakers themselves are doing marketing on their websites and Facebook pages. Someone from the *Cascadian* will be here to interview Scott and Genevieve. So hopefully, we'll get a good turnout for these films."

"I can tell you," says Genevieve, following up on what Ellen has said, "that I'm hearing good things about the Summer of Film from the folks I know in the Seattle film community. Many are out in their communities promoting the films we'll be showing."

If I didn't know Genevieve better, I'd question how effective that kind of promotion can be.

"That's why we wanted to have local filmmakers involved with the Summer of Film," says Dad. "If we're supportive of local filmmakers, they'll likely become another source of good word-of-mouth advertising for the theater.

"And thanks to Raji for bringing to our attention the local filmmaker whose thriller we'll be screening at the end of July."

Raji smiles and explains, "I knew this guy because I crewed for him a couple of weeks last summer when he was shooting in Seattle."

"I think Rick is well-known in the local film community, and I believe that we will see a good turnout for his film," adds Genevieve.

"Can staff watch some of the films, as long as it doesn't impact their work?" Clarice asks.

"Most of you will probably want to come to films on your days off. All films are free for staff, and we're designating three seats in the back row as staff seating.

"But if you're scheduled to work on a particular day, you'll need to stay in the concession area or the office, unless the house is very small, and then you'll need to check with either Jackson or myself before you go into the film."

Dad's obviously trying to be diplomatic on this point. But he really expects staff scheduled during the Summer of Film to be working.

"Incidentally, to give this film a decent six-day run, before we start the mini-fest on women directors, we'll be open on Monday, July 29th, and Jackson will be in charge that day."

Yes, my work schedule and responsibilities are going to balloon again come July 5th. Dad made that point when he talked with me about my summer schedule a few weeks ago. So, this doesn't come as a surprise, just a disappointment.

"As our assistant manager," he said, "you'll need to take more responsibility during the Summer of Film. You need to be a model for the rest of the staff, so remember to be positive."

"Also," Dad says as he continues talking to the staff, "when I'm introducing films, like during the documentaries run, staff will want to check with Jackson about minor problems. In fact, Jackson will be your go-to person whenever I'm not in the building or can't be interrupted.

"You should all have your work schedules for July, and I want to have the August schedules out by July twelfth," Dad adds. "Okay then, let's make—"

Before Dad can finish, Eric breaks in with one more question. "So, what's the to-be-determined film at the end of the festival?"

The Summer of Film lasts through the three-day Labor Day Weekend. We're even going to be open on Labor Day. But the program flyer for those last three days just says TBD.

It's Genevieve who answers Eric's question. "It's a film or films we'll announce later in July. Something big, we hope. But for now, I can't tell you more than that. You'll just have to wait and see."

"And that's a good way to answer any questions you get from customers about the schedule," Dad says. "Ask them to be patient and wait, and there will be more information forthcoming later in July."

Scott Ryan
Journal Entry
July 1, 2019

I feel like this could be a make-or-break two months for the Magic Lantern. Of course, I'm being positive, especially in front of the theater staff. But there is a lot riding on us being able to keep the theater seats filled throughout July and August—our financial stability for one thing, and our status as the film center for North Seattle for another.

I haven't been sleeping well. There has been so much to do to get the Gala organized, so many decisions to make about the program, and publicity, and equipment. Genevieve has been great, even when she hasn't agreed with all my decisions. Plans for the movie poster auction are running behind. It's been hard to get information out of the person who is organizing it. I just hope it wasn't a mistake to get him involved in such an important project. He is so excited about helping the theater that he's working cheap. Given what we're spending to bring in Jordan Walters, anything that saves money really helps. Some days I'm so tired I can hardly think by the end of the day.

CHAPTER 22

The Man Who Loved to Show Movies

Ana and I made plans to meet again at the public library for another Spanish lesson. But when she arrives, I can tell that she's preoccupied.

"There are rumors that the government is going to do sweeps in certain cities, places like Seattle that are friendly to immigrants, looking for undocumented people that they can deport," she says.

"Are you worried that they might come after you?"

"We're supposed to be protected from deportations, at least until the Supreme Court rules on this administration's policy on the deportation of Dreamers. I don't know what to think. Regardless, my grandparents and I are scheduled to visit a college in California next week. So everybody thinks it's best if I stay around the house until we leave."

"Oh." I don't know what to say. "I guess there's a lot of stress in your world right now."

"Yes," says Ana, "there is. We hear these rumors all the time, and usually nothing happens. So anyway, I wanted to let you know in person, rather than just calling you. But I'm not going to be able to stay."

I can tell that she's sincere, and I can sort of understand how stressful it must be in her situation. But I was really looking forward to seeing her. I want to ask her if we can plan something for when she gets back, but instead, I say, "I understand. Right now, it's important for you to be safe."

She smiles, and then out of the blue gives me a big hug.

"You're a good friend, Jackson."

Well, I'd like to be a little more than that. But right now that seems like the best I can hope for.

What I couldn't tell Ana was that I'd agreed to go on three college visits—one each in July, August, and September—with Mom. I had wondered how these were going to fit into my work schedule at the theater. But Dad agreed to a plan that has the first two scheduled on Mondays in the third weeks in July and August. The theater will be closed on those Mondays, and Dad will be in charge on Tuesdays.

I also have an appointment to talk with someone in the Admissions Office at the University.

"That's great," Ellen said when I told her. "I think at least investigating college is the right thing to do. After all it's about your future."

Yeah, I guess I can see that.

The Spider Man film we're screening right before the beginning of the Summer of Film has been well attended.

"Why didn't Scott schedule the Spider Man to start the Summer of Film?" Raji asks when he returns from his time off.

"Genevieve did the scheduling," Dad said when I asked him, "and the film was opening at a bunch of other theaters on July fifth, so this gave us a head start on the competition."

Dad also said that this would probably be a plus for the Summer of Film. Because getting big crowds right before the Gala means we've had an opportunity to market to more people who'll now have the Summer of Film on their minds.

I get July 4th off, but it hardly seems like a holiday. Dad is working and Mom is resting. The day before, Ana called me to say that her trip to California had gone well and to mention that her family was having a family-only holiday celebration at their house. So, getting together on July 4th is out of the question. After what happened the last time I saw her, I wasn't surprised. Anyway, I end up going with Ellen and some of her friends to the fireworks display at the lake.

I sleep late on the 5th and just hang around the house until 2:30, when I catch a bus into the U District for the first night of the Summer of Film. On the ride in, I notice how quiet everything seems. There is some traffic, but nothing like a regular Friday afternoon. People are on the street in the District, but the numbers are smaller than usual.

Dad has been at the theater since before noon, getting the Magic Lantern ready for what he hopes will be big crowds coming to see today's film.

We have scheduled three screenings of *The Farewell* on each of the first three days of this film's run. At concessions, I put money in the till, turn on the machines, and then make sure we have Summer of Film flyers in both the lobby and the salon.

Dad opens the ticket window and then unlocks the front door at 3:15, and we wait for the crowd. Nobody shows up until about ten minutes before show time, when a small group of Asian women buy tickets. By the time Dad does his short introduction to the film and the Summer of Film, there are maybe thirty people in the seats. But if Dad feels disappointed in this initial turnout, he doesn't show it.

Raji comes in at six. With just thirty minutes between the first two screenings, we definitely need two people besides Dad on site to get the theater clean and concessions ready.

Attendance at the 6:45 show is about double the first show, and Dad looks almost cheerful when he come out after doing his introduction to the film.

"So the 3:45 crowd was small?" Raji asks Dad when he walks by on his way to do his introduction to the first evening showing.

"It was about what I expected. For the first screening of the festival and the Friday of a major holiday weekend, having thirty to forty people in the seats for the first screening is about what I expected.

"Anyway, I really appreciate your being willing to add shifts, Raji. We're going to have some big crowds. Even tomorrow and Sunday could be big, and we're going to need everybody who can work."

Dad nods and smiles at me. It feels like he's giving me a message—be more like Raji. Then he turns and walks into the screening room.

"Dad's nothing if not an optimist," I say after he is gone.

"Oh, he loves this," answers Raji.

"I know he loves the movies, but running a small theater and not really knowing if you're going to make it financially, that can't be much fun."

"Scott loves running this place," Raji says again. "He's like a showman. He loves showing movies in his movie house, and he wants everybody who comes to see a movie here to leave loving it and the theater."

I don't say anything, but I guess that's true. Dad is a man who loves showing movies.

So it turns out Dad was right, at least initially. We have a much bigger attendance for the Saturday screenings, the evening shows are almost full, and we're busy. Along with Dad, there are four staff in the building: Raji, Ellen, Eric, and me. It is the most staff we've ever had working in the Magic Lantern at one time.

For some reason, having this many people working makes everything more fun. I run the film and help out where needed. Raji and Eric work concessions. Ellen sells tickets and helps clean up between films, while Dad introduces the film and chats with customers as they arrive and leave after the showing.

Between the evening showings, Genevieve stops by to talk with Dad, and afterwards she comes back to the lobby and finds me.

"We had a full house for the 6:45 show."

"Yeah," I say. "Today was much better than Friday."

"Well, first days after holidays, especially one where people usually do something outside or out-of-town, can be slow. But tonight's crowd is encouraging, and Scott said all the comments he'd gotten from people so far were positive."

I nod. "It's a good start to the Summer of Film," I say, sounding unusually positive.

"How are you feeling about having to work more during the Summer of Film?"

"Conflicted," I say. "Dad actually scheduled four of us to work over the weekend, and the work has felt a lot more manageable, even with the bigger crowd, than when there are only two or three of us."

"That's good. He said he was going to schedule more staff, at least on weekends during the Summer of Film."

Dad hadn't said that to me. But it only makes sense, and I'm glad to hear it.

Over Genevieve's shoulder, I see someone who looks familiar going into the theater office.

"There's that odd gentleman. I can't remember his name. You know, the one who was such a fan of the theater. Anyway, I think he just went into the office."

Genevieve looks toward the office and smiles.

"You mean Mr. Belvedere."

"Yes, that's him," I say. "I wonder what he wants with Dad?"

I haven't heard much about the poster auction. It's listed but without a date on the Summer of Film flyer, and Dad mentioned it at the staff meeting, but without any details.

"So there is going to be a poster auction?"

"It looks that way. But I'm not really involved with the planning. Scott's dealing with that," Genevieve says.

"I know he's a collectibles dealer, but what's this guy's connection with movie posters?"

"He's got a store in Bellevue, and a big online site. And according to Scott, one of his specialties is movie poster art."

For not being involved in planning the poster auction, Genevieve sure knows a lot.

"So when is the auction going to be?"

"That's the question. Apparently, there is some difference of opinion on what day to have it. But I don't really know why it isn't on the schedule."

This provides me with an opening to ask again about the TBD film over the last weekend.

"We had a little trouble deciding about what we should schedule, a single film or a retrospective."

"I bet Dad wanted to do another retrospective."

"Yes, he had someone he really wanted to showcase."

I try to visualize the discussions between Dad and Genevieve. Dad can be stubborn, but I bet Genevieve finally got him to come around and accept whatever film she was suggesting.

As people start to arrive for the 9:20 screening, I notice Mr. Belvedere quickly leaving the theater.

"So can you tell me what the TBD film for that last weekend of the Summer of Film will be?"

"Scott's going to make an announcement next week, but it's not going to be a single film."

"It's going to be another miniseries?"

"Another director's retrospective," Genevieve says.

I'm surprised. Actually, I'm stunned. I can't believe Dad's going to run two retrospectives in a row to end the Summer of Film. I'd like to know more, but most of the crowd is seated, and Dad walks by, heading for the screening room to do his introduction.

"Thanks," I say to Genevieve. "I've got to go run a movie."

CHAPTER 23

Topsy Turvy

On Monday, I interrupt Dad in his office at home to mention what Genevieve said about running a second retrospective to end the Summer of Film.

"Yes," Dad says. "We're ending the Gala with two retrospectives. The last one will be a short, four-day retrospective of films by Hirokazu Kore-eda."

Dad loves the films by this Japanese director. According to him, Kore-eda rivals the most famous Japanese directors, with his deliberately paced movies about modern Japanese families and their conflicts.

"This will be a four-film series. The first film will be showing for two days over the holiday weekend. The second film will be *Our Little Sister*. It's Kore-eda's most beautiful film. It will run for three days, end the Summer of Film calendar, and be the first film of our fall schedule. The final two Kore-eda films will follow it and run for three days apiece."

Dad has taken Mom to see every Kore-eda film that's come to town. She particularly liked *Our Little Sister*.

164

He looks at me and offers a bit more detail on why he wants to show these films.

"I believe we'll get an audience for them because we'll have shown Seattle moviegoers throughout the Summer of Film that great films they may not know about are being produced, and the place to see them is the Magic Lantern. The response to *The Farewell* is one indication that we should draw an audience for Kore-eda."

I don't know what to say. Yes, *The Farewell* was popular. And the two Kore-eda films I've seen I liked. One was a quirky film about a down-on-his-luck writer who moonlights as a rather sleazy private eye, and the other was about a murder case in Japan. The film about the private eye was funny, and a little sad because the main character was trying to reconnect with his son, while *The Third Murder* was riveting and had me glued to my seat.

But there were only about twenty-five people in the audience when we saw *The Third Murder*.

"I can't understand why his films don't get a bigger audience in Seattle," I remember Dad saying as we walked back to our car. He was visibly upset by the turnout.

I think Dad sees this as his chance to reintroduce Seattle moviegoers to someone he sees as a major director. But is this the right time to slot in four films by an unpopular director—at the end of maybe the most important event, the Summer of Film, in the Magic Lantern's short new life?

I'm in charge on Wednesday, and when I come back to the office after starting the film, Clarice stops me.

"There's a man waiting for you in the office. He wanted to see Scott, but when I told him that Scott wasn't here, he said he'd wait and talk to you."

"Old or young?" I ask.

"Older."

The man turns out to be Mr. Belvedere.

"Jackson," he says as I walk into the office. "Nice to see you again."

"Mr. Belvedere. What can I do for you?"

He gets this curious look on his face like he's trying hard to remember something.

"Now I remember where I saw you first. Even before we talked after the short films program. It was outside on the street before the theater officially reopened."

Yes," I say. "You asked me if the theater was really going to reopen."

"Oh, yes," Mr. Belvedere smiles wistfully. "What a wonderful day that was."

"So, what can I do for you?" I ask again.

"I have the list I promised Scott."

"The list?"

"Yes, the list of the posters that we'll be selling at the August poster auction."

"Oh."

So, Genevieve was right. There is going to be a poster auction.

Mr. Belvedere hands me a three-page list. There are thirty-five posters listed, arranged by the name of the film and listing the country of origin, along with an estimated value. What I notice right away is that American posters are valued considerably lower than the foreign ones. Then I notice the date. The auction will be on August 16th. That's a Friday.

"Well, this is an impressive list."

"I do hope Scott thinks so. I wasn't able to pick up all the older film posters I wanted, and I just got the German and Japanese *Vertigo* posters and the *Dracula* poster on Monday. So I'm a little late, but I wanted the list to be complete when I gave it to Scott."

I glance back at the list. The first page lists just American posters valued mostly between $20 and $30. The second page is a mix of American and foreign posters, with a few listed as high as $100. Only three posters are listed on the last page: *Jaws* (one sheet, excellent condition), *2001: A Space Odyssey* (one sheet, good condition), and the *Bride of Frankenstein* (Style D, good condition). There are no estimated values listed for these posters.

"So how much do you think we'll make from this auction?"

Mr. Belvedere pauses and sort of shakes his head as if reluctant to give a number.

"Oh, it's hard to tell really. It depends on who comes and how much people are willing to spend. Since it's a benefit auction for the theater, we can expect that there will be some overbidding. But with so many good posters now being sold online, you just never know."

"I see," I say, as I look over the three posters listed on the back page. "So the last three posters don't have a value listed?"

"They're the best of the lot. Any estimated value would be too low. But again, it's hard to tell what someone who really wants a particular poster might pay."

"Well, thanks, Mr. Belvedere. I'll give this list to Dad. Can he call you if he has questions?"

"Oh yes, he has my number. But I know he's busy, so if I don't hear from him, I'll call him or come back by. After all, it's only five weeks until the auction."

He smiles again and his eyes seem almost to twinkle.

"I'm really excited about being able to help the theater," he says.

And then after a slight pause, "Could I take a look at the salon for just a minute before I leave?"

"Sure," I say, and walk with him to the entrance to the salon.

"I remember sitting in here with Jennifer after we'd seen a movie we really liked, and just sitting and talking about the film."

I leave him in the salon, go back to the office, and immediately call Dad to let him know that the poster sale list has been delivered. When I walk back into the salon, Mr. Belvedere has gone.

"I expect a core group of documentary lovers to come to see all the documentaries," Dad says on the first day of the documentary mini-fest. "The question is, how many other folks will show up, and for how many films?"

Eric volunteered to work all six days the documentaries are showing. It turns out that he is an aspiring documentary filmmaker and has an in-progress screenplay about a mixed-race family trying to start a restaurant in a neighborhood in South Seattle.

Each of the six documentaries will show two or three times on one specific day of the mini-fest. With my first college visit coming up on Monday and Tuesday, Mom insisted that we get together to talk about it on Saturday. Because of the visits, Dad has limited my work schedule to Friday, Saturday night, and Sunday afternoon, with me returning to a regular schedule on Wednesday. So Ellen was right, there are definite benefits to going on a few college visits, although they are not necessarily the ones she mentioned.

"*Finding Vivian Maier* ran at this theater for the first time in April of 2014," Dad says in his introduction to the first documentary in the mini-fest on Friday. "It ran for almost a month, and those who saw it then, loved it."

"This was the perfect film to start the documentaries program," Dad told me earlier in the week when I asked him about it.

"It's perfect for our regulars and for artists in an artsy town, for those who saw it before and told their friends, and for those who heard about it from their friends but never had a chance to see it."

"So tonight we thought it would be appropriate to bring this wonderful, award-winning documentary about an eccentric, 35mm street photographer back to kick off our documentary mini-fest."

There are only about twenty-five people at the four o'clock showing of *Finding Vivian Maier* and about twice that number at the seven o'clock showing. Still, almost everybody has a positive comment as they leave.

"Thanks for showing this again," a woman with her husband says. "I remember seeing it here in 2014 and loving it."

"I liked how the filmmakers approached the photographer's story as solving a mystery," an older man with a cane and a big smile says to Dad as he walks out. "A good friend of mine who saw it when it was first shown recommended it, and I'm glad I came."

"It's really about finding out who Vivian Maier is," someone behind the man says. It's Clarice. I didn't recognize her at first. She is always dressed up when she works, but tonight she's wearing jeans, a plain blouse, and a baseball cap.

"Clarice," Dad says, "what did you think?"

"It works for me, both as an examination of her work and a search for her identity."

"Certainly she was an eccentric, but what a talent. Are you a photographer?"

"I do a little," Clarice responds. "I'd really like to see an exhibit of her work. I know someone who works at SAM, and I'll ask her if they've considered showing her photos."

It makes sense that Clarice is interested in photographic art. She's a design student.

After the second show, Dad seems happy with both the turnout and the comments.

"It's a good start," he says as we close the theater. I don't say anything, but I think he was right because, despite the attendance, it felt like the right film to start the documentary mini-fest.

Maybe it's all the positive customer comments on this first documentary, or maybe it's my feelings after my first college visit. But I'm feeling more positive about working at the theater and the Summer of Film.

The next film up, *Honeyland*, a documentary on Europe's last female bee hunter and her efforts to preserve native bees, draws a much bigger crowd when it is shown on Saturday. Even Dad seems surprised at the turnout.

"It was screened at the film festival and it looks like positive word-of-mouth on the film got a lot of people interested."

When I open the theater doors on Sunday, I'm surprised to find Ana, Carlos, Alfredo, and Peter Bergmeier waiting in line to see *Bisbee 17*.

After they get their seats, Ana and Carlos come out to talk with me.

"Any chance after the movie starts you can come sit with us?" Carlos asks.

"Not really. I've got to help Clarice at concessions. But we can talk after the film. I'm only working the matinee today."

"So you're not living here anymore?" Carlos asks sarcastically.

"I'm going to Bellingham College tomorrow on a school visit, so Dad gave me the night off. He's coming in to work the evening show."

"You've decided to go to college after all. That's great," Ana says.

"I've agreed to go on a couple of college visits. That's all."

The theater lights flicker, which means customers have five minutes to get back to their seats.

"It's popcorn time," says Carlos.

He turns to Ana. "I'm getting the humongous size, so everybody can have some. Do you want anything to drink?"

"I'll pass on the popcorn, and I can get myself a diet coke. You'll probably have your hands full getting that much popcorn back to the seats."

Carlos grins. "I see, you want to talk with Jackson alone. Okay."

Ana doesn't respond, but she waits for him to walk over to concessions.

"So you'll have time to talk after the movie?"

"Sure," I say.

"Maybe we can have coffee somewhere. I have a couple of things I want to talk about."

Is Ana asking me out? I can hardly believe it.

"Great. I'll need to hang around till Dad gets here. But he'll probably be here by 6:00. Then we can go over to that bookstore coffeehouse on the Ave."

She smiles. "See you after the film."

Then she goes to concessions to get her drink.

Bisbee 17 is a film about the forced deportation of twelve hundred mine workers from Bisbee, Arizona in 1917. It's a combination of traditional documentary and a reenactment by people who live in Bisbee today.

I step into the screening room for a minute or two about halfway through the show. It's a dramatic story. But my mind isn't really on the movie. It's on Ana asking me to have coffee. Regardless of what she wants to talk about, it seems like a step forward in our relationship.

Dad hasn't shown up yet when the film is over. So I stand by the door thanking those who came, many of whom are talking about the film.

"I've never heard this story," a middle-aged woman says.

"Of course you haven't," the Hispanic man with her says. "This isn't the kind of history Americans, particularly those in power, want you to know about."

As I walk from the front entrance to see how many people are still in the building, two women are standing in front of the stairs to the bathrooms, talking about the film.

"They closed off communication with the outside world until the deportees had been dumped off in New Mexico. Can you believe it?" one of them asks.

"Companies had that much power in the past. What gets me is that the federal government investigated this, but nobody was charged with anything."

When I turn around, I notice Alfredo and Peter talking in the lobby and walk over to them. I don't see Ana.

"I didn't know such things could happen in America," Alfredo says. "I thought it was just the current administration that was so racist."

"This is our history," Peter says as they get to me. "Isn't that right, Jackson?"

I'm not sure what to say. Of course, I know about slavery and the forced Japanese relocations during World War II, along with some smaller incidents like the big Chinese deportation from Tacoma in 1885. Yes, these things did happen in the United States. But I keep feeling that Peter is always recruiting for some cause, and so the story he's telling is how bad things are. But is it really?

"Well, I'd never heard about this incident before," I say, "and I only saw a little bit of the film. But maybe I'll get to see more later and then I'll have an opinion."

For some reason my response sets Peter off.

"You know I talked with Scott about having more social problem films at this festival. I know in the past he's been a bit of a climate activist. But he said he didn't think having more of those films would draw an audience."

"No," I say, "I didn't know that." But I'm not surprised.

Out of the corner of my eye, I see Dad and Ellen come in and walk into the theater office. Peter sees them too.

"Well, before I forget, I'd like you to consider coming with Ana and Carlos to a big demonstration we're having in August at the South Sound Federal Detention Center," he says. "People from all the immigrant rights groups will be gathering there to support closing the center."

"I'm working every day except Mondays until the Summer of Film is over."

Peter frowns. "Is that even legal?" he asks.

I'm starting to feel irritated, and I think Peter can tell that he's pushing me a bit too hard.

"Okay, so just think about it, Jackson," he says, "and talk with Ana about it, too. I'm sure she'll be coming."

Just then I see that Ana is right behind Peter. He realizes it too, so he turns, smiles at her, and then joins Carlos and Alfredo, who are standing by the concession stand talking.

"Was Peter talking to you about the detention center protest?"

"Yeah, and he's getting a little pushy," I say.

"It's really important that people, especially white people, come out and support closure of the Federal Detention Center."

We walk into the salon, which is empty except for a couple of people picking up Summer of Film flyers and a woman who appears to be waiting for someone.

We sit on the couch.

"When is it?"

"It's the last Friday in August."

"That's the beginning of the Labor Day weekend, and the last big weekend of the Summer of Film. There's no way Dad will give me that day off."

"I understand, Jackson. You have to support your dad. But couldn't you just ask? Maybe Ellen could work your shift that day?

"There have been so many horror stories about what's happening to folks being held at the detention center. We're trying to support a proposal in the state legislature to close this facility, and we need to have a big turnout at this demonstration."

I can tell this was important to Ana. But honestly, I'm not that interested in being in another demonstration.

"I'll ask," I say, "but I can't promise anything."

Ana looks a little deflated. But all I can think about is going for coffee.

"Dad's here, and that means I'm officially off. So, let's go for coffee.

She doesn't answer and seems to be thinking, when Dad walks into the salon. He smiles and says, "Hey, you two, what are you doing in here alone?"

Ana livens up. "We're talking about movies, of course," she says.

"So what did you think of this film?"

"It's a real history lesson. I wish more people would have come to see it."

"What was the house?" Dad asks me.

"Forty-five people, maybe fifty. We can get the final count from the number of tickets sold."

"I see Peter Bergmeier is here. Did he come with you, Ana?"

"Yes. Four of us came—Peter, me, Carlos, and Alfredo."

"I should go talk with him," Dad says with shrug. "He wanted me to show more social action films as part of the documentaries, but I thought a variety of documentaries, with most focusing on individuals, would be the best draw."

He seems to be talking directly to Ana. Maybe trying to justify why we didn't have some films on immigrants.

She just nods. But then just when it looks like Dad is going to turn and walk away, she brings up something else.

"I'm doing a report on women filmmakers for my summer arts class, and I thought you might be able to help me."

Dad looks interested. "That's great. Are you going to come to the films by women directors?"

"Yes, as many as I can. But I was also wondering if you could arrange for me to interview Jordan Walters when she is here."

This is out of the blue. I remember Ana saying that she might do her summer school project on women filmmakers. But I didn't hear any more about it. Of course, until today I hadn't talked with Ana for about three weeks.

If Dad is surprised by Ana's request he doesn't show it.

"Sure," he says. "I'll talk to her, and then Jackson can let you know what she says. It's a little late to be changing her schedule, but I think she might be willing to do it for a young woman. In the meantime, I can refer you to some sources that you might be interested in."

Then he turns to me. "Jackson, Ellen is here to update our website. She and I are also going to talk about other ways to publicize the Kore-eda retrospective. I need you to stay in the theater while we are meeting. I doubt it will take more than about thirty minutes."

Before I can say anything, he's gone, heading back to the office. I don't have a chance to protest or, as it turns out, to ask Ana if she can wait so we can keep our coffee date.

"Jackson, let's get together sometime later in the week at the coffeehouse in Wedgewood," she says. It feels like she's had second thoughts about the whole coffee date idea. But what can I do but agree.

"Sure," I say, trying not to sound as disappointed as I feel. "I'll be gone tomorrow and most of Tuesday, but I can call you on Tuesday night."

"Why don't I call you?" says Ana. "I'll tell my grandparents that we're meeting to talk about my summer school report. Then we can set a date."

Waiting for Dad to get out of his meeting with Ellen, I help Clarice clean up the theater. Right now my life feels totally frustrating. I'm going on my first college visit, even though I'm not sure I really want to go to college. I'm working more at the theater again, even though Dad promised I'd be working less. One minute Ana and I are having a coffee date, and the next minute we're meeting sometime in the future to talk about her homework. Everything just feels topsy-turvy.

CHAPTER 24

Friends

It's Wednesday afternoon when Ana calls, and I'm just heading out for my shift at the theater. She wants to meet after we know whether Dad has been able to set up an interview with Jordan Walters, so we decide to get together at the library in Wedgewood on Monday. She doesn't ask me how my first college visit went.

But Ellen does. She's at the Magic Lantern working on the computer when I get there.

"Hi," I say. "Updating Facebook?"

"Hi to you," Ellen says. "And yes, I'm updating our Facebook page with some new information on the Linklater and Kore-eda retrospectives. So, how was the trip to Bellingham College?"

"How did you hear about that?"

"Scott mentioned it to me. I knew you were doing some college visits, but you never told me where or when. In fact, when was the last time we just hung out together? And I don't mean talking here at the theater," says Ellen, rather sarcastically.

"Maybe July 4th," I say sheepishly. She's right, we've only gotten together once since school was out.

"You want to catch a coffee or some food at the Picasso Café tomorrow?" I ask.

"Sure, how about noon?"

"How about 12:30? Mom and I are getting together to talk about the Bellingham trip mid-morning, and I'll need to decompress afterward."

I get to the Picasso Café at about 12:40. The day is warm enough that Ellen is sitting at one of the little outside tables drinking an iced soy latte.

"Sorry I'm late," I say. "I've been walking around the hill since 11:30."

"Was the Bellingham trip that bad?"

"No, it has a nice campus, lots of trees, and it's close to downtown."

"But?"

"They have a BS degree program in physics and astronomy, but it seems like it's heavy on the five basic theories, and lighter on things like astronomical observation."

"Did you talk with anyone in that department?"

"With a grad student, but she wasn't too helpful. I think she was more of a physics person than an astronomy person. She gave me the name of the prof who teaches most of the astronomy classes. Mom wants me to call him."

"What did your mom think about the school?"

"She liked it. I think mostly because it's close to Seattle, and the tuition is lower than at the University."

Ellen takes a drink of her coffee. Then she says, "Maybe it's a school you should consider."

"Yeah, maybe."

"Couldn't you get financial aid?"

"I don't know ... probably some. Anyway, she wants me to apply at the University too. She's even suggesting I live at home."

"Oh," says Ellen. "I thought your parents had a college fund they'd started for you."

"That's what I thought too. Supposedly, they had saved enough money for me to go out-of-state if I wanted to. But when I asked Mom about it, she said that they want it to last for at least my first two years, so it would be best if I go in-state."

"So you should apply at the U."

"Why? The U won't accept me. My grades are too low. And if I do go to college, I want to go somewhere where I can live on campus."

All this college talk is making me nervous.

"Well, you know what I think?" Ellen waits for a response, but none is forthcoming. "I think if Bellingham is your best bet, you should apply there."

"Are you going to apply at the U?" I ask, switching the conversation to her plans.

"Probably. I'd really like to go to California or back East. But the in-state tuition here makes the U more affordable."

There's a pause, and then Ellen asks, "So how are things going with Ana?"

"Not so hot. She seems to be preoccupied with other things, like her summer school class and the big immigration protest at the end of August."

"She's busy alright. There's no chance for the two of you to get together to do something?"

"She's writing a report on women movie directors for her summer art class, and she actually asked Dad to get her an interview with Jordan Walters, the film critic who's coming to speak at the beginning of the women directors retrospective."

Ellen's eyebrows raise. "Wow, what did Scott say?"

"He's going to talk with Walters to see if he can arrange it."

"So that's probably your opportunity to stay connected with Ana. Help her with her report, or join her to see a couple of the films by women directors. And maybe you two could go together to the march on the detention center."

"There's no chance for that. In fact, there's no chance for me to do much at all until after the Summer of Film ends on Labor Day weekend. But we're supposed to get together at the café in Wedgewood once we know whether she's going to get her interview or not."

"Well, that sounds positive," Ellen says.

"I'm not sure if she wants my help with her report, or if she wants to talk more about the march."

"Well, at least you two will have a chance to talk, and that could lead to something else."

"Yeah, maybe," I say unconvincingly.

Unfortunately, I don't know much about women film directors. Dad's the one she needs to talk to. But maybe I can talk him into giving me one afternoon free to see a film with her. Still, the more I think about that, the more I realize even that's unlikely. So right now, I'm feeling pretty pessimistic. It seems like the possibility of us getting together for anything like a date is about zero.

I look at my watch. It's almost 2:00, and I'm supposed to meet Dad at the theater at 2:30. I can only guess what he wants to talk about.

"I've got to catch the bus. You coming to the theater today?"

"Not today. The Astronomy Club is meeting at my house at 4:00," Ellen says.

I haven't been able to attend a club meeting since May.

"So is everybody going to the July star party—everyone but me?"

"Yes. The Seattle Astronomical Society is having a party at the park celebrating the fiftieth anniversary of the Apollo 11 Mission, starting at 9:00 p.m. So some of us are making food to take and share. Then, at dusk, everyone will start looking at the sky."

"Isn't it a full moon this week?" I'm so uninvolved in the group right now that I'm not even looking at the night sky websites to see what's going to be in the sky each month.

"Yes," says Ellen. "But that was on Monday, and the moon is now in a waning mode. Jupiter and Saturn should both be visible once the sky is dark enough."

Then she adds, "If the weather is this nice on Saturday, it will be a great night for stargazing."

"Yeah." After a pause I add, "Say hi to everyone for me. Sure hope I can be more involved again, starting in September."

Sitting on the bus I feel totally dejected.

"So, I'm going to need you to work every day of the Northwest Filmmakers series," Dad says.

I've hardly had time to sit down when he drops this on me. But I'm not surprised.

"There will be filmmakers here each day. They will be introducing their films at the evening showings and taking questions after their movie finishes. I'll have to be with them most of the time, and I'll only be able to check in with you while the film is in progress.

"Both Clarice and Raji will be working Friday, Saturday, and Sunday, and Eric and Raji will be working Tuesday through Thursday. But you'll be in charge each of those days."

As he's talking, I remember what Peter said when I saw him at Ana's party—Dad's working me so much might be illegal. Then I tell myself, this isn't going to help.

Earlier in the week, I heard Dad talking to someone on his cell phone, and I think he said that attendance at the documentaries had been "just okay." That made me wonder if the theater is still making it financially. So now, maybe because I'm feeling angry, or maybe because I'm upset at the pressure I'm getting to decide about college, I just blurt out, "Is this Summer of Film thing working? I mean, are you making money or losing money with it?"

Dad just stares at me for a moment and then says, "Well Jackson, we're breaking even so far, and I'm very optimistic about what we've got coming up, especially the Northwest Filmmakers series and the retrospective on women directors."

I know he's upset with my question. But he doesn't let it show.

"We had pretty good houses for *Honeyland* and the documentary on Tony Morrison."

Really Dad? I know that the film about the female beekeeper did well, and I haven't been keeping track of the audience numbers for the later documentaries. But what I've heard anecdotally from Eric and Ellen is that the house was less than half full for about everything else.

I get up to leave, but then Dad stops me.

"Oh, I forgot. Jordan Walters is fine with sitting for an interview with Ana. She's staying at the hotel on 45th, and she wants Ana to meet her in the coffee shop there on Friday, August 2nd, at 10:30 a.m. Can you let Ana know the interview is on?

"I've also got links to a couple of websites I'll send to your computer, so you can give them to her to look at. The IndieWire list should be particularly helpful. I assume she knows how to do research on the internet."

"Ana couldn't get the grades she gets without knowing how to do research. She's determined to go to college."

Dad looks at me and then smiles.

"Well then, I'm glad that you and she are friends."

I start to ask Dad about getting time off to see a film or two in the women directors series with Ana, but it's definitely the wrong time. I'll have a better chance of getting him to say yes if I can tell him I'm helping Ana with her report. If Dad thinks Ana is a good influence on me, he may be willing to cut me some slack during the women directors retrospective to help me keep the friendship going.

Ana will be excited when she hears she's going to get an interview with Jordan Walters. So now all I have to do is convince her that I really know enough about women directors to be able to help her with her report. And that will be a challenge.

Scott Ryan
Journal Entry
July 20, 2019

We had big audiences for The Farewell, *the documentary* Honeyland, *and the film on Toni Morrison. The other documentaries got respectable crowds. As I expected, the docs that got the biggest audiences were focused on individual people, not causes or history.*

Yesterday's film, the opening film in the local filmmakers series, was almost a full house. People like to meet local filmmakers and hear them talk about their films. The big question is: what kind of audience will we get for some of the quirkier films next week? About 40 people have signed up so far for the filmmakers workshop on the 26th. At $50 a registration, and with five more days before registration ends, I believe the workshop is going to turn a profit.

But we do need, and I am expecting, bigger, more consistent crowds for the Women in Film retrospective. Having Jordan Walters here for the first four days should make a big difference, even if she is expensive. It looks like Ellen's idea of selling a series pass to interested customers will guarantee we have a core audience. I wish I could get these kinds of ideas from Jackson. Still, I'm grateful that he has been willing to work so much over his summer. I really need him to be here when I'm doing introductions to films and dealing with filmmakers.

Apparently, he's interested in this girl Ana, and it sounds like she's more academic, more focused on going to college, than he is. So maybe she will be a good influence.

CHAPTER 25

Local Sightings

The first film in the Northwest Filmmakers series was about the Truman High jazz band. Truman has a nationally recognized jazz band, and it's the pride of the school. I'd hoped I could see part of the film and maybe even hear the director, who is doing a Q and A. But it seems like much of the band's local following turned out to see the film, as both the late afternoon and the seven o'clock shows were essentially sellouts. So between running the film and helping out at concessions, I didn't have much time free while either film was showing.

Saturday's film, *Up, Down and All Around*, is the newest film by Erin something. I can't remember her last name. But Genevieve in the Summer of Film flyer describes her as "a well-known local female director."

She shows up early for the seven o'clock show with two local film critics in tow, to talk with Dad before the screening. I'm not able to see any of her film, but I do catch some of her Q and A afterwards, and she turns out to be this very attractive blond with an infectious smile and a great sense of humor. She seems to love answering questions, and she has some really interesting observations on independent filmmaking. She even hangs around for about twenty minutes after the Q and A and talks with people in the salon.

Dad said that she was very popular with her film crews, and I can see why she would be fun to work with.

She stops me at the door on her way out.

"You're Jackson, right? Scott's son?"

"Yeah, that's me."

"How's the Summer of Film doing?"

I'm hesitant to say anything, but she's obviously expecting an answer.

"I guess we're doing okay. The opening week film, the documentary *Honeyland*, and the first film in the Northwest Filmmakers series did well. And this film—I mean your film—was basically a sellout for both shows."

"This was great," she says. She's obviously happy with the turnout. "And it's good to hear that the Summer of Film is doing well. It can be really hard to get people inside to see films when the weather is nice."

"Everybody says that," I say. But just as I do, Dad and Genevieve show up.

She swings her arms open and says, "Scott, it looks like your big gamble is taking off. I was so glad to be part of the Summer of Film."

She gives Dad a big hug. He looks a little embarrassed and is probably glad Mom isn't here.

"Thanks, Erin. It was great to be able to show your film in the Gala."

A group of customers get Erin's attention and start asking her questions about her film. Dad uses the opportunity to go back into the office, while Genevieve and I just watch. Erin certainly has some avid fans.

As the last of the customers leave the theater, Genevieve and I walk back into the office. Dad is ecstatic, "How about that turnout, Jackson? Four sellouts in two days, and we've got four more super films by local directors set to go."

"Erin was right," says Genevieve. "It's pretty encouraging to see this kind of turnout for two local films. Although there might be a little drop off with the films next week."

The feeling of enthusiasm appears to be contagious.

"Scott's gamble seems to be paying off," Raji says, as I help him and Clarice clean up.

"It seems like his plan is working, Jackson," he adds when I don't immediately respond.

"So far, so good," I say. But does Dad really have a plan, or is this, just like Erin said, a big gamble? Genevieve thought so initially, and it's still too early to tell.

Saturday it looked like the Summer of Film could be the biggest event in Seattle this summer. Then reality sets in on Sunday.

It is clear and sunny when I get up. Mom has gone to church, and Dad is working in his office. And when I take a cup of coffee outside to sit on the front porch, it's already feeling warm. It's going to be a hot day.

With the temperature hovering in the mid-80s, a few folks start to wander into the theater for the 4:30 show. Sunday's film is about a group of pickleball devotees, their lives and loves. Pickleball is very popular in Seattle. There are courts all over the city. But by the time the filmmakers—the director and producer—show up at about 4:20, the theater is still only about one third full.

"I guess a lot of the intended audience is out playing pickleball," Clarice says with a smile. "I know that's where I'd be if I wasn't working here."

"You think so?" I say, with just a touch of cynicism.

The evening show does a bit better. Maybe half the seats are full.

"What's the weather forecast for the rest of the week?" Dad asks as the theater clears out after the second show.

"Hot and sunny, I think."

Dad frowns, and I know what he is thinking. He's afraid we may be hitting the summer doldrums, that part of summer when everybody just wants to be outside, and nobody is really thinking about going to the movies.

With five weeks to go, the Summer of Film still looks like a big gamble.

CHAPTER 26

Film Studies

Ana is waiting for me outside the library on Monday. I'd hoped she would suggest that we go sit on the bench with the view and just talk. But she's got a room reserved, and she's brought along her laptop. So I know she's here to work.

When we get into the room, she turns on her laptop and goes immediately to the Women in Film flyer that she has scanned into a PDF.

"So can you tell me about any of these women?" she asks.

I glance at the flyer. Luckily, I had time to talk with Dad about some of these directors, and I also looked at the list of best films by women directors on IndieWire.

Still, I only know what Dad has told me. But I have seen four or five of the films we're showing, and I can tell Ana a bit about how Dad decided on what we're showing.

"I can tell you a little about some of them," I say. Ana seems happy with that.

"Ida Lupino was a well-known actress, who slowly got into directing in the 1950s. She had her own production company for a while. She directed five features. Her films were considered B movies at the time."

"B movies? What's a B movie?"

"In the 1950s, lots of theaters ran double features. They would show a big budget movie with big stars, and then a second film, usually a western or science fiction story, to fill out the bill. These second films were called B movies."

As we're talking, I realize that one benefit of working so closely with Dad at the Magic Lantern—even if it is a hassle sometimes—is that I've learned a lot about the history of the movies.

"So Ida Lupino was a B movie director?"

"Yes, but during the 1950s she was the most prominent woman director working in Hollywood. She was independent and she wanted to make her own movies. Her films featured stories of social significance, hot button issues like rape and bigamy, and the main characters were usually women."

"Have you seen any of her films yourself?" Ana asks.

"I saw her film about a serial killer who kidnaps a couple of men who are on a fishing trip a couple years ago at the film festival."

"They show old films at the festival?"

"According to Dad, they always show a few. Many long-time festival passholders like to see a few older classics each year. They even show one or two silent movies most years."

"They do?"

"Yes, and they do attract an audience. Until this year, Dad has always attended the film festival and he usually took Mom. Once in a while, when he thought there was a movie I'd enjoy, he'd talk me into going. I saw some interesting films and a few strange ones at the festival."

"How did Scott decide on what he wanted to show?" Ana asks. "I did some searching on the net, and there are a lot more women directors than I had realized."

"There sure are," I say. "Look at the IndieWire list of the best films directed by women and you'll see. Dad says he basically used three criteria: importance of the director, impact on film culture, and diversity. He also said he decided early on that he wouldn't pick any films shown before 1940. He calls this an eighty-year retrospective of women filmmakers."

"What's IndieWire?" Ana asks.

"It's a website on independent films."

"So, how many of these films by women directors have you seen?"

I knew she'd ask me that.

"Four or five."

"Of the ones you saw, which ones did you like most?"

Now I've got to think quickly. Can I even remember any of these films?

"*Persepolis*, the animated film based on a graphic novel about a family in Iran, and *Winter's Bone*—that's an intense movie. It's about a girl in Arkansas looking for her missing father who may be a drug dealer. I remember those two."

"Anything else?" Ana asks.

"*Lady Bird*. I'm not sure exactly why I liked it, but maybe it's because I could identify with the main character."

"That's the only one of the retrospective films I've seen," Ana says. "I want to see as many of the others as I can. But my grandparents are already asking if I need to see all the movies. They don't want me to be out every night."

"Every film should have a four o'clock matinee—I think. So try to find out from your research which films are considered groundbreaking or which directors are the most important."

Ana nods. "That's a good idea. Maybe Jordan Walters can give me some idea about which directors she thinks I should really focus on, and what themes or ideas these women explored in their films."

"It sounds like you've got some good ideas for how you want to proceed."

I'm a little out of my depth talking about film criticism. But I feel like I need to sound positive.

"I can tell you what Dad told me about Agnès Varda," I say. But Ana seems to have lost interest in specific directors.

"Has Scott heard if Ms. Walters is willing to talk with me?"

"Oh, I forgot. Yes, she's agreed to sit for an interview. She'll meet you at her hotel, on Friday, August second, at ten in the morning."

I hand Ana a list made with the information about her meeting with Jordan Walters, along with Dad's list of resources on women directors.

Ana looks at the list. She smiles, and suddenly seems more relaxed.

"Oh Jackson, Scott's list is great. He's given me some websites to check for information, and even a couple of articles on film criticism to look at."

Then she points at the list. "And look, here's a link to the IndieWire list. He's even given me a citation to a *Film World* article on Ms. Walters."

Ana pauses and then adds, "And I've got an interview with Jordan Walters." She's beaming, and I can tell she's really excited.

"I didn't have your email address, so I just printed off the list to give to you."

I'm signaling that I'd like to have her email address, but she doesn't pick up on it. She just reaches across the table to touch my hand.

"Thank you and please thank Scott for me."

"Sure, but you know you will see him a lot at the movies, and I think he'd like to know from you what you think of the retrospective."

Ana pulls back her hand, but she's still smiling.

"Can you help me by reading the rough draft and making suggestions?"

"Sure, I'd love to," I say. I must be crazy. What am I agreeing too? But I just can't say no.

Scott Ryan
Journal Entry
July 29, 2019

Oh, the summer weather. When it's sunny and warm in Seattle, nobody wants to go inside to see a movie. Right now, I may be the only person in Seattle who's praying for a cool and cloudy August.

Our audience dropped off for the last few films in the Northwest Filmmakers series. The combination of quirky films and 80-degree sunny days cut the size of the houses. The same has been true of the eco-thriller we are currently showing. After one good weekend, the audience dwindled. Luckily, we locked in the attendees to the Filmmakers Workshop by having them register in advance. So despite the 26th being the hottest day of the summer so far, the workshop made money.

So I'm staying optimistic. I expect the Women in Film retrospective to be well attended—I'm counting on that. But I'm still not sure about the film poster auction. Winston Belvedere hasn't gotten back to me since he left the poster sale list with Jackson. He wants very much to help the theater, and as a collectibles dealer he knows how to acquire and price movie posters. Also, he was willing to work for just a small percentage of the sale profits, 10 percent. It seems like we can't lose money on the auction, but I'm not sure we will make money either. My fingers are crossed that the next two weeks will be a success.

Chapter 27

The Women Who Make Movies

"Welcome to our Women in Film retrospective," Dad says in his best showman's voice. "We'll be showing films by thirteen major women directors, all of whom made their personal marks on the film-making world, and who contributed to the way we see women portrayed in the movies.

"I know that some of you may be thinking, why didn't we program a film by some other woman director you feel was worthy, or why didn't we choose another film—maybe a favorite of yours—to represent the work of one of the directors we're showing.

"When Genevieve Rolland and I programmed the women film directors series, we tried to look for three things: the importance of the director, the importance of the film in the history of film, and diversity. But this retrospective only runs thirteen days, and so we could only program thirteen films, which means it can't be completely representative of the work of all those talented female directors who have contributed to filmmaking since 1940. Still, we think the Women in

196

Film series will provide you with a good sampling of the work of some of the best women directors."

This introduction is classic Scott Ryan. I'm standing in the back of the screening room, listening to him and realizing how much he knows about movies, and how important sharing these movies with other people is to him.

"Given our criteria, you might wonder why we have chosen a couple of the specific films we're showing. Diversity is one reason, and the other is that as the programmers, we reserve the right to show certain films just because we like them."

There is a murmur of laughter from the sellout crowd.

"So yes, personal bias did creep into our programming just a bit. But I believe you'll agree that any of these films and directors deserve to be recognized."

Ana and one of her friends are sitting two rows from the back of the theater. Sitting up front is Genevieve, and on her right is a woman with short dark brown hair, who is wearing glasses. I assume she is Jordan Walters.

"And," Dad says, "I will be in the lobby after each film to answer questions and hear your ideas about what you liked and didn't like. So, if you don't already have one, please pick up one of our Women in Film program flyers, which are also in the lobby."

He holds up a copy of the program flyer. "It's your best guide to the Women in Film retrospective."

WOMEN IN FILM RETROSPECTIVE

The Magic Lantern Theater

August 1–15 *(Closed Mondays)*

August 1   ***Dance, Girl, Dance*** (1940) – Dorothy Arzner

August 2   ***The Bigamist*** (1953) – Ida Lupino

August 3   ***Cleo from 5 to 7*** (1962) – Agnes Varda

August 4   ***Swept Away*** (1974) – Lina Wertmüller

August 6   ***My Brilliant Career*** (1979) – Gillian Armstrong

August 7   ***Desert Hearts*** (1985) – Donna Deitch

August 8   ***Daughters of the Dust*** (1991) – Julie Dash

August 9   ***The Piano*** (1993) – Jane Campion

August 10   ***Eve's Bayou*** (1997) – Kasi Lemmons

August 11   ***Real Women Have Curves*** (2002) – Patricia Cardoso

August 13   ***Persepolis*** (2007) – Marjane Satrapi

August 14   ***Winter's Bone*** (2010) – Debra Granik

August 15   ***Lady Bird*** (2017) – Greta Gerwig

"So now I want to introduce the other half of the programming team, the Magic Lantern's regular film buyer, Genevieve Rolland, who will introduce our guest, Jordan Walters."

Genevieve gets up and gives the audience a thumbnail sketch of Jordan Walter's career.

"We are so lucky to have one of America's most influential film critics joining us for the next four days to introduce films and talk about the impact of women directors. She is the nationally known film critic of the *Chicago Post*, a long-time contributor to the academic journal *Film Perspectives*, and author of *Film Fanatic*, her popular film blog.

"Commentators have called Jordan the best female movie critic in America. But I beg to differ. I think Jordan Walters is the best writer and movie critic in America today."

It's just what I would expect from Genevieve, opinionated but classy. The crowd breaks into applause.

"So now please welcome Jordan Walters."

The applause continues and gets louder. The critic, dressed casually in a green plaid shirt and dark blue slacks, stands up and steps up to the microphone. She looks relaxed and comfortable, and her glasses give her a definite professional look. I can't really tell how old she is.

"Thanks, Genevieve. I'm so happy to be back in Seattle for this fantastic Summer of Film event. When I was here five years ago to participate in a long weekend of the Film Festival, it was rainy or grey every day. So it's great to be back and to finally understand why so many people have told me that Seattle is beautiful in the summer.

"Scott is starting this retrospective with a film by Dorothy Arzner, a key female Hollywood director of the 1930s and early 1940s in America.

"Actually, there were many women making films during the silent era. Maybe the most important of these was Lois Weber. But for almost all of those women, their careers didn't transition into the talkie era. Weber, for example, only made one talkie, her last film in 1934.

"Arzner was a medical student when she dropped out of the University of Southern California in 1917 and became a typist for Famous Players, the company that would become Paramount. She worked her way up, and by 1922 she was a chief editor. In that role, she was best known for her editing of the famous film, *Blood and Sand*. She spent some time screenwriting and then negotiated herself a chance at directing. Her first feature was *Fashions for Women*, a silent film and a rather conventional 'women's picture' released in 1927.

"She directed Paramount's first talking feature, *The Wild Party*, for which she is credited with creating the boom mike, an innovation which allowed actors and films to have more movement.

"During most of the 1930s, Dorothy Arzner was the only woman directing feature films working in Hollywood. Her films focused on women's friendships, and particularly after she left Paramount, they were increasingly centered on strong, independent women involved in unconventional romances. The clearest example of these films is *Christopher Strong*, which stars Katherine Hepburn as an independent aviatrix who falls in love with a married man with tragic results. Other key films directed by Arzner include: *Sarah and*

Son, *Craig's Wife*, and *The Bride Wore Red*, along with the movie we're showing tonight, *Dance, Girl, Dance.*

"Your first reaction to *Dance, Girl, Dance* will probably be that it feels rather dated. But if you look a little deeper, you'll find a film that has all the key elements of an Arzner movie—two characters who are in the burlesque business, but trying to be independent women and make their dreams come true in a world dominated by men. And if you're looking for an underlying message, it's all there in Maureen O'Hara's speech from the burlesque stage at the end.

"*Dance, Girl, Dance* was a flop when it was first released in 1940. A re-examination of the film first began in the 1970s, and many modern critics have called it a landmark in feminist filmmaking."

Ellen walks in and asks me to come help at concessions. They've had a big rush of customers trying to get food before the film starts.

After the film, there's a buzz as customers leave the showing. Some people are talking about the film, others about Jordan Walters, while still others are stopping to talk with Dad, who seems to be enjoying the whole thing tremendously.

There's another big audience for Friday evening's showing of *The Bigamist*. After the show, I spot Ana in the crowd waiting to talk with Dad. As the crowd thins out, I walk over. They're engaged in an animated discussion about the next film on the schedule, Agnès Varda's *Cléo from 5 to 7*.

"Oh, you've got to see the film by Agnès Varda," Dad says. "She was the major female influence in the early French New Wave, and this film has that New Wave style. Much of her work was considered avant-garde, and she was a pioneer in both documentary and feature filmmaking."

"I want to," Ana says, "but my grandparents don't want me to be out alone on Saturday night in the district." Ana's frowning, and I can tell that this is a real conflict for her.

"Come to the matinee at 4:00," I blurt out as I stop by Ana.

Both Ana and Dad look at me.

"Listen to Jackson," Dad says. "You won't hear me suggesting that very often, but right now that's your best alternative."

Ana shrugs. "I'll talk with my grandparents. I don't know what they'll say."

"If you have to cut something ... " Dad stops to think about what he wants to say.

"I really like all the films we've selected to show. But if you have to cut something, I'd cut *Swept Away*. It's playing on Sunday, so that's a day you spend with your grandparents."

Dad's suggestion seems to perk Ana up.

"Yes, that might be a good trade off, particularly if I can come to *Cléo from 5 to 7* tomorrow afternoon." She pauses and then adds, "And maybe I can get someone to come with me."

I thought she meant a girlfriend. But when she walks into the theater on Saturday afternoon, she is with Carlos. They are among the first customers to come in for the four o'clock show, and they stop at the concession stand to talk.

"Carlos," I say, "I'm surprised to see you at a festival on *mujeres directoras de cine*."

"Amigo, I support the women in my life, like my cute friend Ana," he responds, and then gives me a knowing smile.

"I see your grandparents let you come."

"I emailed Jordan," Ana says. "She had given me her email address, with the understanding that I would not share it, and would trash it when the film series ends."

"And what did she say?"

"She said just what Scott said: 'You've got to see *Cléo from 5 to 7* because Varda is important both as a woman director and as an avant-garde filmmaker. She was a key figure in developing the cinematic voice of women in film.'

"When I told my grandparents what she said, and that I would take Sunday off from the film series to spend the day at home, they agreed—reluctantly I think—to let me come, as long as I got someone to go with me."

"And I'm the lucky somebody," Carlos says.

It's almost four o'clock and the theater is less than half full. Ana and Carlos fortify themselves with coke and popcorn from concessions, and walk into the theater to get a seat.

Jordan Walters walks in. Dad, who had been working on his financial spreadsheet in the office, comes out to meet her.

"It's getting hot again, isn't it?" he says.

"Oh, compared to summer in Chicago, 80 degrees in Seattle is pretty mild," Jordan says. "I've enjoyed my walks from the hotel. This morning I got coffee and walked around the campus. It's a beautiful campus."

"It is," Dad says, and then he adds, "So far, the house is a little smaller than yesterday."

Jordan pulls out her notes and glances at them. The clock on the back wall of the screening room says four o'clock.

"Ready?" Dad asks.

"Ready," she replies.

They follow a couple of latecomers into the theater. The room is maybe 60 percent full. With a smaller crowd and both Eric and Ellen working concessions, Dad relents and lets me sit with Ana and Carlos, as long as I come out before the film ends.

"Good afternoon," Jordan says. "Today I have the pleasure of introducing to you the work of Agnès Varda, a true film pioneer, and a filmmaker who has been called one of the 'greats' of world cinema.

"Many commentators try to define Varda's work by looking at how she supposedly fits into various film movements—the Left Bank, the French New Wave, and feminism—or by her efforts to combine elements of the documentary and photography with fiction elements in her feature films. This is all valid up to a point, but I believe that the best way to understand the filmmaker Agnès Varda is to understand that she is a very personal filmmaker.

"She is quoted as saying that she 'did ... my photos, my craft, my film, my life on my terms, my own terms, and not to do it like a man.'[6]

"The aspects of Varda's work that have been most influential are the centrality of women protagonists and the development of the female cinematic voice in her feature films, and her focus in many of her best films on marginalized individuals and groups.

"But before I introduce *Cléo from 5 to 7*, a bit about Varda's early career.

"Agnès Varda initially worked as a successful photographer, but very early she decided that she'd like to use her photos to make what she called 'compositions,' and this led her to want to make films.

"Varda is often discussed as a key member of the French New Wave, and certainly elements in her films like filming on location, developing her stories around the concerns of contemporary life, and wanting to make films on 'her own terms' reflect the auteur theory that was articulated by the critics and filmmakers of the New Wave period.

"But her initial involvement in filmmaking came in the early 1950s, just before the flowering of the New Wave, a period of experimental documentary filmmaking called Left Bank Cinema. The Left Bank directors were interested in taking the essayistic approach from literature and applying it in a personal way to engage their audience on complex topics of culture and history.

"In 1954 Varda decided to spend a few days filming life in a small French fishing village, La Pointe Courte, for a terminally ill friend who could not return to see the place one last time. Out of this act of kindness came the film *La Pointe Courte*, the first of her major films, and one in which she uses a mix of professional and non-professional actors, character abstraction and symbolism, and an intermixing of still photos and film to create a film critics praised for its totally free and experimental style.

"Some critics consider *La Pointe Courte* to be the first film of the French New Wave, but I would argue that it comes as much from her participation in the Left Bank Cinema movement, and those directors' willingness to weave documentary and experimental style into their filmmaking.

"Despite the accolades by French critics, the film did not do well financially, and Varda spent the next seven years working on documentaries and refining her style.

"Released in 1961, *Cléo from 5 to 7*—the film you'll be seeing tonight—fits squarely into the French New Wave. The story follows a young singer, Cléo, over a two-hour period as she awaits the results of a biopsy and reviews her life while she waits. The audience sees the action through Cléo's eyes and participates in her journey of self-awareness, as she realizes the superficiality of those around her and struggles with the possibility of death. While Varda was not interested in applying strict feminist theory in her films, her work developing her female protagonist's cinematic voice in *Cléo from 5 to 7* makes this film groundbreaking and worth seeing and discussing sixty years later.

"Varda continued to make what I'd call experimental films that can be hard to categorize, focusing on issues important to women and increasingly on marginalized protagonists. If you feel so moved after you see tonight's film, look for Varda's *Vagabond* and the documentary *The Gleaners and I*, both of which showcase her wonderfully original style."

As I expected, Ana doesn't attend the showing of *Swept Away* on Sunday, and when I don't see her again on Tuesday for *My Brilliant Career*, I start to wonder if her grandparents have stopped her from coming. But then I think that if Ana is as excited about writing this paper as I think she is, there's no way she's going to miss being here for most of the films. And sure enough, on Wednesday she comes to *Desert Hearts*.

The lesbian romance attracts a pretty good crowd. Unfortunately, Raji and I are the only two staff working besides Dad, so I can't get away from concessions before or right after the film. Ana and I wave at each other as she is leaving the building.

Thursday night we have a full house for *Daughters of the Dust* by the filmmaker Julie Dash. Luckily, both Eric and Clarice are here, along with Ellen, and that means I don't have to hang out at concessions all the time. So I catch Ana as she comes in for the seven o'clock show. She's with a girl I don't know. It turns out her name is Sally Morales. She and Ana are schoolmates.

"I'm so excited about seeing this film," Ana says.

"It looks really interesting," I say, "with an all-Black cast, crew, and a Black woman director."

"Do you know that *Daughters in the Dust* was the first feature film directed by a Black woman?" Sally asks.

How had I missed this fact in my conversations with Dad?

"No, really?" I say, feeling a little embarrassed.

I'd like to talk more with Ana, but she and Sally are anxious to get seats.

"Will I see you after the film?" I ask, as they turn to head into the screening room.

"I can't hang out tonight. But my grandparents have agreed to let me come to all the remaining films, as long as I attend the four o'clock showings. So maybe we can have coffee after one of the weekend movies."

After Ana and Sally go in to see the film, I'm floating on air. I'd about given up on the idea that Ana and I would be able to get together to just hang out, and now that possibility seems to be alive again.

CHAPTER 28

Finding Her Voice

Dad's idea that the last seven films in the women directors series, which are newer and better known, would bring in a consistently large audience seemed to be born out on Friday when both showings of *The Piano* essentially sold out.

In her final film lecture on the previous Sunday, Jordan Walters had called *The Piano* Jane Campion's masterpiece. The crowds for that film seemed to feel the same way.

I sold tickets and Raji, Clarice, and I worked concessions for both showings. You could feel the electricity in the air before and particularly after each show. After the last showing on Friday, people hung out in the salon until past ten o'clock, talking about Campion and the film, along with some other films in the series that they had seen.

"What a great performance by Holly Hunter," I heard a woman say to two friends.

"Yes, but what a dark film, and it was hard to watch," said one of her friends. "Still I couldn't take my eyes off the screen. I wanted to know what was going to happen to Ada."

That evening I began to understand for the first time what Dad's dream had been when he reopened the Magic Lantern almost a year ago. This film, and maybe the whole Summer of Film idea, was about bringing film lovers together to see and talk about good movies. As he closed the front door that evening, Dad looked tired but happy.

On Saturday the crowds are more normal. We're showing *Eve's Bayou*, about a prosperous Black family living in a Creole American community in Louisiana, with the story being seen through the eyes of a young daughter. As I walk in to hear Dad's introduction, I notice that only about half the seats are filled.

"This movie is a coming-of-age story about the disillusionment of growing up, and the mysteries of family and life in a prosperous southern Black community, as seen through the eyes of a ten-year-old girl. It's about observation, the unreliability of memory, and forgiveness, with a great performance by the film's young lead actress," Dad says in his short introduction at the first showing.

You can tell by the tenor of his voice how much he likes the film.

After I start the film, I go back to the office to get my water bottle. Dad is there looking at the retrospective brochure. He sighs as I walk by him.

"This is such a great independent film," he says, "a little gem. But it's the type of film that most occasional filmgoers have never heard of, as you can tell by the size of tonight's audience."

"It's not that bad," I say. "We're probably half full."

"Well, maybe," Dad says. "I did a quick count before I came out, and I got ninety-five people."

While Dad is giving his introduction at the second showing, Mr. Belvedere walks into the theater, so I leave Clarice at concessions and go to meet him.

"Mr. Belvedere, we haven't seen you for a while."

"Oh, Jackson. Yes, hello. Well, I've been pretty busy, lots to do, and it took me a while—longer than I'd thought it would—to get the posters I wanted for your poster sale."

He sounds apologetic, and I know that Dad has been a little put off by not being able to get him to talk about the set-up and logistics for Friday's poster auction. But I don't say anything.

"Dad is just finishing his introduction to tonight's film. He should be out in a couple minutes. Why don't you wait in the office?"

As Dad leaves the screening room, I stop him and mention that Mr. Belvedere is waiting in the office.

"Finally," he says, as he heads off to talk to him.

Mr. Belvedere and Dad are in the office with the door closed for about twenty-five minutes. After Mr. Belvedere leaves, Dad calls me in and tells me that Mr. Belvedere will be back on Monday to drop off a batch of posters that we'll store in the office.

"And I need you to come in on Monday morning, so there is someone here to let him in and then close up the theater."

This takes me by surprise. I had been feeling better about my work schedule at the theater, and I have plans for Monday. It's my only day away from the Magic Lantern, and on this particular Monday I am supposed to meet Ana to talk about her report.

"I'm meeting Ana at 11:00 at the library in Wedgewood to help her with her report," I say. Dad has been interested in my staying friends with Ana, so maybe he'll agree to meet Mr. Belvedere himself on Monday.

But no, Dad frowns and says, "Just call her and reschedule for later in the day."

Then before I can say anything else, he goes back to looking through the paperwork on his desk. Our conversation is over. But as I turn to leave, he adds, "Remind me to give you the keys tomorrow after we lock up."

It turns out Ana is fine with meeting later. That way she can have lunch at home. Of course, I'd been looking forward to us having lunch together.

I meet her at 1:30, and the first thing I realize is that Ana doesn't really need much help from me with her paper on women film directors. She already has a theme and an outline.

"Something Jordan told me, something that she mentioned in her film introductions, and that I feel came out in most of the films I've seen, is the idea of developing the female cinematic voice. I think that's going to be the focus of my paper."

We go through the various films she has seen. She has already identified some good examples to use in illustrating her theme, the expansion of women's cinematic voice over time.

"Good movie examples of this idea are *Cléo from 5 to 7*, *The Piano*, and *Lady Bird*," she says.

"Don't forget to mention *My Brilliant Career*."

"I wish I hadn't missed seeing that film. Jordan mentioned the Judy Davis character in that film when she was talking about female characters finding their voice."

"It's all about a young woman finding her voice," I say, trying to sound like an expert. "You should try to check out a copy from the library."

"I've got a copy on hold," Ana says. "I'll check the hold shelves before I leave to see if it has come in. But my grandparents don't have a DVD player."

"We have one at home, and you'd be welcome to use it if you need to."

Ana smiles but seems reluctant to accept the invitation. "My friend Maria has one that I can probably use. Anyway, I've got to start writing tonight. My teacher gave me an extension, but he wants the paper by next Monday. I should be able to work in something from a few other films once I have the basic draft done."

"You're going to be busy."

"Very busy, but I'm really excited about this paper."

I can tell that by her body language.

"And I'm so grateful for all the help I've gotten from your dad, Jordan, and you, of course."

"I haven't done that much," I say, which is true—I haven't.

Then out of the blue she asks, "So Jackson, any chance you'll be able to come to the immigrants' rights march on the 30th?"

I had completely forgotten about the march.

"It's being heavily publicized, so we're hoping to have at least 25,000 people. Everybody's meeting at Swanson Park. I'll be going with a group from St. Francis.

Carlos will be there, and some folks from your church, I think, and even Ellen is coming."

"Wow, 25,000 people. That sounds huge."

For a minute, my mind goes back to the other march, the one I was able to go to, and the good feeling of what I guess you'd call solidarity, the signs, the chanting, the singing. And then I hear in my head that song, *De Colores, de colores* ...

I have to catch myself before I start singing. Because I know that going to this march isn't possible. There's no way I can get that Friday off, so there's no reason to even ask. Dad wants me to be there on weekends, including Fridays, and if Ellen has already asked to have that Friday off, there's just no way Dad will let me go.

I think Ana gets the message. Seeing my reluctance to commit, she finally says, "Well, think about it. You've got a few more weeks to decide. Let me know if you want to come. We'll be meeting up at 11:00 a.m. at Swanson Park. It's an easy bus ride, and some folks will be getting rides from St. Francis."

I smile uncomfortably and that's how we leave things.

CHAPTER 29

Poster Art

When people walk into the salon at the Magic Lantern on Friday, the first thing they see is Jimmy Stewart kissing Kim Novak under the Golden Gate Bridge. The big green and red Japanese film poster for *Vertigo*—which Eric and I had somehow been able to put up—hangs from the ceiling in the center of the salon, and all around it on the floor and walls are posters for other movies. The room has been transformed and the poster auction is about to begin.

That poster is eye-catching, but it isn't particularly valuable, according Mr. Belvedere. It also isn't really a film poster, but rather a canvas wall art print of the Japanese *Vertigo* poster.

Four of us, Dad, Ellen, Eric, and I, have spent over two hours setting up for the auction, which officially starts at ten this morning. Mr. Belvedere supervised and spent most of his time telling us which of the posters needed to be especially visible, and which should be put on one of two racks he brought for the "cheapies."

"We'll be lucky if we get $10 apiece for the cheapies," he says.

Some of the most interesting posters have been hung around the salon using special poster holders. We have a limited amount of wall space because of the windows on the east wall, so many posters end up being propped up on chairs or just leaning against a wall.

The table that normally holds the theater information has been moved next to where people walk into the salon and made into a purchase table, overseen by Mom, who has come in to help with the financial stuff.

It feels like the salon has become a showcase for movies of the past. There are posters for movies from the 1950s and 1960s, films that Dad always refers to as classics: *The Searchers*, *Rear Window*, *2001*, *Invasion of the Body Snatchers*, *Jaws*, and even some real oldies like the *Wizard of Oz*, along with a few other films I've never heard of. One that catches my eye is a poster showing a nun ringing a bell in a huge tower against a backdrop of snow-capped mountains for a film called *Black Narcissus*.

"It's an old British film about some overheated nuns in the high mountains of India," Raji said when he saw the poster in the office earlier in the week. "It's from a book and my mother is a real fan of the author."

Just before we open Mr. Belvedere gets the four of us together to explain how the auction will work.

"When people come into the salon they will be given an auction catalog."

He holds up the catalog. He seems pretty proud of it. I guess that's because he designed it and had it printed. Dad thought Ellen could put one together, but

Mr. Belvedere insisted we needed one that looked "professional."

"Raji, I want you to hand out auction catalogs at the door. There will be thirty-three posters listed in each catalog, each will have a number, and thirty of these will have a minimum price—a price we won't go under—listed along with some additional information on the condition of the poster. I expect most of these posters to sell for between $20 and $50, and if we get lucky, we might sell one or two for more. I've listed poster number twenty-nine, *Jaws,* and poster number thirty, *2001, A Space Odyssey*, as having a minimum price of $100. These are probably the best of this group, and they could sell for considerably more.

"There are three other posters listed in the catalog, numbers thirty-one to thirty-three. These are the 'specials.' There is no minimum price listed for these posters, and it is my hope that one or two of these nice posters will sell for a four-figure price."

I glance at my copy of the catalog. Poster number thirty-one is *Anatomy of a Murder* (one sheet, Style B, black and white, very good condition with some minor fading), poster number thirty-two is *Casablanca* (Italian rerelease 1953, limited number, good condition with small blemishes and tears), and poster number thirty-three is *The Bride of Frankenstein* (one sheet, Style D, good condition with some wear and color fading, rare).

The first two of these posters I don't remember seeing on the list Mr. Belvedere gave to Dad.

"And oh, if anyone asks you about the specials, please have them see me. I'm hoping to see some real collectors show up, and they're the ones who are most likely to be interested in the specials."

"I hope you're right about those four-figure prices," Dad says.

Listening to Mr. Belvedere, Dad seems to get nervous. I imagine that's because there seems to be no way to predict how much any of these posters will sell for.

"If people want to bid on a particular poster, they write their name, along with their bid on the four-inch by six-inch card that will be sitting by each poster. A small number of posters will be auctioned off, starting with poster number one, at each round of bidding. A bidding round will be done each half hour, beginning at eleven o'clock. The three specials will be sold at the 3:30 auction. I'll be the auctioneer and will mention this periodically.

"Scott, will you pick up the auction cards for the appropriate posters right before each bidding round and give them to me. Jackson, will you be prepared to step in and help Scott as needed. There is likely to be a lot of activity and noise on the floor as we move along into the afternoon, with people talking and asking questions, so be aware of what's going on and stay in touch with each other. Besides the posters listed in the catalog, there are two racks of 'cheapies.' We are pricing these at $10 apiece. After three o'clock, we'll sell these posters for whatever we can get."

"But don't tell customers that until 3:00," Dad says. I know Dad wants to get around $250 from the sale of the cheapies.

But Mr. Belvedere seems to be more concerned with selling as many as we can. "Ellen, you'll help Laura on the purchasing table."

Mom shows up at 9:45, and the theater doors open at 10:00. But there will be no sales, except for posters from the cheapie racks, until 11:00 which is good because the first few customers, two men, don't arrive until almost 10:30. One of the men stops to talk with Mr. Belvedere—maybe he's one of those collectors?

"I think that guy runs a collectibles business somewhere in the city," Dad says, as we stand around waiting for more people to arrive.

Right before eleven o'clock the salon starts to fill up. But bids have only been made on three posters. Two are sold at the eleven o'clock round of bidding for $25 apiece. Apparently, someone filled out a bid card for the third poster because no one bids on it.

Dad has given Eric and me name tags, and we wander around trying to answer questions. The most frequent questions are: "Where is the bathroom?" and "This poster doesn't have a price on it?" Some people conveniently miss seeing the sign on the cheapies poster racks that says $10 apiece. Also, even though everybody has a catalog, they don't seem to know that the catalog is where the minimum price for priced posters is listed.

Getting nervous, Dad takes the opportunity to make a pitch for more sales, and to also make sure that everybody knows the final sale will be held at 3:30 and the auction will close promptly at 4:00.

Business picks up at noon, and suddenly the little salon feels very crowded. I end up helping Mom and Ellen at the purchasing table, mostly putting posters in clear plastic bags or in poster boxes that Mr. Belvedere brought, so that we don't have to roll up any of the pricey posters. By 12:15 we have sold seven of the priced posters, the biggest sale being for $40.

Ellen spells Mom on the purchasing table at 1:15, so that Mom can eat lunch. Just as Mom is leaving, Dad comes over to check with her about our sales so far.

"We've sold less than half of the priced posters, and more than half of the cheap posters from the racks," she says.

She takes a quick glance at her tally sheet. "I'd estimate we've made about $750 so far."

Dad frowns. He's not happy with that figure.

"A number of buyers have said that there are better deals on eBay," Mom adds. "But they want to help the theater, so that's why they're here."

Dad walks back over to talk with Mr. Belvedere. They are in rather intense conversation when a customer interrupts them with a question.

At one point, before he knew exactly what we'd be selling, Dad said he hoped we could make $5,000 from the auction. Seven hundred fifty is a long way from five thousand.

The crowd thins out again after one o'clock. I walk around the salon, straightening up, and run into Mr. Belvedere, who seems a little agitated.

"Jackson," he says, "if you see a tall, older man in an immaculate grey suit, or a woman with bright red hair, who are just hanging around, please let me know."

"Somebody you're expecting?" I ask.

"A couple of dealers who I'm hoping will come. So far, I've only seen one other collectibles dealer here, which is a little discouraging. I think Scott is disappointed in the sales so far, but we still have three hours to push our numbers up."

At the two o'clock auction, the *Wizard of Oz* poster sells for $60.

"That's a surprise," I tell Dad between sales. "That's a great looking poster. I thought it would go for more."

"Winston says it's a reprint, and that a lot of those were made. But I was hoping it would sell for a higher price too."

Next, the *Black Narcissus* poster is brought up for sale—the one that caught my eye earlier, and for some reason made me want to see the film.

Mr. Belvedere is looking at the bid cards and he seems a little perplexed.

"We have a tie bid," he says finally. "Both Ms. Jolette and Mr. Gupta have bid $100 for the *Black Narcissus* poster."

Mr. Gupta? Raji? It couldn't be Raji?

"I'm going to hold this poster aside so that we can finish with selling the other two posters we have in this round of bidding. In the meantime, I would like to have the two bidders make second bids on another bid card and then hand them to me."

A woman's voice comes out of the crowd, "Where can we get another bid card?"

Mr. Belvedere quickly scans the crowd for Dad. Apparently, he doesn't see him because he turns around and says, "Jackson, can you give new bid cards to the two bidders on this poster?"

I take some bid cards out of my pocket. But it's too crowded for me to tell where they are. So I say, "Would the two bidders please hold up their hands?"

One hand goes up immediately. It's from a woman at the other side of the salon. I make my way through the crowd and hand her a card. Then I turn around and Raji is standing right behind me.

"Raji," I say, "are you the other bidder?" Then before he can answer, I add, "Isn't it some kind of conflict of interest for you to bid?"

"It certainly isn't," Raji says. "It's blind bidding, and it's my money."

I hand him a card, but he doesn't take it.

"You don't want to up your bid?"

"I can't," he says. "One hundred dollars was my limit."

After he auctions off two more posters, Mr. Belvedere comes back to the *Black Narcissus*. He glances at the one bid card he has been given.

"I only have one bid card. Does the other person—Mr. Gupta—want to make a second bid?"

Raji doesn't answer.

"Okay," says Mr. Belvedere, "So I have a bid of $125 for this stunning poster for Michael Powell's masterpiece *Black Narcissus*. Do I hear a higher bid?" He pauses and looks around the room one more time. Nobody raises a hand or speaks up.

"Sold! This beautiful poster for the film *Black Narcissus* is sold to Ms. Jolette for a bid of $125."

I walk back to the purchasing table to help the buyer put the poster into one of the special poster bags.

"I am a fan of the director Michael Powell," the woman says as I hand her the poster bag. "I have posters for a number of his films. I wasn't planning to buy anything here. But when I saw this poster, I knew I had to have it."

As she leaves, Raji comes by the purchasing table. He looks pretty unhappy.

"I really wanted that poster," he says, "I was going to give it to my mother. She loves the novel."

"That's a shame. You couldn't top the other offer?"

"One hundred dollars was my limit. From what Winston told me, I didn't expect anybody would bid more than about $50 for it. I guess it's not that rare, although it's in great condition. So I thought I had a real chance to get it for $100."

I feel bad for Raji. It sounds like he really wanted to buy the poster. But we are here to make money for the theater. I guess he understands that.

"You'll be back to help with the take down?"

Raji nods. "I'm going over to the Ave to get a pizza. I'll be back by 4:00."

Everything feels awkward for a moment.

"Sounds like you need some comfort food."

"I tried," he says, and then he turns and leaves.

Sales pick up with the 2:30 bidding round. Dad seems more relaxed, as the number of posters selling for over $35 increases. Then someone bids $250 for a good quality, black and white original poster for *The Searchers*, and the mood in the salon changes. You can feel a kind of nervous energy in the room.

"They're going to start bidding now," Mr. Belvedere says with a smile. "I can feel it."

At three o'clock three of the four posters up for sale, including the *Jaws* poster, sell for $75, $90 and $125, respectively, and the fourth, an original poster for the classic B movie *Attack of the Fifty-Foot Woman*, sells for $500. When Mr. Belvedere says "sold," several people in the room applaud.

The focus turns immediately to the final bidding round and to the most expensive posters, the three specials, along with an original poster for Stanley Kubrick's *A Clockwork Orange*, number twenty-eight in the sale catalogue. Dad stands next to where the three specials are on display, making sure nobody touches them. They can ask questions, but Mr. Belvedere says no one is to touch any of them before they come up for auction.

"The basic information on all these posters is in the catalogue. Nobody needs to handle them before they are sold."

By 3:25 the salon is buzzing with people talking about what they think of this last batch of posters, and what they believe individual posters will sell for. But the room quiets down as Mr. Belvedere starts the final bidding round.

When the *A Clockwork Orange* poster sells for $350, there's another murmur from the crowd. Some people are obviously expecting bigger sales for the three specials.

"These final three posters are truly 'specials,'" Mr. Belvedere says. "They're either originals or from a foreign country. There's a limited number in existence, and/or the condition is very good to excellent. The first of the three is for the film *Anatomy of a Murder*. Do I hear a bid of $250 for this wonderful movie poster in very good condition?"

The bidding goes quickly and the poster easily sells for $500. The crowd applauds again when the sale amount is announced.

"I want to say word or two about the final two posters we have to auction today," says Mr. Belvedere as the crowd quiets down. "First, there is the *Casablanca* poster, made for the rerelease of the film in Italy in 1953. One of a limited edition, it is considered to be among the most beautiful posters for this film. There are a few small tears and some blemishes on the bottom and upper right-hand corner of this poster. A copy in excellent condition sold at auction a few years ago for $200,000."

An audible murmur runs through the crowd when he mentions a price of $200,000 for a poster. I look over at Dad—I can't tell what he's thinking, but $200,000 for a movie poster seems unbelievable.

Mr. Belvedere glances around the salon, and then says, "So, let's start the bidding on this poster at $2,500."

After a slight pause, a hand goes up in the back of the room. It's a tall, well-dressed man with greying hair—maybe one of the collectors Mr. Belvedere mentioned.

"I got here late and would like to take a closer look at both posters. Could you give those of us who haven't had a chance a few minutes to examine them?"

Mr. Belvedere looks at Dad, who joins him at the front of the room.

"You can have five minutes to look at both posters," Dad says. "We have to get the salon emptied out and the theater cleaned before our regular film showing at 6:45."

Four people, including the distinguished older man, come up to the look at the *Casablanca* poster. He seems to be looking for faults.

"What do you think, Ira?"

Mr. Belvedere knows him. This guy is definitely a collector.

The man looks over at Mr. Belvedere.

"One of the tears is fairly big, and there is some yellowing on the bottom. But it's probably the best looking of all the *Casablanca* posters. It's the first one I've seen for a while."

Two women, one a middle-aged redhead in a colorful blouse and pants, the other much younger and wearing a Nirvana tie-dye shirt and blue jeans, stand by Ira. The older woman bends down to take a closer look. She mentions a few things about the poster, talking softly to the younger woman.

"It's such a beautiful poster," the young woman says.

While the women look at the *Casablanca* poster, Ira turns his attention to the *Bride of Frankenstein* poster. A short, muscular, younger looking man, who has been standing behind the women, walks up and tries to look over Ira's shoulder.

"This is amazing," Ira says, "and it's in very good condition."

After a moment, the older woman joins them. There is a bit of jostling, and the younger man steps to the side. He's apparently most interested in the *Bride of Frankenstein* poster.

"Only a few small tears, a little fading, and a slight bit of bleeding," the older woman examining the *Casablanca* poster says.

"Time's up," says Mr. Belvedere. Ira and the women move away to stand by the auctioneer's podium. But the other younger man, now by himself, continues looking at the *Bride* poster.

"Sir," says Dad, "we need to start the bidding."

The man nods. He looks very determined as he steps back into the crowd.

"So do I have a bid of $2,500 for this beautiful *Casablanca* poster?"

The tall man raises his hand.

"We have a bid of $2,500 for this beautiful poster. Are there other bids?"

A thin woman in a grey blouse and slacks raises her hand and says, "Three thousand."

The young friend of the older woman who had examined the poster so closely quickly raises her hand and says, "Three thousand five hundred."

Mr. Belvedere pauses.

"So, we have a bid by this young lady of $3,500. Do I hear other bids?"

The tall older man's hand goes up. "Four thousand," he says in a confident tone.

Immediately, the young woman raises her hand and says, "Four thousand two hundred and fifty."

There is a murmur from the crowd. I think people are surprised that this young woman is continuing to bid.

"We have a bid of $4,250," Mr. Belvedere says. "Does anyone want to top that bid for this beautiful *Casablanca* poster?"

He looks over at the tall man who seems ready to make a higher bid, but then doesn't raise his hand.

The auctioneer turns and looks down at the young woman standing just in front of him. She appears to be literally holding her breath.

"Sold to the young woman in blue jeans for $ 4,250," he says.

The crowd breaks into applause.

"That is a beautiful poster," Mom says as she chats with the young woman buyer while I'm putting her poster into one of the special poster containers to keep it from being damaged before she gets it home.

"Yes, it is."

"Are you a collector?" Mom asks.

"I'm an Ingrid Bergman fan. She's so great, and the film is so romantic."

This sale is good news for Dad and the theater. But what I'm wondering is how this young woman can afford to buy a movie poster for so much money.

Mr. Belvedere moves quickly to auction off the final poster, *The Bride of Frankenstein.*

"This final poster is a one-sheet original in Style D, very rare, and in good condition, except for some minor tears, blemishes and a little bleed-through in one spot. So, given the expected value of this poster, I'm suggesting that we start the bidding at $5,000."

There's an audible murmur from the crowd when Mr. Belvedere announces the starting price. I look at Dad and even he looks surprised. What is Mr. Belvedere doing? Can we really expect to get $5,000 for a movie poster, even a rare one?

Immediately Ira raises his hand.

Then before Mr. Belvedere can say anything, the older woman, who bid on the *Casablanca* poster, ups the bid. "Five thousand five hundred," she says.

Ira counters with a bid of $5,750, and the older woman counters his bid with one for $6,000.

They go back and forth, until Ira finally bids $10,000.

"We have a bid of $10,000 for this rare and wonderful *Bride of Frankenstein* poster. Do I hear another bid?"

The room is silent, as the crowd waits to see if the woman will make a counter bid.

"Ten thousand once, ten thousand twice ... "

Mr. Belvedere pauses. He looks like he's about to close the bidding when someone else raises a hand. At first, it's hard to tell who it is. But it's not the older woman. Finally, the younger man, the quiet one who had only seemed interested in the *Bride* poster, steps forward.

The room is silent.

"Do you have a bid, sir?" Mr. Belvedere asks.

"Yes," the man says, but he hesitates to say a figure.

"Sir, I'll have to close the bidding if you don't make a specific bid."

"Okay, okay, I bid ... I bid $15,000."

Someone gasps in the crowd. I glance at Dad. For a moment it looks like he's frozen, as if he can't believe what he's just heard, and then his whole body relaxes.

"Sold," says Mr. Belvedere. "Sold to the gentleman for $15,000."

PART 4

The Story Goes On

Scott Ryan
Journal Entry
August 30, 2019

What a month it has been. We had good crowds for many of the films in the Women in Film retrospective. People were energized, and after certain films we had people hanging out to talk about what they had seen. It felt like the Magic Lantern was finally becoming the place I'd dreamed it could be. Jordan Walters, our main speaker, was a big draw for the first four films, and even with her fee and expenses we still made money on the retrospective.

On the other hand, we barely broke even on the Richard Linklater series the last two full weeks of August. Linklater is a major American director and film innovator, so I thought he might draw an audience of younger filmgoers and professionals. But the two weeks before Labor Day are always tough for theaters, and this year was no exception. The screening room was seldom more than half full for any of his films, even for his classic, Boyhood. I guess it's too long for a general audience, particularly when it's sunny and 80 degrees outside. The final six-day run of his newest film based on a book by a Seattle author barely broke even.

I always bet on Seattle audiences to be discriminating and interested in the films of major directors. But sometimes they disappoint me.

The poster auction took a lot of time and energy, but people came and bought posters, and that's what we needed. I don't know what to say about how it ended. A latecomer to the auction, J. J. Gittes, bid $15,000 for a *beautiful* Bride of Frankenstein *poster. And then he didn't have the money to pay for it. We're still holding onto it and waiting for our money.*

CHAPTER 30

Cinema is a Strange Creature

"**I** can't replace you on Monday," Dad says.

I'd just told him I want the Monday holiday off so that I can attend the party at Ana's.

"We're on the verge of a big success with the Summer of Film."

"We are?" I ask, trying not to sound sarcastic.

"Yes, except for this mess at the end of the poster auction, we've done fine. But now we need all hands on deck to get us through this last big weekend, and you want Monday off?"

"We're usually closed on Monday, that's normally my day off, and I've been invited to an end-of-the-summer party at Ana's."

"We're moving to a different staff rotation on Wednesday," Dad says, "and you'll be back to having Wednesdays and Thursdays off, along with most Saturdays. But I really need you to work this week-end."

Suddenly I feel very angry. I worked here all summer. When other staff took time off, I filled in. I could count my days off on one hand, and even two of my Mondays were taken up with school visits. I had no real summer, no trips, no star parties, no ballgames, and if it hadn't been for her summer school project, I wouldn't have seen Ana at all.

"Sure, when school starts, I'll have two, maybe three days off a week instead of just one. Big deal. I need a day off before school starts," I say, raising my voice.

Dad frowns. He's not happy with my response. And I can see that he's not going to change his mind. He's been distracted and cranky since the auction.

It's Friday afternoon and the Kore-eda series, the last event in Magic Lantern's Summer of Film, will be starting with a matinee in just a half hour. Dad's probably worried about who'll show up. Maybe it's a bad time to ask for another day off. I sigh and that's the end of our conversation.

Back at concessions, I glance at the back page of the Summer of Film flyer and think back on how the poster auction ended. As I recall, Mr. Gittes waited until everybody else had left the theater. He stood by his $15,000 poster as if he was guarding it. Dad sent me over to watch him, while he went to stand by the theater door to thank those who had come to the auction.

Gittes is a stocky man, average height but pretty muscular, and for some reason he reminds me of a certain movie actor whose name I can't remember. Maybe it's his smile, the smile of someone who knows something other people don't.3

Mr. Belvedere and Mom stood by the purchasing table just watching. Eventually Dad came back into the salon, and Mr. Gittes walked over to talk with him.

I expected Dad to motion for me to bring the poster over to where they were talking. But then I noticed the serious look on his face, and after a few more words, Mr. Gittes turned and walked out of the salon.

Then all of us gathered at the purchasing table.

"He's going to have to get the money and bring it back to me next week," was all Dad said.

"I don't understand," said Mr. Belvedere, who looked upset.

It felt like all the air had been sucked out of the room.

"I guess he doesn't carry $15,000 around with him," Dad remarked.

"He doesn't have a checkbook?" Mom asked.

"Apparently not," Dad responded. "He's going to bring me a cashier's check next week."

I had other questions, and I bet I wasn't the only one. But before anyone asked anything else, Dad thanked everyone and asked Mom to bring the sales register, and then they went into the office. Dad was irritated, I could tell, but what else could he do except wait?

Little did we know that it would be two weeks before Dad would hear from Mr. Gittes again.

"It is really too late to be making any changes for a holiday weekend," Dad says when he comes back from introducing *Like Father, Like Son*, the first film in the Kore-eda series.

"But if you can get Ellen to work the Monday matinee, you can have the afternoon off. Just as long as you're back to work the evening show."

His suggestion of a compromise comes as a shock. Maybe he's feeling bad because he wouldn't let me attend the big immigration march a week ago. But the party is in the afternoon, and I can probably get back in time to work the evening show. I've got to take this offer.

"Okay, I'll talk to Ellen."

The house for the first showing of *Like Father, Like Son* is maybe fifty people. Hirokazu Kore-eda is a favorite director of Dad's. He wanted to have a big retrospective of the director's major films in the middle of the Summer of Film. But he suddenly changed his mind—or was talked out of it. I'm not sure which. So he cut the retrospective back to four films at the end of Gala. It looks like he was right to do that.

Raji makes things worse when he stops Dad as the film is letting out and asks him what's happened with the sale of the *Bride* poster.

"You know as much as I do," Dad answers, with some obvious annoyance.

Then he turns to me and says, "I've decided to take the poster home tonight. I think it'll be safer there than here in the theater."

With that Dad walks back to the office.

"Scott seems kind of out of sorts," says Raji. "I guess he's worried about getting the bid money for the *Bride* poster. Is he worried that the bidder won't show up?"

"Maybe, partially, but he told me the theater had done okay at the auction, even without the $15,000. So I think he's more upset about the small crowd for tonight's film."

"What's the deal with Kore-eda?" Raji asks. "Is he a favorite of Scott's?"

"Yeah, and I think it bothers him when we show films by directors he likes and they don't get an audience."

"I've never seen a film by this guy."

"That's amazing," I say. "I thought you'd seen everything."

"I'm hoping to see *After the Storm* and maybe *Shoplifters*," Raji says.

"I liked *After the Storm*," I respond.

"Is *Shoplifters* a crime film?"

"No, according to Dad, it's more about a Japanese family surviving by being small time crooks. Apparently, it won some big prize at the Cannes Film Festival."

First thing on Saturday, I call Ellen and she agrees to work my afternoon shift on Monday. It seems her family doesn't celebrate Labor Day.

Saturday afternoon the audience is bigger than the showings on Friday. When Raji and I come back from having a pizza between shows, I notice Genevieve talking with Dad at the door to the office. They've probably been meeting. It's only 6:30, but people are already coming in for the evening show. So I walk over to the new ticket booth in the lobby. During the Summer of Film we set up a ticket booth in the small lobby between the office and concessions. Nobody likes it except Dad. He thinks it keeps the office area more private.

"Hi, Jackson," Genevieve says. "How are things going?"

"Okay," I say. "I'm looking forward to school starting because I'll be working less hours."

"You didn't have much summer, did you?"

"Not really. But Dad's given me tomorrow afternoon off so that I can attend a Labor Day party."

"Oh, that's nice. Where's the party?"

"At Ana's. They have what they call a traditional Labor Day celebration."

"How's she doing? She attended a lot of the films in the women directors retrospective."

"She was writing a summer school report on women directors. I haven't seen her since I helped her with her report."

"Do you know a lot about women film directors?" Genevieve asks with a smile.

"After the Women in Film series I do."

"How did she do with her report?"

"I don't know. Hopefully, I'll find out on Monday."

The line for ticket buyers is growing, and then the theater lights flash to let folks know that it is five minutes until show time.

"You staying for the second show?" I ask, trying to sell tickets and talk with her at the same time.

"Yes, it's the one Kore-eda film we're screening that I haven't seen."

"Dad really likes this director."

"He's probably the most accomplished of the current crop of Japanese directors," Genevieve says. "He started as a documentarian and still mixes documentary and feature film techniques. Like Yasujirō Ozu, his big interest is the Japanese family, both conventional and unconventional. But Ozu was an artist of film composition. Kore-eda's films focus more on characters and Japanese society today."

"Do you think it was a mistake to have this guy's films closing out the Summer of Film?"

"Not really. I know Kore-eda's films have not always done well in Seattle. But the Summer of Film has already been a success financially, and I'm optimistic that at least two of the Kore-eda films will be well attended. The end of any Gala should probably feature films that the programmer likes, and the driving force behind the Summer of Film was Scott."

For a moment, I stop talking to sell an Asian couple two tickets. Then I turn back to Genevieve and say, "Sometimes I don't understand Dad. I guess the Summer of Films has been a success. But he often seems to promote movies that very few people would want to see."

"Cinema is a strange creature. Movies can get into your blood, and if you like a director's work, you can feel like it's your duty to show his or her films, particularly if those films haven't seemed to find an audience."

I'd like to ask Genevieve more questions, but now the lobby is full of people. So I have to stop talking and focus on selling tickets. I notice that Raji and Eric at concessions are getting flooded too. We may have a full house for the Saturday night showing.

"Talk to you later," Genevieve says, and she heads in to get a seat.

On Sunday I have one thing on my mind: seeing Ana again on Labor Day. Still, after the matinee, I can't help but notice people seeking out Dad to thank him for showing *Our Little Sister*, the second film in the Kore-eda series, which Dad describes as a joyous examination of sisterhood.

"What a sweet little film."

"Very charming."

"The four actresses are fantastic. The director couldn't have picked a better group to be in his film."

"I'm going to suggest that my daughters come see this film before it is gone."

Dad, too, seems a bit surprised at the reactions. But later, when it is clear that the evening show was a sellout, he's ecstatic.

"Maybe it was that good review in the *Times*," Clarice, who is working with me at concessions, says.

The local newspaper has been regularly reviewing films shown at the Summer of Film, and the reviews had been uniformly good.

"I'm sure that helped," I tell Clarice. But it feels to me like something else is happening.

I could feel the energy of the people as they arrived to see this film, and again when they left the theater and had so many positive comments. I felt that same energy sometimes during the Women in Film retrospective. Something else is happening, and maybe that means Dad's been able to sell Seattle filmgoers not just on Kore-eda as a director, but on the idea that the Magic Lantern is a place they can trust to show movies they'll want to see. And when I think this, to my surprise, I feel good.

CHAPTER 31

Lady Bird

When I arrive, the big backyard at Ana's house is filled with people. I notice a lot of students, probably from St. Francis, and a few I recognize from Peter's church, along with a few older people, who I suspect are either teachers or family members of Ana. I hear music. Somewhere people are singing.

Somos el barco, somos el mar
Yo navego en ti, tu navegas en mi [7]

Hearing that song takes me back to the May Day immigration march, and for a moment I remember clearly the huge crowd at that march singing another song, "De Colores," in unison.

A couple of picnic tables have been set up, and at one end of the yard, a small group of guys who look familiar are sitting around in a semi-circle, playing their guitars and singing. I spot Carlos, who is one of the singers. This must be his group. I heard them once before at church.

Just past the picnic tables, someone is setting up two barbeque grills. I look for Ana, but the whole yard is now filled with people. Then I hear her voice.

"Jackson." I look back toward the singers and then see Ana weaving her way through the crowd toward me.

As she gets to me, she exclaims, "I got an A on my report about women directors!" And then, out of the blue, she gives me a big hug.

"Jordan said she would write me a recommendation if I apply to a journalism program. Thanks for all your help, and please thank Scott for me."

Ana is really happy. I smile, partly embarrassed about the hug, but happy for Ana too.

"Nice party," I say after a minute, trying to sound cool.

"Sí, it's a great turnout. I was afraid a lot of kids would be out of town with their families. But most of my friends are here."

I look around, but still only recognize a few people.

"Mi amigo." It's Carlos. "Did you survive the big summer film festival?"

"Sí, Carlos," I say with a smile. "But I'm really looking forward to school starting."

"Me too."

"That makes three of us," Ana says. "So Jackson, did you hear that Carlos got arrested at Friday's demonstration?"

Carlos laughs as though it was nothing.

"You got arrested?" I'm shocked.

"No, not arrested. Three of us got stopped because we fit the description of some guys the police thought were trying to break into the federal building."

"So what happened?"

"They stopped us, and took us to a patrol car where they took our names and phone numbers. Then they let us go."

"Is that going to cause you any trouble?"

Carlos shrugs.

Ana's body language says she'd like to say more, but she doesn't.

"I don't know," Carlos says. "But I'm not going to worry about it. Today I'm here to party, and tomorrow I'll start thinking about what colleges I want to apply to."

"So where do you want to go?"

Carlos isn't a brainiac like Ellen. But he works hard and gets good grades, and I expect he'll get invitations from a number of schools if he doesn't run into trouble because of his status.

"Some place with a good baseball program. Most likely the University, but if some of those good California schools make an offer, I just might say yes."

"I just hope your *desgracia* at the march doesn't get you into trouble," Ana says.

"I'm not worried," Carlos says. Then out of the blue he says, "It might not matter anyway, as there may be a Supreme Court ruling on DACA this fall."

"Oh," I say, not knowing what, or if, I should ask what he thinks is going to happen. But I don't have to decide because Carlos quickly changes the subject.

"Come sing with us. We're singing mostly songs you'll know from church."

I look at Ana. She waves her hand and says, "Go, go! But come over to the food line when you get hungry. I'll be working on the line, and we can eat together. Okay?"

"Okay," I say, even though I'm reluctant to leave her. I bet there are a lot of other guys here interested in getting to know Ana.

Carlos is right, I know most of the songs the guys are singing, even some of those in Spanish. There are five of us. Carlos and another guy have guitars, and one has what he calls an African drum. I thought we would probably just provide background music for the big crowd that is milling around in the backyard, drinking soda or iced tea, talking and laughing. But as it turns out, most of us have sung in choirs or small groups or, at least, with our families, and the singers aren't the only people who know the songs. Most of the crowd knows them too, and some sing right along with us.

Sometimes Carlos passes out the words for a particular song, and I notice that for a couple of the songs someone, maybe Carlos, has changed a few of the lyrics to make them more relevant to the immigrant experience. Sometimes that doesn't really work for singing, but once in a while it does, like when the lyrics in "A Simple Song of Freedom" about people not wanting the Vietnam war were changed to "Let the immigrants come through the door."

Between songs I look around to see if I can find Ana, and I finally notice her standing with a rather stern looking, grey-haired older woman, probably her grandmother, over by the grills.

"Last song," Carlos calls out as people slowly head for the food line, and all of us guys start to sing, "Sit at the Welcome Table."

"All kinds of people at the welcome table ..."

The words are from a liberal version of an old African-American spiritual that everybody seems to know. We've sung this version at church. Many people in the crowd join in the singing, and some start to dance and clap their hands as they move toward the food. We sing it twice, and as we finish, there is some spontaneous applause.

Ana is helping at the food table, and I'm suddenly very hungry and also really wanting her company. I grab a plate and get into line. Then immediately somebody else calls my name.

It's Peter Bergmeier, who is right behind me in line.

"How are you, Jackson?"

"Fine," I say. "I'm looking forward to going back to school."

"I guess you had to work at the theater most of the summer."

"All of the summer," I say with emphasis and without really thinking.

I guess Peter can hear the sarcasm in my voice, because he hardly waits for me to stop talking before he responds.

"That's too bad, and that's why, I bet, you couldn't come to the immigration demonstration on Friday."

I nod. "There's no way I could take Friday off on the last big weekend of the Summer of Film."

"So how did you get off to come to the barbeque today?"

"I got someone to take my afternoon shift, and I have to be back to work for the evening show."

"I never see Scott anymore. He seems to have left the church. It's too bad. He was a big part of our climate group."

Peter pauses and then adds, "And I'm wondering if all this emphasis on his theater is keeping you and Laura away too."

"We've all been pretty busy."

I'm starting to feel a little uncomfortable with this conversation. I glance ahead. The food line is moving slowly as people are chatting, laughing, and talking to the servers.

"It's a shame, a real shame, you know. Don't get me wrong. It's great you're helping your family, but I wonder if you're not learning the wrong thing by being so focused on Scott's business."

"The wrong thing?" I ask.

"Young people have to nurture their social consciences, and that means finding a cause and getting involved, marching against injustice, writing letters, and working with other young people to make the world a better place."

Suddenly, I feel I have to defend Dad.

"It's more than a business for Dad. It's his dream."

"Well yes, but I wonder if Scott hasn't become a little obsessed with his theater dream and is making you, and Laura, too, work to fulfill that dream while taking you away from other things that might be just as important."

I never remember that Peter is Mom's brother. They just don't seem that much alike to me. But he always mentions Mom whenever we talk.

He pauses and then adds, "What do you think? Is that fair to you?"

"No," I say without hesitation, only to immediately wonder if I should have answered the question at all. Is it wrong for people to follow their dreams and work to make them come true? I start to qualify my answer, but Peter responds immediately.

"No," he says, "it isn't. You should be working toward your own dreams."

But what are my dreams? Do I want to go to college? It doesn't seem like I have a dream, at least not one like Dad's dream of running the Magic Lantern, or Ana's dream of full citizenship.

"Do you have a dream, Jackson?"

"Maybe going to college." That's all I can say. I'm second in line to get some food, and I'm feeling like I really want to get away from Reverend Peter.

"You know what you need?" he asks.

"I need to get something to eat," I say, and I pick up a plate and turn toward the food table.

Then over my shoulder, I hear Peter say, "You need to get involved in something like marching for immigrant justice, and you need to feel the fire of commitment that those marchers feel, especially the young people like your friend Carlos. You need to find a cause."

I look at the food on the table. I can understand why Ana and Carlos are committed to getting their citizenship. But which is more important for me, marching for the Dreamers or helping Dad make his theater dream come true?

"I'm not sure it's that simple," I say, speaking more to myself than to Peter.

Then I turn and there's Ana smiling at me.

"What's not that simple?" she asks.

I smile and forget that Peter is behind me.

"It's nothing," I say, and then I add, "With all this tempting food, how can I decide what I want to eat?"

The food is a mixture of traditional American and Latin American food: hot dogs and beans, tacos and tostadas, corn chips and salsa, mustard and relish, soda and iced tea. And everything looks great. Finally I just fill my plate.

Now Peter is talking to someone else, which gives me a chance to leave the food table with Ana. We walk over to where some folding chairs have been set up.

Knowing that the subject is going to come up, I ask her about Friday's demonstration.

"It was good. There was a lot of energy and solidarity. Everybody, the Dreamers and others, is waiting to hear what the court is going to decide. Everybody is afraid the administration might start mass deportations in the run-up to the next election."

"Are you afraid?"

"I guess I'm focused on getting into college. But I'm a little worried now for Carlos. Given what happened Friday, what if they find out his status? But what about you? How did that August school visit go?"

"Actually, I liked the campus. It's small and it's easy to get around."

"It's in Tacoma?"

"Yes, Rainer College. The campus is in the north part of the city. They have a nice library and a big science building, and it's close, but not too close to home. Apparently, the faculty is very accessible, and the classes are relatively small."

"That sounds great."

"The only thing is, it's pretty expensive. I guess everybody there gets some kind of aid."

"You could probably get aid."

Could I? I wonder.

"Probably, but not enough to cover living on campus."

"You could commute."

"No, I don't want to commute, and besides I don't have a car."

"Can't your parents help? They want you to go, right?"

"I've got a college fund, or at least I think I have one."

Ana looks confused. "Don't you know?"

"We haven't talked about it for a while."

Not since Dad started working on reopening and running the Magic Lantern, and I guess in the back of my mind I've wondered if he might have used that money to help buy the Magic Lantern. But I could be wrong, and I don't mention this possibility to Ana.

"I need to ask my parents. We're getting together next weekend to talk about visiting campuses and applying to some colleges. I'll find out."

"So are you getting more interested in college, now that you've visited a few schools?"

"Maybe," I say. "The truth is, I'm still not sure. I could see myself going to a smaller school like Rainier. But I still don't have a real reason to go. What will I major in, and what is my career goal? I don't know."

"You know, going to college can change you," Ana says. "You might grow up and find your own dreams."

I wonder.

"But shouldn't I have a dream before I go to college? You have a dream. Ellen and Carlos have their dreams."

"Maybe going to college will help you find one," says Ana. "Every time I talk with you about college I think about that movie *Lady Bird*, the movie that ended the women directors series. Did you see it?"

"I saw it when it came out," I say. I laugh and then add, "Actually, Ellen took me to see it because, even then, she was trying to get me interested in the idea of going to college. But I was too busy working to see it again at the Summer of Film."

Ana gives me a knowing look. "Remember how in *Lady Bird* Christine had a dream about leaving home and going to college. But her mother didn't think that dream was possible and tried to talk her out of it."

"I remember." But I'm not sure why Ana has brought this up.

Now Ana laughs. I've never seen her laugh, really laugh out loud, before.

"Jackson, you're just the opposite of Lady Bird. Everybody wants you to go to college. Everybody except you knows that if you go to college, you'll have to start thinking about your future. You'll have to get yourself a dream, or at least some goals, even if you don't have any now."

I look at Ana, and then think about Ellen and Mom, and I wonder if they are right. Maybe just going to college would help me decide what I want to do with my life.

"Do you think that Dad has been unfair in making me work so much at the theater?" I ask Mom after she picks me up to drive me back to the theater.

I keep thinking about what Peter said, that Dad was not being fair to me when he made me work so much at the Magic Lantern.

But Mom doesn't immediately respond. Then, when she stops for a light on 75th, she says, "Jackson, I know those first few months the theater was open were pretty rough for you, juggling school and work. But then Scott hired more staff, and this year you'll only be working two days a week once school starts."

"Isn't that because you've insisted that I have more time my senior year for schoolwork?"

"Both your dad and I agreed on cutting your hours, and you'll be having Saturdays off so that you can do social things, like with the Astronomy Club."

For some reason, this answer only makes me feel more upset.

"I bet if you hadn't pressured him, he would have kept me working four days, even though it affects how much time I have to study."

We drive into the little parking lot on the west side of the Magic Lantern, and Mom parks the car.

"Jackson, Scott really does care about you, and we were aware of the stress it might put on your grades having you work so much. But you actually did fine."

"That's because when I wasn't working at the theater, I was studying."

"The theater budget was very tight for a while," Mom says.

"So that's why he couldn't hire enough staff before he opened the theater? He didn't have the money?"

"Yes, and we talked a number of times about whether or not we should expect you to work and how many days a week. But after renovations, Scott barely had enough money to open the theater doors, and it wasn't until after the theater was up and running that he felt like he could hire more than one extra person."

"It's hard for me to understand why Dad is so obsessed with running this old theater."

I enjoyed working at the Magic Lantern more during the Summer of Film gala—really, it's all I had to do—and I've also grown more interested in movies. But I can't see it becoming the whole focus of my life.

Mom sighs. "It's Scott's dream, Jackson, and he always throws himself totally into whatever he decides to do. Someday, hopefully, you'll have such a big dream. I hope you will, and then maybe you'll know a bit about how he feels."

"Yeah, I can see that he's worked very hard, and it was more fun working at the theater over the summer, but I could never make it the center of my life the way he has."

Mom gets a perplexed expression on her face, but says nothing.

Then I remember what Minister Peter said.

"But I still think it wasn't fair that I had to work so much at the theater my whole junior year, to lose most of my free time. You know, socializing is important for teenagers," I say.

Now I can tell that Mom is struggling to find something to say that will placate me. But I don't feel like being placated.

"It feels really unfair, and ... and Peter thought so too."

"Peter? Your Uncle Peter? When did you talk with Peter about this?" Mom asks.

"At the party. He was at the party, and he asked about how things were going, and I told him, and he said that he thought Dad was working me too much at the theater."

Mom glances at me, and I can tell she isn't really happy with what's she hearing.

"I think Peter overstepped himself talking to you like that."

She pauses and then adds, "I think he has become a bit obsessed himself with social action. He wants to be a change agent, and I think he feels he hasn't been successful at it. So now he's trying to make his whole congregation into activists, especially the young people."

"But don't you think it was unfair? I mean the amount I was having to work. Don't you?"

"Scott and Peter haven't always seen eye to eye on things. When we were going to church regularly, Scott essentially took over the Climate Action group, and I think Peter didn't feel like Scott was open to his input on the direction of the group. He called a meeting of the team to speak with them directly, and Scott responded by leaving the church."

Wow, that's why Dad quit going. It seems a little extreme to me.

"I think Scott and Peter are both dreamers, Jackson, and in certain ways their dreams have clashed. Scott believes in doing what he loves. He loves movies and old theaters, so naturally now he's trying to run one. Peter believes in working to change the world, so he became a minister in a liberal church. But unfortunately that work has only made him frustrated."

"Why is that?" I ask.

"I'm not sure exactly, but my guess is that it's because the work he's chosen is never really finished. Anyway, for now, Jackson, I'd like you to just concentrate on your schoolwork and on deciding which colleges you want to apply to. And remember we need to work together as a family so all our dreams can come true. We can talk more about this later. But you'd better get into the theater so that Scott knows you're here."

I get out of the car and as I watch Mom drive away, I think about what she said. So both Dad and Uncle Peter are dreamers. Maybe that's why I sometimes feel uncomfortable around them.

CHAPTER 32

After the Storm

Ellen is working on the website when I walk into the theater office.

"So, how was the house for the first show?" I ask.

"Maybe three quarters full," Ellen answers. "I think Scott was right about *Our Little Sister* drawing a crowd."

"I guess."

"He seems to be pretty happy," she adds. "Oh, and he also wants to talk with you after the film starts."

I wonder what he wants.

"How did the visit to Rainier College go?"

"It was fine. I liked the campus. It's small and they have a big science building with an observatory on the roof."

"It sounds great. Do you think you'll apply?"

"I don't know. I'm still not sure I want to go to college, at least right now. But this place would be easier to get used to than one of the big state schools and—"

"Jackson, you should apply!" Ellen says, interrupting me before I can finish my sentence. "I don't know what's holding you back. But whatever it is, you need to get over it."

Ellen and I have talked about this so many times, and she's right, something is holding me back, and I don't know exactly what it is, except that I'm not sure I belong in college. Unlike Ana and Ellen, I don't seem to have a college dream, and I can't really see myself anywhere but in Seattle.

"Maybe I'll just go to the community college here."

Ellen is about to say something when the first customers arrive to buy tickets.

"We can talk later," I say.

"I'll be here. I'm hanging out until you and Scott have your meeting. I'll be helping Raji at concessions."

As the film starts, I close the thick red drape that covers the door to the screening room and walk back to concessions to talk with Raji and Ellen. But almost immediately Dad comes out of the projection booth, and we walk back to the office.

Dad's smiling, which lessens my fear that he is going to tell me he can't give me more days off.

"Good news, Jackson," he says. "The guy who bought the *Bride of Frankenstein* poster, Mr. Gittes, called me this afternoon to let me know he will be coming by on Friday afternoon with his cashier's check."

"Wow, that is good news."

"You'll be here Friday. If Mr. Gittes is here right before the first film—which I expect he will be—I'll want you to run the film for the four o'clock show. I'll be bringing that poster back from home, and I'd like you to help me get it into the office. So I'll pick you up at Truman at three o'clock."

Luckily, Friday is a day I can leave right after my two o'clock class, rather than Thursday, which will be this school year's first meeting of the Astronomy Club. I'm determined not to miss a club meeting this year.

"So, have you hired the new staff?" I ask. I know he has been interviewing, but I haven't heard anything about new hires.

"I've got one good candidate, but I want to hire three new people to cover most of your hours and to give me a little more free time. Eric and Clarice are quitting on the 22nd."

This comes as a shock. No one has mentioned leaving to me.

"Actually, Clarice has agreed to work through Wednesday the 25th. Apparently, her classes don't start until Thursday. But don't worry," Dad says. "I'm committed to getting you your days off, so you can keep your grades up. And since this will be your last year at Truman, I know you'll have other things you want to do."

Boy, this sounds different than anything Dad has said to me since he opened the Magic Lantern.

"So how was your visit to Rainier College? Your mom said she thought you were more comfortable there than at Bellingham."

"Well, yeah, I guess." Talking to Dad about my future, I'm suddenly lost for words.

"It's a small campus. They have a big science building and a nice library. The girl who showed us around the campus said the classes are small and it's easy to talk to your professors. She said that was one good thing about Rainier."

Dad's actually looking at me and seems to be interested in what I have to say.

"So this might be a school you'd like to apply to?"

"Maybe ... I don't know. They actually have an observatory on the roof of the science building, and the girl who showed us around said physics students can use it if they're doing research. But I'm still not sure I want to go to college. At least, I'm not sure I want to go right after high school."

"I see," says Dad. "Well, what would you like to do?"

"I don't know. I like to write and I love to stargaze and talk about astronomy. But I don't see myself going to graduate school."

"Is that why you're taking Advanced Math and AP Calculus this fall? Trying to bulk up your science credits just in case you do want to apply to some place with a strong science program?"

"Yeah, but that AP class is going to be a stretch. That's one reason I really need more time to study."

Dad smiles. It's been a long time since we had a talk about anything that's important to me.

"Being an astronomer, now that would be exciting," Dad says.

"Yeah, but it seems like such a dream."

"Maybe that's your dream. You know, the one you haven't been able to find."

I just stare at Dad, and then I ask him the question I've wanted to ask for a while. "When did you decide you wanted to buy a movie theater?"

For a moment this question seems to stymie Dad.

"I'd thought about running a small neighborhood theater for a while, at least since I was in my late twenties. All the time I was running the consulting firm, when Laura and I would go to see a movie, I'd look at whatever theater we were in and think, what would it be like to own a theater? And over time I came to love these smaller independent houses, the ones that run all the independent and foreign films. You know, it became something that I was going to do after I retired, and at that point it was truly just a dream.

"Then Laura and I came to the Magic Lantern two days before it closed, and all the customers were talking about what great memories they had of seeing movies here. As we left the theater that night, I felt so sad and couldn't stop thinking about how wrong it all seemed. I started driving by the theater after it was closed, and one day I parked and walked over and stopped by the steps. And as I stood there, I realized it was waiting for me, and throughout all those years of dreaming I had been waiting for it."

Dad's eyes are shining as he talks about finding the Magic Lantern.

"Back in the 1980s, PBS ran a series with this philosopher named Joseph Campbell, who talked about finding your bliss. He said that to be happy people needed to follow what he called 'their bliss' and that if you did, you'd find the people to help you, and you'd be able to achieve whatever you wanted to accomplish.

"I know this idea sounds simplistic. But that's what I believe, Jackson. It's always worked for me, at least so far. I've never worried about following my dreams. That's what I do."

"So how do I find my bliss?"

Dad smiles. "Find what you love to do, and you'll find your bliss."

J. J. Gittes comes in right after we open the doors on Friday for the four o'clock showing of *After the*

Storm. I remember who he reminds me of when I see him again. I help Dad get the poster from the locked room in the basement, and then head for the projection booth to run the film. By the time I come back to the office, Dad is sitting alone looking at the schedule of films we'll be showing for the next six weeks.

"How did it go?" I ask.

"It was anti-climactic," Dad says. "He came in, gave me the cashier's check, we shook hands, and he took the poster."

"Did he say why it took him so long to get the money?"

"No, and I didn't ask. The only other thing he said was that he'd been looking for a copy of this poster in excellent condition for years and was very happy to find one."

"Are you sure the check is good?"

"I checked with the bank, and there should be no problem with the cashier's check," Dad says. "Anyway, I'm taking it in to deposit right now. So you're in charge until I get back."

"It's kind of strange that it took so long for him to get the money," I say.

"Well, it's a lot of money. The thing that bothered me was that he didn't get back to me for so long after he bid on the poster."

I guess there's no mystery here, and even if there is we'll never know the whole story.

"I'll be talking with staff, as soon as I get a chance, to let them know how successful the Summer of Film was. But just between you and me, with the check from Mr. Gittes, any financial problems are over for the Magic Lantern, at least for now."

Scott Ryan
Journal Entry
September 4, 2019

It feels like we've turned a corner and are finally on solid ground. Even with summer being a tough time to get folks to come inside to see a movie, I feel confident in calling our Summer of Film gala a big success. The Farewell *started us off with a bang. Then the independent film workshop, the Women in Film retrospective, and the poster auction all made money, and I believe helped fix in the public's mind that the Magic Lantern is the place where big things are happening film-wise in Seattle.*

We lost money on a couple of the locally produced films and two films by Richard Linklater. We're doing fine so far with the Kore-eda film series, breaking even on two of his films, while Our Little Sister *drew big crowds. I'm not surprised at that. His latest film,* Shoplifters, *which has already won numerous international awards, will run five days and both close our Summer of Film gala and start our fall film program.*

Our fall schedule is strong, thanks primarily to Genevieve's hard work. The Summer of Film took most of my time and energy, and I had to depend on her to draft the fall film schedule. I'm starting a new staff member on Friday, and hope to hire two more before the end of the month.

Had a nice talk with Jackson yesterday. We should talk more. I know he's still angry about having to spend so much time at the theater, especially this summer. I think cutting back his hours his senior year is the right thing to do. I know he'll work hard, and I hope he can get some enthusiasm about applying to colleges. He doesn't seem to know what he wants to do after high school.

I've been very tired off and on since the poster auction. And I'm hoping I'll be able to take a few Sundays off after I get everybody hired and trained.

CHAPTER 33

Things of Importance

School started on Wednesday. It was good to see everybody again, especially the members of the Astronomy Club. But chairing the club meeting again felt awkward. The club has two new members, and I'd never met either one. When members started talking about what they had done over the summer, I realized how out of touch I had been. Three had gone to Dark Sky sites on their vacations and had brought pictures on their cell phones and stories about what they had seen. Me, the April star party is the only stargazing I'd done all year.

Even worse, after only two days, I'm already up to my neck with school assignments. So it's hard for me to have much energy to work at the Magic Lantern on Friday.

When I show up, Dad is in his office with a smallish African American girl.

"Jackson," Dad says, as I come into the office to leave my coat. "This is Saffaire Brown. She's going to be the newest member of our team."

The girl jumps up and extends her hand before I can say anything.

"Hi, Jackson," she says.

"Hi," I say and shake her hand.

"Boy, how does it feel to be the assistant manager of a movie theater when you're in high school?"

There's that assistant manager stuff again. I feel like I should ask Dad to stop calling me that. But he saves me from having to answer the question when he says, "Saffaire is going to be working with you on Fridays and with Raji on Saturdays. I've given her the tour and talked with her about what she'll be doing in general."

"I'm excited about working here," Saffaire says without any prompting. "I know how to use a cash register, and Scott showed me the concession stand. So I hope I won't have too many questions."

"So you're working with me?" I look at Dad and frown. Once again, I'll be training new staff. It will be just the two of us working concessions for the early show, as Clarice will only be working the evening show today.

"This was a good day for Saffaire to start," Dad says. "I'm expecting a smaller crowd and I'm not do-ing an introduction to the film this afternoon. I'll start the film and then come by concessions to see how everything is going."

The crowd for the four o'clock showing of *After the Storm* is in fact small, maybe forty people. So we have some time to talk after the film starts, interrupted just occasionally by customers wanting to buy something or looking for the bathroom.

It turns out Saffaire is a drama and literature stu-dent with lots of opinions and questions. She likes

Spike Lee, but doesn't think much of Denzel Washington, particularly playing Malcolm X. Luckily, most of her questions are about how we select films, and for those answers I mention Genevieve and then refer her to Dad.

After the first show, we clean up the screening room, and then Saffaire goes into the office to eat the food she brought with her in a big brown bag. I sit down in the salon to read, and later, when I walk by the office on my way out to get a piece of pizza for dinner, I notice Dad and Saffaire are talking.

The audience is larger for the seven o'clock show, so it's lucky both Saffaire and Clarice are here. Saffaire seems like a quick study. She can talk to anybody and she does. So, a couple of times I have to step in and help customers who have been waiting too long at concessions.

"Another drama student," Clarice says when Saffaire leaves to take her break. "They like to talk."

"You're leaving?" I ask.

"Yeah. This is my last year at the U, and I'm starting a design internship in a couple weeks, so I just won't have time to work here."

I never talked much with Clarice or most of the other staff, except Raji, but she has been a good worker, always on time, and never asked too many questions. So I'm sorry to see her go. But it sounds like she is following her own dreams, her bliss. So I wish her good luck.

Sunday, Ellen is again working on the computer when I arrive at the theater. Dad was feeling tired, so I'm in charge until he comes in for the evening show.

"Working on the website again?" I ask.

"Yeah, I'm trying to get the site set up so Scott can just add information himself."

"Why would he be doing that when you're around?"

"I'm not going to be able to work at the theater anymore. My parents and I had a talk. It's important that I do really well my senior year, and—"

"You're already a straight-A student—how much better can you do?" I say, interrupting her before she can finish talking.

"I'm taking three AP classes the first semester. I want to apply to four or five top colleges, which means I'm going to have to concentrate on other activities that will show my community spirit. So besides the Astronomy and Math clubs, and now the Honors Society, I'm going to volunteer for the teen feeding program in the University District."

I've never thought of Ellen as someone who does a lot of volunteering. But, she's right. That will look great on her resume.

"I kind of expected that you might be dropping some of your work hours this year. But I thought you'd stay on to help with the website and tech stuff."

"I just can't continue to work," Ellen says. "I got one B last year, and my parents weren't happy, especially since it was in American History. They've been talking about it all summer, and now that I'm going to apply at Berkeley, Harvard, University of Chicago, probably Princeton, along with Stanford, I just can't be doing things that don't relate to my college plans."

"Boy, I can't see Dad working on our website very much."

I know what that means. With Ellen leaving, it's likely Dad will expect me to help out again. But maybe there's a way I can stop him from asking me to work any more hours. If I decide to apply to some colleges, and I get really serious about doing well my senior year, he'll have to find someone else to take that time.

"So what do you think about the referendum?" Ellen asks.

"What referendum?"

"The one giving citizenship to the Dreamers."

I vaguely remember Mom saying something about this.

From high school history, I know that the main way our Constitution can be amended is by a national convention. The states had called one, but after five years of wrangling, nobody thought it was going anywhere. Then, out of the blue, the convention passed a proposal to allow voters to pass constitutional amendments by a 60 percent majority, and it was approved by two-thirds of the states in just six months.

"So that effort to get a vote on citizenship for the Dreamers is going to happen?"

"They're calling it the Dreamers amendment, and Congress passed it Friday night, so it could be on the ballot in November," says Ellen.

"Wow." I can hardly believe it. Immediately, I think of Ana. This is big, really big, and if it passes, it will change the lives of so many people.

CHAPTER 34

The Road Ahead

Everybody at school is talking about the Dreamers Referendum. Will it pass? And what will it mean? But in our house, my parents are focused on something else: getting me to apply to two or three in-state colleges.

So, when I tell them that I've decided to apply to Rainier College and probably the University, they are ecstatic. Mom immediately starts talking about my applying to other schools like Bellingham College and Central Washington, while Dad simply calls it "the right decision."

"Maybe the first year you can live at home, and even work a shift or two at the theater," he says. "You'll need gas money if you're commuting to Tacoma."

When I mention that I'd like to live on campus, he doesn't respond. But as soon as I say it, I realize that if I go to Rainier, I'll likely have to live at home and commute for at least the first year. And then my enthusiasm begins to fade.

We run a science fiction film starring Brad Pitt after the Kore-eda mini-fest ends, and then *Judy* starts the last Friday in the month. Before the staff meeting that day, I notice that Dad is acting kind of strange.

"Not getting enough sleep," he says when I ask him if he's feeling okay. I wonder if he's getting the flu. It's strange because Dad is one of those people who seldom gets sick. I know he got his flu shot. Mom hounded him until he did. But he's obviously not feeling well, and he sends me out to get him a big cup of coffee.

Dad introduces Saffaire and the other new hires at the beginning of the staff meeting. Berkeley Macintosh and Michael Skarsgard are replacing Eric and Clarice. Berkeley is a design student. Michael has a double major in computer engineering and English literature. Go figure that. To my surprise, Ellen is at the meeting and so is Genevieve.

"All in all, the Summer of Film was a big success," Dad says. "And I want to thank all of you who worked here over the summer. I mentioned this to both Eric and Clarice before they left. Thanks to everyone on the staff for all your hard work.

"The opening night film for the Summer of Film, the documentaries, the filmmakers workshop, and even the final Kore-eda mini-fest made money. The women directors series was big, a real game changer, as was the poster auction. There were some disappointments, but mostly from individual films that didn't get the expected audience."

Dad stops for a moment. He seems to be having trouble staying focused. He takes a big swig of his coffee and perks up.

"So, the bottom line is that the Summer of Film made money, and because of that we are now on a firm financial footing. And I feel like we are well on our way to establishing the Magic Lantern as the theater where people in North Seattle go when they want to see a great movie."

Dad pauses and shifts in his chair as though he is uncomfortable.

"Now I'd like to have Genevieve tell us about what we'll be screening this fall. But first, for those of you who are new to the team, let me say that Genevieve is our wonderful film buyer, and much of the success we've had in bringing the Magic Lantern back to life is due to her hard work."

"Thanks, Scott. What Scott hasn't said is that we got really great coverage of the Summer of Film by local media, and we also got great word of mouth in the larger Seattle film community, especially about the Northwest Filmmakers series and the Women in Film retrospective.

"So now let's talk about our fall film schedule. Starting tonight we'll be showing *Judy*, a film about the final London tour of Judy Garland, starring Renee Zellweger."

"She's the front runner for the best actress Oscar," Dad says, interrupting Genevieve. "I'm expecting a big audience for the film's two-week run."

"Next up," Genevieve says, "we've got a Korean satire about two families who take the class struggle in South Korea to new heights. It won the Grand Prize at the Cannes Film Festival in May."

"And," Dad interjects, "it will be a U.S. premier, because Genevieve was able to schedule our showing of *Parasite* for its initial run in the U.S. And that's a real coup for us."

It's hard to stop Dad from talking movies, but now I notice that he's wiping his eyes feverishly and rubbing his back like it's bothering him. He really is sick. I think Genevieve notices it too because she speeds up her review of the fall schedule.

"After *Parasite*, we'll show a feature on Harriet Tubman, the famous conductor of the Underground Railroad. Then we'll be showing Almodóvar's newest film about an aging choreographer, an out-of-work singer, and an LGBT band, who travel from Spain to France to participate in a music contest."

"I love Almodóvar films," Berkeley says. "They're so colorful."

"There you go," says Dad, trying his best to look relaxed. "And I've been told this film is very funny."

"And then," says Genevieve, "we'll be screening the new Noah Baumbach film for a month, starting November 22nd."

"Whatever happens with the other three films, I'm counting on that film to bring in the crowds," Dad says, this time a little too loudly.

"Any questions?" Then, after a quick look at everyone in the room, he closes the meeting.

"Is Scott feeling okay?" Raji asks as we stand on the sidewalk in front of the theater.

"I don't know. But I think I'd better check in with him before people start to arrive for the four o'clock show."

I am not fully through the theater door when Dad comes out of the office and asks me to close tonight.

"Feels like I've got a touch of something. I've got a whopper of a headache, so I'm going home. Ellen has agreed to stay and work the four o'clock show with you and Saffaire. Unfortunately, you two will be on your own for the second show."

I start to protest—if there's a big crowd, two people won't be enough—but before I can say anything, he thanks me for stepping in to take over things when he needs me to.

"And I should have said this more often, but I appreciate everything you've done over the past year."

He sounds so sincere that all I can say is, "Thanks, Dad."

He gives me a half smile, then turns and walks back into the office. I notice him grab what looks like a pill bottle off his desk, and then he leaves.

I join Ellen and Saffaire at the concession stand.

"I thought you'd quit," I say to Ellen.

"I'm still on payroll until the end of the month. So I told Scott I'd be willing to work a few shifts until the newbies are trained," Ellen replies.

"Can you stay to help during the second show—that way you could take me home—and maybe work tomorrow if Dad can't come in?"

We exchange smiles.

"Sorry, Jackson, I won't be able to chauffeur you home, as much as I would like to. We're filling out college applications tonight and tomorrow and probably also next weekend. So I won't be able to work tomorrow either. I hope Scott feels better."

Suddenly Dad reappears at concessions.

"Laura will pick you up at 9:30. Call her if you're not going to be ready."

Later, as we are cleaning up between shows, Ellen asks me if I've decided to apply to the school in Tacoma.

"I guess so. I told my parents I would apply. But it's really expensive, probably too expensive for even my parents."

"Your parents' college fund can't help?"

"Oh, it can help. They have put away almost $20,000 for me to use."

It's hard for me to imagine how they did that, particularly with Dad not working for about three months between the time he quit working at his consulting firm and when the Magic Lantern opened.

"See," Ellen says pointedly, "they didn't use your college money for the theater."

"I guess I was wrong to think they might have. But still it costs more than that for just one year's tuition at Rainer College, and room and board would be extra."

"Well, college is expensive," Ellen says, sounding a little surprised.

"Yeah, maybe too expensive."

"So you're not going to apply?"

"Yes. No. I don't know. I'd like to go to a smaller school. I think it would be cool to have a telescope on campus that I could use. But the cost ... "

"Have you talked to the financial aid person at Rainier?" Ellen asks.

"Just over the telephone. But Mom's going to schedule another trip to the campus to talk to the financial aid person, and I'll probably decide after that visit."

"Remember, tuition at the University is just $11,000. Your college fund would cover all of that, plus you'd have enough for books and materials, with a big chunk left over."

Ellen's right. The problem, I just realized, is that I don't really want to go to the U. If I go to college, I want to go to a smaller school, away from Seattle.

"If I apply and get accepted, my parents have promised to buy me a smart phone," I blurt out.

"Well, there you go. If you're undecided, wouldn't it be nice to finally have your smart phone, especially if you actually do go to college? Every college kid has a phone."

"Yeah, I guess. If I don't have a college dream, at least I can have a smart phone. Anyway, if nothing else changes, maybe I'll be able to improve my grades this year, and then maybe I can get enough financial aid that I'll be able to go to Rainier."

Chapter 35

The Unexpected

Fall is here. Most of the leaves on our bigleaf maple have turned yellow or tan, and there are now piles all over the yard. Dad started to rake them up, but then stopped. So I'll probably have to finish that job this weekend.

It feels like I've basically settled into a normal routine. My classes are going well. I'm back to running the Astronomy Club meetings, and I've even been asked to write a couple of science articles for the school newspaper by the paper's new student editor, Ellen.

Now that I'm only working two days a week at the theater, it doesn't feel like it's dominating my life like it was my junior year.

The financial aid officer at Rainier College says I should be able to get enough aid to pay my first year's tuition. Room and board, along with books, would still have to come out of my college fund. But knowing that I can afford it makes the idea of going to Rainier College feel a lot more doable.

Dad is back at work. The doctor says his headaches and eye problems were something called a migraine. His blood pressure was a little high, so he's started taking a pill. He continues to get tired though. His doctor suggested he get more exercise and lose a little weight. Dad used to swim a couple times a week, but after he bought the theater, he couldn't seem to find the time.

At some point in October, I noticed he had brought in a folding cot and set it up by the far wall of the office.

"It's in case I need to lie down," he told me when I asked what it was for.

I'd been trying to talk myself into calling Ana to ask her about the Dreamers amendment referendum. For a while, I thought she might call me. But she hadn't. Then one Saturday afternoon I take a walk and end up at the coffee shop in Wedgewood, the place where we went after my Spanish lessons at the library. And there, standing in line to buy some coffee, is Ana.

"Ana, what a nice surprise," I say.

"Jackson," she says. I notice that she looks tired.

"I've got my grandparents' car," she says, and points at an older blue Kia in the parking lot. "I've just been out driving around."

"That's great." I'm envious. "Want to sit down and talk?"

For a moment she doesn't respond.

"Sure," Ana says finally.

We look around, but all the tables are full.

"Let's go outside," she says. "It's too noisy to talk."

We end up on the bench where we sat in the spring, the one with the view of the Olympic mountains.

Although today they are partially obscured by clouds, and it's a lot cooler.

"This is where you read me your poem."

"Yes," Ana says, and I notice a faint smile. But I can tell that something else is on her mind, and it feels a little awkward.

"I've been totally focused on classes, and when I'm not studying, I'm working with the St. Francis group supporting the Dreamers Referendum."

"I was wondering if you'd gotten involved in the referendum effort."

"I meant to call you," she says. "But everything has happened so fast, and I've been so busy. The whole Dreamer community has been mobilized to get out the message. Carlos is the chairperson of our group, and we're working to canvas North Seattle to get people information on the referendum—there's so much misinformation out there, so many lies about what the referendum would do if passed—and also to ask people to please vote in November."

"You look tired," I say. "Are you getting enough sleep?"

"Probably not. I've been so worried. The latest polling shows the referendum with barely 50 percent support, nowhere near the 60 percent it needs to pass."

Ana pauses and takes a drink of her coffee.

"And I'm worried about Carlos. He seems to feel that if the referendum doesn't pass, the Supreme Court will rule the DACA program illegal by the end of the year, and then we'll all face deportation. So he's speaking out. He was on the local television news last week, and I'm afraid he'll get himself in trouble. I mean he is technically illegal."

"Aren't the Dreamers still protected?"

"Yes, but only until the Supreme Court rules on the legality of the program or the referendum passes," Ana answers.

"I guess the situation is pretty scary."

"It's frustrating, and I'm not sure exactly what I should do. My grandparents don't want me to get too involved. They want me to stay focused on getting into college, and not draw too much attention to myself. But everybody I know at school is speaking out, and there is now a statewide Pass the Amendment committee."

"Well, if you need some help," I blurt out, "you can count on me."

Ana smiles. "Thanks, Jackson. Have you made any decisions on applying to colleges?"

"It looks like I'll apply to the U and probably to Rainer College."

"That's great. One big school, one smaller one."

"I think Rainer College is more my size, and it's not in Seattle, but still close enough for me to come back to visit when I want to. I like the campus and everyone there seemed helpful."

"It sounds like you've already made up your mind about where you want to go."

"Well, there are a couple of problems."

"Like what?" Ana asks.

"I don't have a car, and Rainier is expensive."

"Can't you get financial aid?"

"Yes, probably some, but I'm not sure if it would even cover tuition, and everything else will have to come out of my parents' college fund. Mom wants me to apply to Bellingham College as an alternative to the U, but it's almost as big a school, and there isn't even regular bus service to Seattle like there is from Tacoma."

"Well, Jackson, now that you're interested in going, I really hope that you'll apply and get accepted wherever you'd like to go."

It feels nice when she says it. I get that feeling again, the one that says, go ahead and ask her for a date. But I know with everything that's going on it's really not the right time.

She looks a bit sad, but then she perks up and smiles.

"You know, I want to see the film on Harriet Tubman that will be showing at the Magic Lantern at the end of the month. Why don't we meet at the theater on the afternoon of the 26th. We'll see the movie together, and then you can come by my house, and we can sit in the backyard and talk."

This is not exactly what I had in mind. But I can see that Ana is excited about the idea.

"Great," I say. "Just the two of us, right?"

Ana gives me a very sympathetic look, and then she responds. "Just the two of us ... and all those other people in the theater, and my grandparents at home."

For about a week, I'm flying high. Everything seems to be going well. I've sent early applications to the University and Rainier College and, at Mom's insistence, to Bellingham College. Mom and I just got together and did them. I'm going to the October star party, the first one I've attended since April. And in just eight days, Ana and I will be getting together to see a movie.

"Things are looking up," I tell Raji when he shows up to see the Korean film.

When I come in for my Friday shift, Dad calls me into the office. Genevieve is there, and Dad is looking upset.

"Hi, Gen," I say. "What's up?"

"What's up is that we're not going to be allowed to have the new Noah Baumbach for as long as we wanted," says Dad. He sounds angry.

"Why?"

"The distributor is only offering it to theaters for a limited period of time because it was financed by a streaming company."

"It's called a limited release," says Genevieve, "and it's for a month, starting November 6th and ending December 5th."

"We were planning to run *Marriage Story* from right before Thanksgiving until five days before Christmas. But to get more dates during the limited distribution period, we'd have to drop the Almodóvar film."

"You couldn't just reschedule it?"

"No," says Genevieve. "I checked with the distributor. It's too late to make a change, and if we cancel, we will have to pay a penalty."

We don't regularly run films for more than two weeks, and during the Summer of Film gala most of the films only ran for two or three days. How important is it to have a film for a month?

"So how long will we have the Baumbach film?"

"Two weeks," Dad says.

"That's a normal run for us, isn't it?"

Dad frowns. "With a four-week run this film would have made us money. But now with just a twelve-day run, we'll barely have enough time to build up an audience, and now we have a big two-week hole in our schedule in early December."

"I think we can get a decent audience with the time we have," says Genevieve, seeming to contradict Dad. "But we are going to have to go all out with our publicity and—"

"One thing is for sure," Dad breaks in, "we can't depend on word of mouth when we only have this film for two weeks. Folks will know that they can stream it starting December 6th, and that is an incentive for them to not go out to see it. But I want to see this theater full, at least over the Thanksgiving weekend, which means we have all got some work to do.

"This change also means we'll have to print new schedules for November and December, and I'm going to need to update our website as soon as possible."

"Being at the end of the release period means the major reviewing sources will have already printed or posted their reviews of the film," Genevieve says, trying to sound as positive as possible.

"You know as well as I do, Genevieve, that when a first-run film is going to be streamed, theaters have to sell their customers on the idea of seeing it in a theater. And they have to do that before the run, so people can plan in advance on seeing the film at their local theater."

I've never heard Dad speak to Genevieve that way. He's really worked up.

"Damn it, these streaming companies are killing movie theaters."

"I know," Genevieve says. "But the only thing we can do is to make this change work for us. I'll start calling around to see what else is out there for us to show in early December."

"Michael is scheduled to work tomorrow, and I'm going to call him to ask if he can come in early to talk about ideas for the website," Dad says. "Jackson, I need to have you come in to help with Saturday's matinee. I'm sorry, but the website has to be updated, and that means I'll need to have you here to run the film and deal with any problems."

I look at Dad, but don't know what to say. Just when it looks like my life is getting back to normal, something unexpected happens and I get pulled back into working more at the Magic Lantern. It's frustrating. But for now all I can do is sigh.

CHAPTER 36

Falling Apart

Since it became clear that our run of the new Baumbach film is going to be restricted, Dad's been a different person. He's grumpy a lot of the time, especially with staff, and he spends less time at the front of the theater greeting and thanking customers.

"He's not getting enough sleep," Mom tells me after Dad leaves the house on Tuesday. "And he's having headaches again."

Another reason for Dad's crankiness is the attendance for *Parasite*. Despite winning international awards, our audience for the Korean thriller has been much less than Dad expected.

"Less than half the seats have been filled for most of the weekday showings," he tells me one day when I see him at home.

"It's too dark for most American audiences, and they don't know much about South Korea or Korean filmmakers," Raji says when I mention the meager audience at some of *Parasite*'s showings. "Of course, if it had won an Academy Award, it might be different."

Why has the low turnout for one film irritated Dad so much? And why haven't we heard what the Christmas holiday films will be? Anyway, as the days go by, my mind turns more and more to getting together with Ana on Saturday.

Then, just a few days before our big movie non-date, Mom knocks on my door while I'm sending an email to Astronomy Club members about our October meeting.

"I thought you should know, in case Scott brings it up, that he got a letter from some local ministers asking him to donate the theater on Monday nights, so they could show what they describe as meaningful movies."

"What are meaningful movies?" I ask.

"I think that they're documentaries on social issues."

"Dad would never do that," I say. "It would require someone from our staff to be there to open and close, and his working another night is out of the question."

"Yes, and it's really a bad time to even bring this up."

"This sounds like something Uncle Peter would propose."

"His name, along with the names of six other ministers from churches in North Seattle, is on the letter."

"Is Dad upset about the letter?"

"He said he was going to call Peter when he got a chance."

Friday is the first day of *Harriet*'s run. I'm surprised to see Genevieve in the office again, talking with Dad.

"You're hanging out here a lot these days," I say when she comes out of their meeting.

"Yes, we're trying to figure out how to fill the rest of the holiday schedule. Not being able to show the Baumbach film well into December means we've got to schedule something else for two weeks, and we don't have a lot of choices."

"Does Dad seem tired to you?"

"A little. I know he's upset. We had our film schedule planned into January, but now it's being disrupted at a time when theaters can usually count on making money."

"Mom says he hasn't been sleeping well, and it seems like he's having trouble with his eyes."

"It sounds like stress to me," Genevieve says. "I'm sure he'll be okay, once we get past these two unexpected problems."

"So do you know what movie we'll be showing over Christmas?"

"It's a Tom Hanks film about Mr. Rogers."

"Oh. That should draw an audience."

"With Tom Hanks," Genevieve says, "I think it will. But we've still got to fill a big hole in our December schedule."

"Dad seemed really surprised that the houses for the Korean film were so small. Was that such a big surprise?"

"Not totally."

There's a pause and Genevieve seems to be thinking about what else she wants to say.

"The film has been a big international success. It's doing well in L.A. and New York, and I think Scott thought it would be a great bridge between *Judy* and *Marriage Story*."

"So he just read the Seattle movie audience wrong?"

"I think when your dad talks about the Seattle movie audience, he's really thinking about an audience of the '70s, '80s, and '90s. Much of today's audience wants to see their movies at home, the younger filmgoers especially. They like the convenience of the streaming technology. There is still an audience for movie theaters, but it's much smaller than it was. Action films and big Hollywood films get the biggest theater audiences."

"So what does that mean for Dad's idea of reviving this old theater and making it work financially?"

Thinking that she might not answer such a direct question, I'm surprised when she immediately responds.

"Scott has saved this theater, Jackson. It may only be for a while. But he has done it. It's just that you can't count on an in-theater audience anymore, even for a really good movie like *Parasite*, especially if it's a dark satire and a foreign film, and as more people use streaming, the streaming companies have more and more say on how films are distributed."

I glance at my watch. It's time for me to open the door for the four o'clock show.

"I'll walk with you to the door," I say to Genevieve.

"Oh, I'm going to use the restroom, and then I'm staying for the matinee."

"Somebody's a movie lover," I say, with just a touch of sarcasm.

Genevieve smiles and says, "I'm guilty."

Harriet turns out to be a pretty popular film, with the main actress being a standout. Ana certainly liked it, and after it was over she really wanted to talk about the movie.

"I felt such a kinship—is that the right word?—with her."

"I can't imagine how it would feel to be a slave," I say. "She must have been very brave."

"Yes, brave and desperate," Ana says. "But she also had a dream of something better."

We talk about the film all the way to her house. This is the kind of conversation Dad wants to see people having after they see a film at the Magic Lantern.

At Ana's, we're greeted by her grandfather, a tall, slightly stooped man with bright eyes and an infectious smile. I guess that smile runs in her family. He speaks broken English, but as Ana tells him about the film we've just seen, he smiles and shakes his head, and when I mention something funny, he laughs.

After a few minutes, Ana's grandmother appears. She's a small woman, more talkative than her husband, and less stern looking than she was at the Labor Day party. Her English is better too. She invites me to stay for dinner, and then Ana and I go out into the backyard. October has been warmer and drier than usual. So I feel comfortable sitting on an old sofa someone has put on the back patio, although Ana puts on a sweater to keep warm.

She immediately starts talking about her college plans and then asks again about mine.

"I'll go if I get accepted. Hopefully, I'll get accepted somewhere."

"What will you major in?"

"I'm not sure. I'm not sure if I'll even have to declare a major before I can get accepted."

Ana smiles knowingly.

"When you're admitted you have to have a pre-major in something. I'll be a pre-major in journalism. But I plan to declare a real major once I get accepted and have talked with my advisor at whichever school I attend."

I hadn't realized that.

"So, where are you applying?" I ask her.

"Besides the University here, the University of Southern California and some of the other state schools in California that have journalism majors. But I plan to take a number of political science and English classes too. At some point, I'll probably declare a minor in either or both of those subjects."

"You have to declare a backup major, too?"

"It's not really a backup major. It's more of a secondary subject you're interested in, and you don't have to have a minor, or you can declare one later after you've taken a few classes."

"Your situation has made you interested in politics?"

"Yes, kind of." Ana pauses, and then adds, "I think I'd like to combine my journalism, my writing, with an interest in politics, and get a job reporting the news on public television or at one of the big newspapers."

"Wow, you are ambitious."

Ana smiles.

"Are you nervous about getting accepted?"

"Not really. I know I'll get in somewhere. I just hope it's a college with a good journalism program. I'll have to get financial aid, too. But there seem to be a lot of aid programs for women and minorities. So I'm pretty confident I'll be able to get some money to go wherever I get accepted."

We sit there for a minute just looking at each other and enjoying the late afternoon light.

"It's nice here."

"Yes, *mi abuelito* works hard to make the yard look nice. He really seems to enjoy it. He says that they never had a real yard before they came to the United States. They love this place."

Then Ana's expression changes from happy and relaxed to serious, and I immediately get an unsettled feeling.

"The thing is, Jackson, regardless of what happens with the referendum, I really need to put all my energy into keeping my grades up, so that I can get into a good college. My grandparents have done all they can do, giving me a safe place to live in America and setting up some rules that have helped me be successful in school. But now it's really up to me. And that means ... no dating. Friends are okay, but no dating. Nothing that could derail my college dream."

I feel my heart sink. I wonder if she's been working up to this all the time we've been together today.

"I get it," I said. "I know you've said that you can't date. But I just like spending time with you."

"So, friends are okay. Today was fun. I'd like you to stay for dinner, but we can't date and I can't see you all the time."

"Okay," I say, trying to sound sincere, but I can hardly get the word out of my mouth because it's not really okay.

Apparently, Ana can tell that I have mixed feelings about being just friends.

"Oh, you look a little sad," she says. "We can still be friends, and I can still tutor you in Spanish if you want me to."

"I do understand," I tell her, less than convincingly.

"Good," Ana said. "You want to stay for dinner?"

At dinner, most of the talk is about college admissions. I try to sound upbeat, but I'm pretty sure that Ana's grandmother realizes that I'm not quite at Ana's level academically and might have trouble just getting into a four-year school.

It's only at the end of dinner that the topic of the referendum comes up, and Ana's grandmother is the only one to say much.

"We're concerned about people, our friends, who are supporting this referendum very publicly, people like Ana's friend Carlos. They may face problems if it fails," she says. "But Ana is a good girl, and she is keeping her focus on getting into a good college. That is where we think she needs to put her time and energy."

Scott Ryan
Journal Entry
October 31, 2019

Since Judy ended, we've been struggling. For each of the last two films—a Cannes grand-prize winner, and a well-made and acted feature film about Harriet Tubman, attendance dropped off after the first weekend of the run.

Genevieve says it's theater fatigue. Too many people saw films here in the run-up to and during the Summer of Film, and now they just want a break from seeing movies. But I don't buy that. Fall is usually a good time for people coming back to the movies, and we should have more regulars after the success of the Summer of Film. What's happened to our regulars? Some were here to see Judy and some showed up for that first weekend of Parasite's run, but after that it's like they've mostly disappeared.

We paid for some ads on Harriet to run in community newspapers in South Seattle. Some folks from the south end attended that first weekend. A few even stopped by as they left the theater and had positive comments about the film. I thought Harriet was going to be a big, big box office for us, but after that first weekend attendance dwindled.

In talking with other theaters, it seems like fall audiences are down across the city this year. If independent theaters can't count on big houses during the fall and around the holidays, and can't schedule good films when and for how long they want them, it's going to be a struggle for us to stay open.

CHAPTER 37

Brainstorm

Dad says he's feeling better, and he's been working overtime to build local interest in *Marriage Story*'s short run. That's in addition to working with Genevieve to get another good film to fill out our schedule in December.

"He's still not sleeping well," Mom tells me one morning at the end of October. She sounds worried.

"Scott was on the telephone when I got up this morning," she says, "talking to someone on the East Coast, and the conversation sounded pretty tense. He's got to be tired. He's moody and still having those headaches."

It sounds like this theater thing is consuming Dad.

"Have you talked to Ana lately?" Mom asks.

"Not since we saw *Harriet* together. I think she's totally involved with her classes, applying to colleges, and supporting the Dreamers referendum."

"I guess the polls show the yes percentage is climbing," Mom says.

"Oh, that's good." I should call Ana.

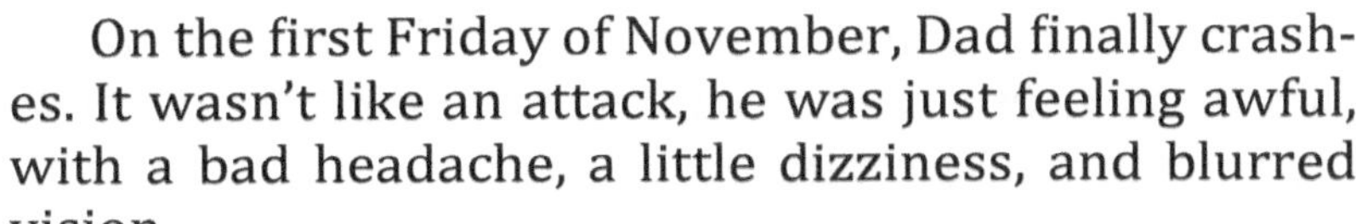

On the first Friday of November, Dad finally crashes. It wasn't like an attack, he was just feeling awful, with a bad headache, a little dizziness, and blurred vision.

The second show was just starting. I hadn't seen him for almost an hour. I'd been working on concessions. A bunch of latecomers showed up while the previews were on, and everyone wanted something to eat.

When I finally go back to the office, I find him slumped at his desk.

"Jackson, can you close up? I'm feeling awful and I want to go home."

He looks awful. "Sure."

"I'm going to call Laura to pick me up. I don't feel like driving, so I'll leave my car and you can drive it back home."

When I agreed to apply for college, my parents bought me a new iPhone as a surprise. I'm still not totally sure how to use all the features. But it comes in handy when I get a call from Mom just as the show is letting out.

"I'm with Scott and we're at the Urgent Care clinic. You're okay getting home?"

"Sure. What's going on?"

"Scott's having trouble with his equilibrium, so I thought, with the weekend coming up, he should be seen by someone."

There is a long pause. "This sounds serious," I say.

"Let's not get worried until we know what's going on," Mom responds in her usual steady way. "There's a lot of people waiting. So we could be here a couple hours. There's food in the fridge if you're hungry when you get home."

I'm in bed but not asleep when Mom comes home. I go downstairs to see what they found out, and the first thing I notice is that she's alone.

"Where's Dad?"

"He's been put into the hospital for observation and tests."

"What's wrong with him?"

"They aren't sure."

"Don't they know anything?"

"I don't want to get into a big discussion right now, Jackson. I'm tired and I'm hoping he'll be back home tomorrow."

She really does look tired.

"Now I just want to get to bed, and you'd better get to bed yourself. Tomorrow's going to be a busy day."

I'm not surprised when I get up the next morning, and Mom has already eaten and is on the telephone, talking to someone about Dad.

"That was your grandmother," Mom says after she finishes. "I wanted to let her know what's happened.

"We need you to work today along with tomorrow at the theater. Raji will be there today so you should be okay. I'm going to call Raji and Saffaire from the hospital to see if either one can work Sunday with you."

"Will Dad be back to work on Tuesday?"

"Jackson, we just don't know right now. We'll have to talk about it after we know more about what's happened."

"I hope Scott is all right," says Raji when I talk with him at the theater during the first Saturday show. "Without him, this place would have folded and been torn down last year."

"You don't think someone else would have bought the place and remodeled it just like Dad did?"

"No way!" says Raji. "Your dad saved the Magic Lantern from the wrecking ball."

"Yeah," I say. "I remember when the movie house on 45th had its roof collapse. The story made it onto the front page of the paper."

Raji shakes his head, as if he's trying not to remember the shocking pictures of the theater in the *Cascadian*.

"The owner said it was the city's fault, and the city fined the owner for not maintaining the building properly."

When I get home after closing the theater, Mom is lying down on the sofa.

"How was the theater?" she asks.

"Okay. The matinee audience was small, but the evening show was over half full. Dad would have been happy. How is Dad?"

"He's sitting up and talking. But they think he's had a small stroke, although they're not 100 percent sure. So, they're keeping him in until Monday just to check a few more things."

Mom sits up. She looks beat.

"We're going to close the theater starting Monday, and then we'll open up again on Friday," she says.

"Without Dad?"

"We talked about it. This is what he wants."

"So who's going to be in charge?"

"You'll be in charge on Fridays and Sundays."

"And the rest of the time?"

"I'll be in charge on the other days."

I don't know what to say. Mom's going to work at the theater and at her shop, too. How's that going to work?

"I'm still working out the details, Jackson. But I think it will be easier this way for now. We've got enough staff to pull it off—that is, if Scott's not off work for more than a few weeks."

"But you don't know how long he'll be gone?"

"No, not yet."

A lot is unclear, and I don't see how we can keep the Magic Lantern open for long without Dad. But I don't say any more because I know Mom's got a lot on her mind.

"We'll go by the hospital tomorrow morning, and you can talk to Scott yourself."

I was really apprehensive about seeing Dad. But when we walk into his room at the hospital, he's just sitting in a chair by his bed and chatting with a pretty nurse.

"Hi, Jackson," he says. "Sorry ... "

Immediately, I notice Dad's speech is halting.

"... if I scared you any on ... Friday. But we didn't really know ... what was going on."

"So, you're okay?"

"Yes ... they think it was ... just a small stroke."

"A stroke. Isn't that pretty dangerous?"

"Well, it can ... be, but it can also be ... almost nothing. The doctor is coming ... to see us in ... a few minutes. I'm speaking a ... little funny. But I'm hoping ...

with some rest ... and medication that ... I'll be back at work in a couple ... weeks."

It's then that I notice that he's having some trouble flexing his right hand, which looks sort of limp.

Dad notices what I'm looking at, and then realizes what I'm thinking.

"Yes." He pauses, and then says, "I'm having a few ... problems with my hand. That probably means I'll ... have to do some physical ... therapy for a while, but that's pretty common in these cases."

Just then a woman in a white coat comes into the room. Another nurse? No, it's the doctor.

Mom hands me a five-dollar bill and asks me to go downstairs to get her a cup of coffee. I'd rather stay and hear what the doctor has to say. But I can tell she wants me to leave. They'll tell me what they want me to know when I get back.

The hospital seems huge, and Dad's room is on the second floor. At first, I just wander around, but finally I find the cafeteria. By the time I come back with the coffee, Dad's back in bed and he and Mom are talking.

"Good news," says Dad. "I'll ... be released tomorrow to come ... home, and will start P.T. on ... Thursday."

Then he reaches for me with his left hand.

"Jackson ... I know I can ... count on you when we ... have a minor setback like ... this to help out at the theater ... "

He pauses like he's trying to find the words to finish his thought, and then he adds, "and to also ... stay focused on ... your schoolwork."

I try to smile, but for the first time I realize that Dad is really sick. Sure I'll help out, what else can I do? But I wonder how this is going to affect everything we've been doing and talking about doing because Dad's rehabilitation is going to take some time.

"I have complete confidence ... in your ability, Jackson, ... to run the theater and ... to deal with any problems ... that arise, and if you have questions ... you and Laura can talk, and ... she will talk with me about ... anything she needs to."

Dad's back home, but he's still spending a lot of time in bed. I'm told that after he gets his exercises, he'll be spending a lot of time doing those.

Mom and I make a nice sign for the theater about the temporary closing, which I post on the front door after we close on Sunday.

VALUED THEATER PATRONS:
THE MAGIC LANTERN WILL BE CLOSED
FOR THREE DAYS BECAUSE OF A FAMILY
EMERGENCY. WE WILL REOPEN
AGAIN ON FRIDAY, NOVEMBER 8TH.

Michael posts a similar note on the website.

I try to stay focused on my classes. I've got some big exams coming up. But then it's Tuesday, and Tuesday is election day. That evening, as the election returns come in from the East Coast, it remains unclear if the referendum will pass.

When Mom and I finally go to bed at 11:00 p.m., the Dreamers referendum seems to be stuck at a 59 percent yes vote.

On Wednesday morning, public television has the referendum ahead with 61 percent of the vote. But about ten states are still counting their votes, and there are a lot of absentee ballots out in some places. So nothing is final yet. But I still call Ana after I get home from school.

"Oh Jackson," she says, "I'm so excited and so scared."

"Hang in there. The referendum is ahead, and that's a good sign," I say, as if I know something she doesn't. But really, since this is our first national referendum, nobody knows what to expect.

It doesn't take long for Dad to want to get back involved with the theater at some level. With Mom's help, he is able to make a cell phone call to Genevieve about the films to be scheduled for the beginning of the new year. Then on Friday, I meet with Genevieve at the Magic Lantern.

"I was shocked when Laura called me about Scott's illness. But when I spoke with him on the telephone, he sounded okay. His speech was a little halting, but he sounded clear and lucid."

"You wouldn't notice much unless you saw him. But he's having some problems using his right hand."

Then I add, "As you'd expect, he is anxious to get back to work. But I'm not sure they know how long his rehab is going to take."

"He told me that he wants to be back in the theater by the 22nd, the start date for the *Marriage Story* run," she says.

That seems awful early to me, but I say, "I guess we're trying to be optimistic."

"That's good. I can't see Scott being happy if he just has to sit around," she says and hands me an envelope.

"It's information on films I'm planning to schedule for January and February."

"Isn't this pretty late to be scheduling for the winter?"

"We got a bit behind because of the *Marriage Story* confusion. But I think the films I'm going to schedule will be fine. Please give it to Scott as soon as you can.

"This is going to be a lot of stress on you and especially on your mother. So tell Laura that I'll be happy to help in any way I can."

"I will," I say.

Genevieve looks at me and I can tell she's concerned.

"You know," she says finally, "a few of us have almost as much invested in this dream of restoring and operating the Magic Lantern as Scott does. Your Dad has done something wonderful here. And I know that I don't want to see it end, not yet, anyway."

She pauses and then adds, "But if the work starts to be too overwhelming, I think everyone will understand if Scott and Laura decide they have to close the theater."

CHAPTER 38

Judgment Day

When we reopen on the second Friday of November, it seems like every other person who buys a ticket has a question or something to say about the theater closing for three days.

"Why were you closed? I really wanted to see the film about Harriet Tubman before it ended."

"I'm really looking forward to seeing the new Baumbach film here. The website says you'll only be showing it for two weeks. Why the change?"

"We're planning to bring our kids here to see the film on Mr. Rogers with Tom Hanks. I hope you're still planning to show it."

"I have some ideas for films you should try to get. Where's the manager? Scott, I think is his name. I'd like to talk with him."

"It's great to see you back open. I hope everything is okay."

Mom and I decide to make a short announcement at the beginning of each screening about the schedule change for *Marriage Story*. We continue to get questions about the closing, but Mom refuses to say anything about Dad yet.

For some reason, Genevieve's comment about closing the Magic Lantern upset me. Yes, it's Dad's dream and it will hurt him the most if we have to close. But after all his and Genevieve's work, and after our keeping it going for so long and actually making it successful, and when I think about all those people who have come here to see movies, and remember their comments, after thinking about all the time, and energy, and hopes—yes, hopes—that have been put into this place, after all that, I suddenly realize I don't want to see the Magic Lantern close either.

I'm standing outside the front door of the theater. The four o'clock show has just started. It's the first day of the run of Pedro Almodóvar's film, and the audience is pretty small. But I'm thinking about just one thing. How can we keep the Magic Lantern open if Dad has to spend months doing rehab?

Then a familiar figure appears at the bottom of the stairs.

"Jackson."

It's Mr. Belvedere.

"Mr. Belvedere."

He starts up the stairs. He's wearing a new suit, but one that looks very much like the one I remember him wearing when I first saw him outside the theater fourteen months ago.

When he gets to the top, he stops to catch his breath and then he asks the question that I know is coming.

"I heard the theater was closed. What happened?"

"Let's go inside," I say.

When we get to the office, he's looks around and then asks the next obvious question. "Where's Scott?"

"Dad had a stroke last Saturday."

"Oh, my god, no," Mr. Belvedere says, now visibly shaken. "Is he going to be okay?"

"It was a small stroke. He can walk, but his right arm—his hand in particular—has been affected. His speech is a little halting."

Sometimes Dad has to stop to find the words he wants to say. But I don't tell that to Mr. Belvedere.

"He wants to be back in the theater when we run *Marriage Story*. But I don't think we know yet when he'll be back full time, or what he'll actually be able to do," I say.

The older man seems distressed. So I have him sit down, and I sit down across from him in Dad's chair at the office desk.

"Is there anything I can do?"

"No, we'll know more as things progress."

"Can I send him a card, or a note?"

"If you want to get a card, you can send it to me here at the theater, or you can leave it with the person who's working that day. They'll get it to me, and I'll get it to him."

Sitting there, Mr. Belvedere seems to visibly shrink. He stares at me for a moment, and then says, "Scott's done such a wonderful thing reopening this theater, and I know he couldn't have done it without your help, Jackson. So I just want to say thanks to him and to you."

He grabs my hand. His hand feels soft and warm. He starts to leave, then pauses and says, "Tell Scott I'll see him at opening night of *Marriage Story*."

"Sure," I say.

Dad has thrown himself into his physical therapy. He's exercising twice every day for about an hour each time. So far what this routine mainly does is tire him out.

He wants to come back to work slowly over time, starting on the 22nd. Mom will be filling in for Dad during the week, and she has given day-to-day operation of her shop over to her assistant. Other theater staff will hopefully pick up some additional shifts here and there, particularly around the holiday. I'll be working all weekends until Thanksgiving. I'm willing to do it to help keep the Magic Lantern open.

At the Astronomy Club meeting on Thursday most of the talk is about exoplanets, and the two guys who discovered the first such planet orbiting around a Sun-like star and won the Nobel Prize in Physics.

After the meeting, Ellen asked me about Dad. "Raji called me and said Scott had a stroke. Is he okay?"

"It was a mild one, and we're hoping he can get back to work before Thanksgiving."

"Is that possible?" Ellen asks.

"We're being optimistic."

"Does that mean you'll be working more at the theater?"

"I'll work weekends through Thanksgiving. But Mom says that they're looking at other temporary solutions, and she is going to be taking Dad's shifts during the week for a while."

"I hope this doesn't impact your effort to improve your grades."

I don't say anything because I can't say anything. I don't know what this means, or exactly how it is going to affect me, or our family, or the theater.

There is a big crowd for the first Friday night showing of *Marriage Story*. Mom drives Dad over for the showing, and he insists on saying something before the film starts.

"Good evening," he pauses, "and welcome everybody to ... the first day of our screening ... of the new Noah Baumbach film ..."

It's like he's having trouble pushing the words out of his mouth.

"... *Marriage Story*. I wanted us ... to get this film ... since we knew it was coming out. And ... thanks to our fantastic film programmer ... Genevieve Rolland, we were able to do just that.

"As you may have heard," Dad pauses, "the theater was closed ... for a few days. But now we are back and ... and we'll be here whenever you want ... to come to see us through the ... holidays.

"So thanks for coming ... and if you like ... the film ... please tell your friends."

When he finishes, Dad smiles and then sighs. He doesn't say anything about the director or any of Baumbach's other films, something he would have in the past. He stumbles a bit as he walks up the theater aisle. I'm with him and I grab his arm. But he pushes me away after a moment, regains his balance and continues walking out of the screening room. It was an upbeat introduction, and Dad seems happy when he sits down.

Dad and Mom get up before the film is over and go out to the lobby.

"Is Scott going to try to stand by the door to talk with the customers as they leave?" Saffaire asks.

"I guess," I say, feeling both wonder and fear.

The second person out of the screening room when the film ends is Mr. Belvedere. I saw him come in for the show, but we didn't speak. As he walks up to Dad, it appears he pours out all his feelings.

Dad puts his hand on Mr. Belvedere's shoulder, and the big man seems to calm down.

I walk over by Mom. Now there is a line of people passing by the two men. Some folks say things to Dad, others just smile.

"Great film!"

"We love this place."

"I wish you'd remodel the bathrooms."

Dad smiles when he hears that remark.

"Thanks for keeping this theater open."

"We're looking forward to the Tom Hanks film."

Finally, Mr. Belvedere leaves, the crowd dwindles, and Dad starts to slump.

"You're getting tired, aren't you?" Mom asks.

"Yes," Dad says finally. "But this was great ... almost a sellout. We can hope ... that the rest of the run will be ... as good."

"This is the best little movie theater in Seattle," says the male member of a young couple, the last customers to leave, as they walk out of the theater.

"Thank you," Dad says, as if all his energy has suddenly come back.

Dad and Mom come by the theater again on Sunday. Dad does another film introduction for the matinee crowd. Then for a few minutes we talk in the office.

"*Knives Out* ... is going to be the follow-up ... film to *Marriage Story*," Dad says. "It's an ... Agatha Christie-type mystery ... and we're lucky we've got it.

"I talked with Michael," Dad says, "about keeping up the website. But he doesn't think ... he has the time to do it. I guess ... he has some major mid-term exams ... coming up. So Laura talked with Ellen, and ... she has agreed to come in one ... Saturday a month to work ... on the site until we can find someone else ... to do it."

That's a surprise.

Pretty quickly Dad tires out and he and Mom leave.

It doesn't look to me like Dad is going to get back to working regularly at the Magic Lantern for a while. After a family meeting, we decide that Thanksgiving isn't going to happen for us this year. Dad wants to conserve his energy. My parents usually prepare the meal together, and Mom doesn't want to cook it all herself—not this year.

I don't really mind. I spend most of the holiday writing a report for school. I call Ana, but we can only talk for a few minutes because they are having a big family dinner, and she is helping with the preparation.

"We're going to have a family meeting on Sunday," Mom tells me as I'm leaving for the theater on Saturday.

I'm guessing that this will be about the theater, and I keep wondering all afternoon what's been decided. Then I wake up early on Sunday. I can't sleep. I have to know what's going to happen.

"So, Jackson ... I'm thinking," Dad says when we sit down in the living room to meet, "that I'm not going to ... be ready to come back to the theater ... full time until January. Are you okay with that? ... Because it will mean that ... you'll be working mostly three-day weekends ... until the new year."

"Sure," I say, without even thinking about my answer.

"And Jackson, we promise you that you'll be able to go back to Fridays and Sundays only in January," Mom adds.

"Here's the list of the films ... Genevieve has scheduled for ... the first two months in 2020 ... and I'd like you to mention ... these to staff. Ellen will add them to the website."

Dad's still struggling with his words, and immediately Mom breaks into the conversation to allow Dad to take a rest.

"I'll do that for the staff I see during the week," she says. "So Saffaire, and maybe Raji, should be the only staff members you'll need to talk to about the winter schedule."

With that the meeting ends.

Ellen comes in to work on the computer after the first show starts on Sunday, and I take the opportunity to talk with her.

"Ellen, how did you get roped into working on the website again?"

"Your mom was pretty persuasive, and she agreed that I'd just be doing design update work, and only one Saturday a month."

"But today is Sunday?"

"Yeah, I know," Ellen responds with a sheepish look on her face. "I just had some free time and wanted to help out. You know, now that Scott is sidelined for a while."

Ellen is concerned about Dad too, and she's also concerned about the theater.

"My parents weren't thrilled," she says. "But I told them I could list this work on my resume as website design work."

I must look amazed when she says this because Ellen suddenly gives me her 'I'm not stupid' look.

"I'm caught up with all my schoolwork, and I thought I'd come by and just look at the site again, so that I'm familiar with it, and then brainstorm an idea or two with you, Mr. Jackson Ryan, assistant manager."

We both smile.

"Well, I'm not sure I'll be much help brainstorming design ideas. But thanks for agreeing to help out," I say. "Dad thinks it's really important to keep the website up-to-date."

Ellen nods her head in agreement.

Ana and a couple of her friends show up for the seven o'clock show, and we talk for a few minutes afterwards about Dad and about the referendum.

"Congratulations on the passage of the referendum," I say.

Ana smiles. "We kept waiting and waiting for the results to become final. One state would finalize its vote and the yes percentage would drop below 60 percent, and then another state would finalize its vote and our vote would go back over 60 percent. But finally after almost two weeks, it is all over. And we won!"

"So now it's official?"

"Yes, the final yes vote was 60.45 percent."

"Wow. How does it feel to be a citizen?"

"Well I'm still not officially a citizen," Ana says. "We have six months to formally apply, beginning January

2nd. Then it will take some time for our applications to be approved."

"But it's going to happen."

"Yes," Ana says. "It's going to happen. And for me it is a dream come true.

"So how's Scott?" she asks.

"He's doing okay. So far, the prognosis is good."

"I really respect your father," Ana says. "He's worked so hard to make his dream come true, and I think it is really great that you and your mom are helping him keep the theater open. I bet he will recover."

"We hope so," I say. "But that's going to take a lot of time and work on his part."

What I don't say is that there is no plan to keep the theater open for more than a couple months.

"But I also hope that this won't stop you from going to college if that's what you want to do."

With Dad recovering and the future of the Magic Lantern in doubt, is that what I want to do? Maybe I should just put off college for a year. I'll still have to work hard and get good grades my last year in high school. But maybe I'll be more ready for college after I've done something else for a while. Still, I've already applied to some schools, so maybe I've already made my decision and I just don't realize it.

CHAPTER 39

The Dreams We Bring

Effectively, Mom is running the theater Tuesday through Thursday, and on Saturday, and I'm in charge on Friday and Sunday.

Dad was at the theater again the last weekend of the *Marriage Story* run. He introduced the film each night, said a little more about the director, spent some time looking through the mail for bills, and on Saturday night stayed until the film ended to listen to customers comments. But by Sunday he was again exhausted. Raji stood with him while he did his film introductions.

Dad's speech is improving, but he still seems sometimes to be searching for a word or words, and it's difficult for him to use his right hand for much. He still gets tired when he exerts himself, so since *Marriage Story*, he's only come into the theater on Friday afternoons to look at the mail and receipts, and when he needs to talk with Genevieve.

But somehow, we've kept the theater running. The only close call was the print of *Knives Out* getting to us in time for its first showing. It was delivered one hour before the Friday matinee. I'm not sure what I would have done if it hadn't showed up. But I'm glad that I didn't have to call Dad.

Classes end early the Friday before the Christmas break. When I get home Dad is resting, but Mom sits down by me as I eat lunch.

"I'm planning a party for your dad at the Magic Lantern on the last Monday of the month. With school out, I'm expecting you'll be able to help me set up," she says.

"A party?"

"Yes, I want this to be a celebration of all Scott's work making the Magic Lantern such a success. I'm inviting most of his friends from the local film community, a couple of local film critics, the theater staff and, of course, Genevieve. She's getting a mint quality print of *Vertigo* that we're going to show. Oh, and Peter wants to come by."

"Are you going to invite him?"

"We had a nice telephone talk right after Scott's attack, and I really feel like he wants to show support for Scott and our family right now."

"And you're going to show a film?"

"Sure, it's one of Scott's favorites. We couldn't have a party without showing a film. We're also going to have a luncheon buffet, a tour of the theater for those who are interested, and then we'll show the film."

"Wow. This sounds like a big deal." Immediately I wonder if they are going to announce that the theater is closing at this party.

"I hope it will be, and I'm going to need your help to make it work."

"Sure," I say. It's great Mom's planning a celebration for Dad. He really does deserve one.

"I'll want you to lead the building tour, and before we show the film, I'd like you to say a few words about your dad and the theater."

"Well okay, but why me? I'm not really a speaker. Can't you say something instead of me?"

"I will be saying something, Jackson. But you know more about this theater, the staff and customers than anyone except Scott, and you know how much of himself he has put into keeping the Magic Lantern going. After all, hasn't Scott always called you his assistant manager?"

I remember how much I've hated that title. Now it doesn't seem quite so awful. But Mom wants me to make a speech to help in recognizing Dad's accomplishment.

I have worked a lot at the theater, and I know all the staff. But still, I'm not sure I'm the one to make a speech, or even to just say a few words. I've had pretty mixed feelings about working at the Magic Lantern. Sometimes I felt like a casualty of Dad's theater dream. But now, I'm beginning to realize what an accomplishment reopening the Magic Lantern has been.

Confused, I blurt out the first thing that comes into my head. "Are we going announce you're closing the theater?"

"No, Jackson, that would be a last resort, and I don't think it's going to come to that. But even if we were, having this party to recognize what Scott has accomplished would be just as important, maybe even more important.

"Right now, what's important is Scott's recovery, and recognizing what he has done could be as important as his rehab and meds."

A few days after Mom and I talk, I run into Ana at the coffeehouse bakery in Wedgewood. It's so cold outside that we end up sitting at a table by the window. The conversation quickly moves from Christmas to Dad's party.

"And your mother is organizing all this?" Ana asks.

"Yeah. She's working three days a week at the theater, paying all the bills, and touching base with the person who is temporarily running her shop while she also takes care of Dad."

"How is your dad doing?"

"He's spending his time doing physical and voice therapy."

"Is he able to talk?"

"Yes, he can talk, but sometimes it's like he's having trouble getting his words out," I say, and then add quickly, "But you can understand him."

Ana sighs. "Scott's really a brave person. I felt that when I met him, and he told me about his dream of reopening the Magic Lantern. But now he's in an even tougher battle, and he's not going to let it defeat him."

"His biggest problem is that he has limited use of his right hand, like he has trouble writing. He's been to the theater and he's still working with the programmer. But Mom's the one who is mostly holding things together."

"Your mom and you," Ana says sympathetically.

I smile. I'm glad she thinks I'm doing something significant.

"Oh, I've got some news too. I've been accepted at USC."

"Congratulations. I bet your grandparents are proud of you."

"Yes, but they're concerned about me going so far away from Seattle. I'm hoping that now, with the referendum passing, they'll be a little less concerned."

"Will you go to USC?"

"I want to go to a college with a strong journalism program, like USC. But I also want my grandparents to be comfortable with my decision. So we'll see where else I get accepted."

"You're so amazing," I say. "Day after day you have to live with the fear of being deported, and yet you keep on working, confident that everything is going to work out."

"This is my country now, Jackson, and I have to believe that once I'm officially legal, all those days of worrying are going to be behind me."

Ana stands up. She's ready to go.

"A party to celebrate Scott, what a great idea," she says. "Can I come?"

"Do you want me to ask Mom?"

"Is it during the day?"

"It starts at noon on the 30th."

"How long will it be?"

"There will be a lunch, and people will be talking about Dad and all he's accomplished. I'll be giving a tour of the theater, for anybody who wants to come, and then we'll be showing one of Dad's favorite films."

I don't say anything about my giving a speech.

"I remember the tour you gave me," Ana says smiling. "But it sounds like this is going to last the whole afternoon."

"Pretty much," I say, and then add, "but you don't have to stay for the whole thing."

"Could I just stay for lunch, and maybe say something to Scott?"

"I'm sure you could. Let me talk with Mom."

"Would I have to bring a gift?"

"No gifts. It's all just to celebrate Dad for what he's done with the Magic Lantern. Mom thinks it will be good for him to know that other people appreciate what he has done."

"Will there be any speeches?"

"Not speeches exactly, just a few people saying nice things about Dad."

"Are you going to talk about working for your dad at the theater?" Ana asks.

"Mom wants me to, but I don't know. I wouldn't know exactly what to say."

"Oh, Jackson, you'll be great. You know so much about the movies and the Magic Lantern."

"I don't know," I say.

"Just tell everyone about your experience working with Scott at the theater and what it did for you."

Mom said that and now Ana, so I guess that's what I should try to do. Tell everybody about my experience working at the Magic Lantern.

The Saturday before Christmas Genevieve shows up for the matinee. I see her come in and we nod to each other. It's the second day of the run of the film about Mister Rogers and there's a pretty big crowd. So I have to help Raji at concessions until about ten minutes after the show starts.

"Big crowd for a matinee," I say to Raji.

"Everybody wants to see Tom Hanks playing Mister Rogers," he answers.

Genevieve stops to talk with me after the film.

"How's the planning going for Scott's party?"

"Mom's doing most of the planning," I say.

Then I add, "All I have to do is give anybody who's interested a tour of the theater, which should be a snap, and then make a speech about Dad and the Magic Lantern."

"Are you working on your speech?" Genevieve asks.

"Not really," I say.

Genevieve looks at me for a minute. I think she's a bit surprised that I'm not preparing my talk about Dad.

"Having a little trouble?" she asks.

"A little. I'm not much as a speaker."

"Well," she says finally, "just talk about your experience as assistant manager, and how hard you saw Scott work to keep the Magic Lantern going."

She smiles and then adds, "Try to focus on what you've learned working with Scott and you'll do fine. I know Scott will really appreciate whatever you say."

Genevieve's advice makes sense. But when I try looking back at the last fourteen months and my work at the Magic Lantern, I remember that at first, I didn't really want to be here at all.

Mom and I get to the Magic Lantern at 10:00 a.m. to start setting things up for Dad's party. Raji and Ellen come in about a half hour later, and Saffaire sometime after that.

The caterer, who is a friend of Mom's, brings in the lunch at 11:30. The food tables are set up in the salon, and then I finish setting up chairs while Mom, Ellen, and Saffaire put out the food.

At 11:50, Mom sends me to pick up Dad, who thinks we are having a meeting with Genevieve at the theater.

The parking lot is almost full when we get back to the theater.

"What's going on?" Dad asks as we park.

"I don't know," I answer. It feels odd to be lying to Dad. But what can I do?

It's only when Dad sees all the people, and simultaneously notices the THANK YOU, SCOTT banner hanging over the doorway of the salon that he realizes what's happening.

Mom comes through the crowd. She's dressed up and looks great.

She smiles at Scott.

"A few friends came by to celebrate your fourteen months as a theater owner," she says.

Now he smiles.

Then, for a moment, Dad seems speechless.

Mom takes his arm and they go into the salon. People keep stopping Dad to speak with him, but eventually they find a seat, and Mom goes over to the food table to get them both some lunch. My guess is that Dad doesn't want his friends seeing how clumsy he is when trying to use his right hand to help himself to food. Somehow, he's trained himself to eat very slowly with his left hand.

I notice Ana in the corner. I wave at her, and the next time I look she is over talking with Dad.

People continue to wander over to talk to Dad, but eventually, as people finish eating, Mom stands up. She thanks people for coming and says, "We're here today to celebrate Scott's success in renovating and operating the Magic Lantern theater," which she calls "the first independent movie theater to open in Seattle in over ten years."

"Scott's always been a dreamer," Mom says. "He's one of those people who grabs onto something and won't let go until it is accomplished. And that's one of the reasons I love him so much. I know his dream for the Magic Lantern was to create here in this theater a movie-going experience that's second to none in Seattle. His goal was to make the Magic Lantern the theater Seattle filmgoers go to when they want to see a good movie."

Mom pauses and then adds, "And I think he has done that."

Then, to my surprise, Mom asks Genevieve to say a few words.

Genevieve is the person who should be talking about Dad and what he's accomplished at the Magic Lantern. She was part of his team from the beginning, and I think she loves the old way of seeing movies as much as he does. Maybe if she talks a lot, I won't have to say much.

"When Scott and I talked about my being the film buyer for the Magic Lantern, I realized that he didn't just want to renovate an old theater that had fallen on hard times. He wanted to try to recreate a feeling of film culture based on independent neighbor theaters that we seemed to have lost. Scott's work here hasn't been just about restoring an old building. It's been about restoring an older way of doing things, about enjoying a movie in a special space with other people. And when I heard him say that, I just knew I had to be part of his dream."

Genevieve looks out across the room and then adds, "Scott always realized that you have to dream big to accomplish anything meaningful. We make a mistake when we don't support the dreams that dreamers bring to us because it's dreams—theirs and ours—that make life exciting. So my thanks to all of you for being here today to celebrate Scott and his dream."

As she finishes, I can feel my stomach tighten. I'm next up, but how can I top what Genevieve has just said? I've got some notes, but as I stand up, I can't remember a word of what I've written.

It's only when I stand up that I realize that there are a lot of people here, and it seems like they're all looking at me.

"I didn't really have any idea about what Dad's buying the Magic Lantern would mean when I first heard he was going to do just that. He showed me around the theater right after he'd bought it. I remember thinking, 'This place is a mess. How much is it going to cost to renovate? Will you ever be able run it and make any money?'"

The crowd is very quiet. Somebody coughs. I pause and take a big breath.

"Right from the beginning, Dad talked about his dream, and how he wanted to renovate an old movie house and run it so he could prove that, at least in Seattle, seeing movies in the dark of a theater with other people was not a dead idea.

"After he completed the renovation, and he asked me to come help him and work at the theater, I didn't want to do it. At that point, it wasn't my dream, it was his, and I thought that it wasn't going to be a success, and that it would be a waste of my time."

The room is completely quiet, and I see that Mom is looking at me and frowning. Keep going, I say to myself. Just keep going.

"Those first couple of months, everything seemed really tenuous. Attendance was up and down. Some people told us that they were glad to see the Magic Lantern open again. But nothing felt solid, nothing felt secure. And then there were the setbacks, like the Woody Allen fiasco. Remember that, Dad?"

I look over at Dad who, to my surprise, is nodding his head and smiling.

"And the award-winning Lebanese film that only a few people came to see, and the snow storm that killed even that audience for the last six days of its run. It seemed like we never knew for sure which films were going to get an audience and which weren't. A lot of the time, things were just beyond our control.

"And there were building problems like the leaks in the bathroom that customers still complain about, even though we've replaced most of the plumbing."

I pause. You could hear a pin drop the salon is so quiet.

"Somewhere along the way, Dad named me his assistant manager. I never asked for that job, but I guess he felt he could count on me, and after a while I began to kind of enjoy having some responsibility."

I feel like I'm rambling. I'm not sure what to say next. I look over at Mom. Now her face is completely blank. But I can tell what's she's probably thinking, "Jackson, don't mess this up."

"But then there were the surprises, like the turnout for the film *Roma*. Early on, customers who came to the new Magic Lantern seemed grateful that it had been reopened, and we developed a small but loyal group of regulars who'd come once or twice a month to see a movie. Still, attendance was up and down, and there were many times that I felt it was only a matter of time before Dad closed the theater.

"Then Dad and Genevieve went out and got a one-week spot for the theater as a venue for the film festival. And if that wasn't enough, Dad announced that the Magic Lantern would be hosting its own film festival, a Summer of Film, in July and August.

"Dad, I thought the Summer of Film idea was crazy. Nobody goes to the movies in the summer in Seattle. But you proved me wrong, because the Summer of Film was a big success. What I didn't realize was that to keep this theater dream alive, you had to keep upping the ante. You had to push us to do more things, so that, as you put it, 'the Magic Lantern would be seen as the one theater in town where people came to see great movies and have a great theater experience.'

"Today I can see something that I couldn't see when you opened the Magic Lantern, or even last spring. I can see that if you have a dream like Dad's, you have do everything you can to keep it alive, even things that defy logic or conventional wisdom, and if you do that, there's a good chance you'll succeed."

Then I turn toward Dad and say one last thing.

"So thanks, Dad, for letting me be part of your dream, and for teaching me that having dreams, whatever they are, gives our lives meaning."

Someone standing by the wall in the salon starts applauding—it's Peter Bergmeier.

"Bravo, Scott," someone else yells, and the whole room bursts into applause.

I feel a little disoriented, kind of dizzy, and as I step back towards Mom and Ellen, I almost fall. Mom catches me, and as I turn to look at her, I see that her cheeks are wet.

She doesn't say anything, just gives me hug. Then she announces that those who want a tour should gather in the far corner by the windows.

I guess I'm up, so I'd better get myself together.

Just then Dad appears at my side.

"Thanks, Jackson," he says with a big smile. "Thanks for believing in my dream. It's good to know," he says and pauses, "... you finally understand."

"Yes, I finally got it."

We both smile.

"And remember the setbacks ... like the ones you mentioned, make success even sweeter when it comes. And also ... I want you to know ... I couldn't have done it without you."

I notice that about ten people have gathered for the theater tour. Dad notices them too.

"I know you'll do a ... good job with the tour. But I'm going to ... sit here for a while. I'm a little tired ... and I'm really looking forward to seeing *Vertigo* again." Dad pauses and then adds, "So I want to be able to stay awake."

The tour turns out to be easy, and I surprise myself by how much I do know about this theater and the films we've shown. When the tour is over, I decide to get a soda and go sit in the salon for a few minutes.

As I go in, I see Ana and Dad sitting together talking.

I walk up to where they are sitting, and Dad sees me and gets up. He seems to have renewed energy.

"I want to get my favorite seat ... before anybody else takes it," he says.

"What's your favorite seat?" Ana asks.

"The seventh row back in the middle."

He excuses himself, and I sit down.

Before I can say anything, Ana says, "This was great. And I could tell that Scott was really happy with your speech."

"You think so?"

"Yes. He told me it was great to know that you finally got it."

I must look a little confused because then she adds, "About having a dream. Now he knows you understand how it is to be a dreamer."

"Oh, yes," I say, feeling a little embarrassed.

"So anyway, I can't stay for the film. But I wanted to tell Scott how much I respect him for what he's done."

"I'm sure he appreciates that."

"He congratulated me on the referendum passing."

For a moment she seems to be thinking about what else she wants to say.

"So now that I know you understand what it means to be a dreamer, and why I have to do everything I can to get into a good college without any strings, maybe we could see a little more of each other. You know, just as friends."

"Sure ... great. I'd like that."

We both smile.

I walk her down the steps from the theater. She's catching a bus back to Green Lake. We say our good-byes, and I watch her walk away. Then I look at my watch. It's almost 3:00 and the movie will be starting soon.

Just as I get to the door, I run into Ellen, who's coming out.

"Not going to the movie?" I ask.

"No, I've seen it a couple times. This was a great party, though. I think Scott felt very appreciated."

"I hope so," I say.

"Have you decided about college yet?"

"Not really."

"So, what are you going to do then?"

"Work hard to finish out high school with some good grades, and then, if I can't decide what I want to do, maybe I'll just hang around here, take some classes at the community college, and see how this theater thing turns out."

Ellen sighs. "I thought you might be thinking along those lines."

Mom sticks her head out the door.

"The movie is starting in five minutes, Jackson. Scott has saved you a seat next to him in the seventh row."

"I've got to go," I tell Ellen.

"Me, too," she says.

"How about getting together for coffee on New Year's Day? The Picasso Café will be open from 10:00 to 5:00."

"You've got a date," Ellen says. We both smile. "I'll call you tomorrow."

The lights dim and the movie starts. Saul Bass's title art appears on the screen and then you see two men chasing someone across city rooftops. One slips, grabs onto a piece of gutter and hangs in midair. You can see fear in his eyes. The other man reaches down to help him, and then he falls into the ally below. The first man remains hanging, his face full of fear, trying his best not to look down. Even though I've seen this opening many times, it still shocks me and leaves me thinking—wow, what's going to happen next?

Credits

[1] Daris, Manohia. "*Roma* Review: Alfonso Cuarón Masterpiece of Memory," *New York Times*, Nov. 20, 2018.

[2] William F. Schulz, "Affirmation # 459," in *Singing the Living Tradition: Affirmations, Covenants, and Confessions* (Boston: Beacon Press/Unitarian Universalist Association: 1993).

[3] Tom K. Reynolds, "Un Lugar Sin Muerte," an unpublished poem. November, 2023.

[4] Jonathan Poppele, "The Spring Sky," in *Night Sky: A Field Guide to the Constellations* (Cambridge, MN: Adventure Publications, 2010), pp. 34–91.

[5] "De Colores," in *Rise Up Singing*, edited by Peter Blood and Annie Patterson (Winona: Hal Leonard Publications, 2004), p. 152. This is a traditional Mexican song, and a favorite of the United Farmworkers.

[6] John Wakeman, "Agnes Varda," in *World Film Directors*, vol. 2 1945–1985 (Hw Wilson Company: 1987), pp.

1142-1148. Cited in *Wikipedia*, "Agnès Varda," n. 9. <https://en.wikipedia.org/wiki/Agn%C3%A8s_Varda>

[7] Lorre Wyatt, "Somos El Barco," in *Rise Up Singing*, edited by Peter Blood and Annie Patterson (Winona: Hal Leonard Publications, 2004), p. 242. ©1984 Lorre Wyatt (performance rights held by BMI).